KAYENTA CROSSING

A CHARLES BLOOM MURDER MYSTERY

MARK SUBLETTE

JUST ME PUBLISHING

Copyright © 2013 by Mark Sublette
Author's Note by Mark Sublette Copyright © 2013

All Rights Reserved. This book may not be reproduced, in whole or in part, in any form, without written permission. For inquiries, contact: Just Me Publishing, LLC., Tucson, AZ, 1-800-422-9382

Published by Just Me Publishing, LLC.

Library of Congress Control Number: 2013938147
Kayenta Crossing / Mark Sublette
ISBN 978-0-9855448-2-9
1. Fiction I. Title

Quantity Purchases
Companies, professional groups, clubs, and other organizations may qualify for special terms when ordering quantities of this title. For more information, contact us through www.marksublette.com.

Cover painting: Ed Mell, *Heart of the Storm*
Jacket and book design: Jaime Gould
Author photo: Dan Budnik

Printed in the USA by Bookmasters
Ashland, OH · www.bookmasters.com

Author's Note

The books in the Bloom murder mystery series are all works of fiction. The most significant real-life artist reference in KAYENTA CROSSING surrounds a rug woven by the late master weaver Daisy Taugelchee, to whom this book is dedicated. Her amazing gift from Spiderwoman was the inspiration for this book.

All the characters are fictional as are all the art galleries, artists, and art dealers. The Native American characters in my books are fictional and any resemblance by name, clan, or description to real life is pure coincidence.

The Toadlena Trading Post, a central component of all the Bloom books, is a real-life working trading post that exists as described on Navajoland. This historic post specializes in Toadlena/Two Grey Hills weavings and is well worth the effort to visit. I would like to thank its proprietor, author Mark Winter and his wife Linda, for their invaluable insight into the world of the weavers.

No book is complete without a great cover and I'm most appreciative to Ed Mell for so graciously allowing me to use his painting HEART OF THE STORM to capture the essence of Northern Arizona and to Jaime Gould for her graphic design skills.

All the photographs are taken by me and serve as points of reference that correlate to each chapter. Hopefully they help to give the reader the sense of place or moment in time that I experienced when I took them.

Finally I wish to thank my late father, whose encouragement of my writing never flagged and whose love of books continues to inspire me.

PROLOGUE

NO NEW TRUCK

Randal Begay's vision was strong. The sweat lodge's medicine had done the trick. Now he could journey down the correct Diné path, in step with his ancestors' beliefs. The hard decision to return the money was clear in his mind. For the first time in months he felt at ease and in balance.

His grandfather, a respected medicine man, had recommended the sweat treatment to help him resolve his inner conflict. It had worked, empowering him with a newfound courage, something he had lacked for too long. Randal knew he must break his deal with the *bilagaana*. If not, he would never walk in beauty. A bad choice had been made eight months earlier by accepting the $10,000 down payment. He would not compound the mistake tomorrow. The $25,000 in cash that was to be paid to Randal for finishing the project was a deal he must back out of. If he completed the transaction, he would never be able to live the life of a good human being by Diné standards. He also might end up in jail if the truth became known. Or maybe worse.

Randal had expressed deep concerns earlier in the week to the old rancher William "Buck" Wilson, his trusted friend whose family had lived near the Begays for two generations. Buck had relieved Randal's conscience at the time. He told Randal he didn't see any problem with his arrangement with the *bilagaana*. He assured Randal that it was an honorable transaction, and no laws were being broken. Buck had influenced Randal by reminding him of his family duties, pointing out, "The money will get your clan back on their feet. Besides, there's no harm being done. You're a Navajo and you are just taking advantage of the talents your grandmother taught you. You have nothing to worry about, son."

Randal had wanted to believe Buck, but Buck was also a *bilagaana* and didn't understand the essence of what it meant to be Diné. Despite his serious trepidation, Randal had continued working to complete his commitment. The outcome was amazing, even in Randal's eyes. He was gifted, yet must destroy what Spiderwoman had helped guide him to complete. It could never be sold or he would be doomed.

Tomorrow would be a better day even if he would be poorer. Randal would face the man with the orange hat and explain why he must back out of his obligation. The man would be very angry no doubt, and demand his $10,000 back plus interest. The money was gone, but fortunately Randal had not wasted it. He had purchased a good truck. He would sign over the vehicle's title and make it right somehow, giving the man whatever was required. Randal would not cause the gods to punish his heart. Navajo spirits are not to be tested. They can destroy a man. He saw this now.

Come clean, change his ways, and have his grandfather perform a Blessing Way ceremony to cure him of his poor judgment and the *chindi* that were haunting his subconscious. So Randal vowed now. He had been sleeping poorly, his appetite nonexistent as he neared the completion of his long ordeal. Now he knew the right road. It was not too late to change, or so he thought.

Steam rose off the hot sweat-lodge rocks, producing a fine ribbon of white clouds that hugged the open mesa's horizon, the lodge's calling card visible for miles. The temperature outside was near freezing, but inside his cramped juniper hut it was well over 100. At just five-foot-six with a slim build, Randal had nonetheless been required to squeeze himself into the space. One more cup of water, and Randal would be fully prepared to handle the anger of the man in the orange hat with the bleached white teeth.

Randal tossed his loose black ponytail over his shoulder and stuck his head out of the hut's opening, searching for the plastic jug of water. He was ready to complete his treatment. His unadjusted eyes were temporarily blinded by the late evening sun, which caused him to reflexively turn his head away from its glaring golden light.

The last memory he had before all went dark was a flash of white and an image of Black Mesa in the distance, its sacred voice calling him home.

CHAPTER 1

YOU AIN'T IN KANSAS ANYMORE

Carson Riddly's last week as a family practice resident should have been full of excitement and joy. Three hard years of training were finally behind him and he could start living again. The lifestyle of a medical resident is not dissimilar to that of a prisoner, only a lot less fun. In prison you're allowed adequate sleep and occasional recreation. A medical resident is not awarded those little life pleasures. For a doctor in training it is constant work with absolutely no free time, ever. Your average workweek is 80-plus hours, and that's a normal week. If you are covering obstetrics, it could easily be over 100 hours. No sleep, just delivering babies and writing notes. Life as a resident means work, no socializing, and little money.

The goal of the family practice residency is to train doctors in a large area of subjects but not in depth. You need to be a jack-of-all-trades and a master of none to be a good family doctor. This means rotations in a variety of areas in medicine including pathology, hematology, oncology, general surgery, dermatology, and obstetrics. Areas of special interest also can be explored like sports medicine, nutrition, geriatrics, and radiology, depending on the individual physician's interests.

Dr. Riddly particularly loved dermatology and loaded up on additional rotations in the field. Dermatologists often like a good murder mystery. The subtle rash not carefully examined or a poor patient history can lead to misdiagnosis and the patient's demise—or just more ointment needed. Life, death, itching, hives, it was all in a day's work. Carson Riddly loved the challenge of a difficult skin rash.

Carson had considered trying to switch over to derm (as doctors call the study of dermatology) during his second year of family practice residency. A particularly grueling surgery rotation at the V.A. Hospital in Tucson had almost broken his spirit. Seeing old vets who had no money and rarely had taken care of themselves all day made him wonder if he had what it took to be family doctor. Carson liked a more cultured patient. He knew this was shallow of him and un-doctor-like, but fortunately he did at least recognize this defect and had come to grips with the fact that this was a negative part of his personality that still needed work.

When he rotated through the dermatology department it was fun and interesting; he looked forward to going to work every day. The nature of always trying to figure out an unknown problem allowed Carson to use his astute deductive reasoning. Deciphering some unknown blob or bump and relating its worrisome presentation to the disturbed patient's history was gratifying. Each case had its own unique parameters and if not analyzed properly the medical puzzle could not be completed. Carson's mind set up perfectly for answering a question that had no obvious answer. The fact that his patients generally had money and rarely died from a dermatological complication was an added bonus. There are only a couple of true medicinal emergencies in dermatology, like the well-publicized flesh-eating bacteria that most veteran derm guys had never even seen. The best part of derm was there were no night calls. All patients could wait until morning. Unfortunately, dermatology was a highly sought-after residency and the probability of Carson securing one of the coveted spots was pretty slim. He had been a good medical student, but his love of fishing, girls, and golf had brought his grade point well below what was required to be competitive in derm. He had decided if he couldn't hack family practice after a couple of years during his Indian Health Service commitment, he would try to switch fields and apply for dermatology again.

More importantly, his inner voice kept demanding, "Why did I take that damn Indian Health Scholarship?" The recurrent thought was permeating every idle moment of Carson's day and creeping into his subconscious sleep patterns in the form of disconcerting dreams.

Sleep was no longer enjoyable but an odd unpleasant mixture of daily doctor duties and a scene out of some horror movie. In a recurrent nightmare he saw himself showing up at an empty trailer in a remote place and knocking on a beat-up aluminum door. When the squeaky door finally opened, his old I.H.S. recruiter jumped out. He was smiling back at Carson with blood dripping from an open head wound. He whispered, "Welcome to Kayenta, Dr. Riddly," and started laughing hysterically. Carson turned and tried to run but couldn't move, his feet spinning like an old cartoon.

Carson Riddly now knew he had made a huge mistake committing to the Indian Health Service seven years ago when he entered medical school. He had wanted to prove to his father, the successful surgeon, that he could take care of himself and didn't need any family money to pay for school; he was young and made a rash decision. By signing a contract with the I.H.S., he had committed to servicing their needs for two years as a doctor on an Indian reservation after his residency graduation, and the government had in turn paid all his school bills including books. His two-year payback was about to begin. Carson had been terribly naïve when it came to understanding what he was committing himself to. He was 21 and it seemed like a challenge at the time, and such a long time before he would have to go anywhere.

The convincing I.H.S. recruiter had shown him pictures of nice new hospitals and city shots of Santa Fe, and promised him there were plenty of good spots for doctors, especially native Arizonans. "No problem, they'll find you a place you'll like near your current home or in Santa Fe." Carson could still hear the recruiter's words. He was now sure the recruiter had been a full-blooded Indian that had it in for rich, white kids like him. He remembered thinking at the time the guy's hair seemed long for a recruiter. Carson was about to get to know intimately what an Indian looked like close-up.

His assignment location had finally come through for what would be his new life. A minimum two-year position and it wasn't good. In fact, it was shit. He had been planning for Santa Fe, NM, hoping for the Indian Hospital as a first choice, or a nearby pueblo like Santa Clara or San Ildefonso as choices two and three. Easy access to the big city, art, food, music, golf, and of course, girls. The girls and golf he had almost completely missed for the last three years of his residency. Carson knew all of Santa Fe's stats: when the last freeze day was, May 15th; how many nearby golf courses, 10; and 200 art galleries.

His fourth choice was Phoenix at the Indian Hospital there, and fifth was near his current location of Tucson, where he had just finished his residency at the large University of Arizona Medical Center. The Tucson location would be the Tohono O'odham reservation in the town of Sells, which was thirty minutes outside of Tucson; with this position he could have kept his apartment. If all else failed, his sixth choice was the Indian Health Board in Seattle, Washington.

He had assumed all along one of these sites would be his. The form to request a duty assignment was known as the wish list. There were blanks for six possible locations. Carson had even hand written in two additional choices. He figured it never hurt to give those in charge a couple more possibilities just in case. He had spent months researching the different cities and associated clinics he could possibly end up at, and was ready for any of the possibilities.

He was shocked by the results in the government form letter, which had ordered him to report July 1st to Kayenta, Arizona!

Opening the white and green envelope with its fancy government emblem had been exciting. He could hardly wait to see how close his clinic would be to Santa Fe. Seeing the words Kayenta, Arizona Clinic stunned him.

"Where the hell is Kayenta? This has to be a mistake, must be two Carson Riddlys," Carson muttered to himself in disbelief as he examined the letter as if it were some rare disease, incomprehensible to his brain's data base, an unknown horrific malady he had somehow missed learning about in medical school. "Maybe this is some sick joke from one of my friends. They're screwing with me, that has to be it!"

He immediately called his I.H.S. representative, who assured him it was very much for real and no joke. Apparently the fact that he had added the two additional possible choices to the form which allowed only six possibilities had not sat well with the rigid officer in charge of clinic location decisions, who decided to give him the least desirable position currently available in the entire doctor pool. After all, it was in Arizona and his recruiter had promised an Arizona boy would get something close by. There was no way to challenge this new duty station. He was stuck and the reality had just started to sink in of his upcoming hardship somewhere in far northern Arizona. He would be starring in his own John Ford movie as its main character, a poor bastard lost to the Navajo Nation for two years.

The little information Carson could find on the web about Kayenta was not reassuring. It was 20 miles south of Monument Valley, a classic stark landscape of what the West should embody. Many early westerns had been shot there. This looked promising on the surface but a little deeper searching revealed his worst nightmare. The town had only 5,000 residents, almost all Indian. No nightlife to speak of, a few fast food restaurants, a half-dozen motels, and the nearest golf course was three hours away. There were two medical clinics: the main facility was a cluster of trailers that served as the primary health clinic and also occasionally as a makeshift hospital and morgue. A large modern regional hospital was being built east of the city, but it would be a couple of years before it was finished, assuming the money didn't dry up. If he were really unlucky, he would end up in the secondary clinic that the official web site listed as "no photo available."

For Carson Riddly, a good-looking single man in his late twenties, it felt as if he had been given a death sentence. Two years of isolation in the backwoods of Arizona. Kayenta!

CHAPTER 2

FATHERS AND SONS

It had been two weeks since Carson had graduated from the University of Arizona's family practice residency, and he had used his remaining time to clean out his one-bedroom apartment, go dancing, and overindulge in alcohol and golf. He had hoped for a quick tryst with one of the nearby U of A sorority girls he had had his eye on for the last six months, but honestly, golf—even in a searing Southwest summer—trumped young women in the short time of freedom he still had left.

His head was aching and his stomach in knots as he drove the boring two-hour trip from Tucson up to Paradise Valley just north of Phoenix, to visit his parents who were just entering the last half of their lives and retirement. Making up for lost time, Carson had played 12 rounds of golf in 14 days, which had done in his back. Tucson's average daily high temperature in June is well over 100. Add to this the nightly alcohol binge and it made for one severely dehydrated individual, even if he did possess an athletic build. Blonde hair under his baseball cap, he pulled the brim down low now and pushed his sunglasses higher to block the Arizona sun.

Trying to find a comfortable position as he drove his pride and joy—a turquoise blue 1968 Mustang convertible—was nearly impossible. If he put his right leg into the passenger side, it helped decrease the lower lumbar muscle spasms, but it also required him to use his left leg for both the gas and brakes. Physicians are supposed to know better than to put themselves in unsafe situations, but the shooting pains in his back overrode common sense.

Carson knew that last day of golf was too much and he should have rested, but he was crushing his drives. Any golfer can tell you hitting a 275-yard drive in the sweet spot is the same feeling as a heroin addict gets when they first shoot up. Dr. Carson Riddly would have scolded his patients if they had come into his office with his own irresponsible injury history, and he hoped he didn't have to explain his limp to his own father the physician, who would reconfirm what he already knew—it had been a bonehead move.

His thoughts lost in space during the mind-numbing drive, he tried to distract himself from his pounding head and aching back. This brought him back to how he had got into his overall life predicament to begin with. It all started with his dad, he figured. Carson loved and respected his father tremendously, but he could also anticipate his voice when he walked into their house: "Well, son, I told you to just let me pay for school. It was a state school, for god's sake, and not that expensive. Now you're stuck in some two-bit, hole-in-the-wall town for two years. Say goodbye to your golf game."

Dr. Mark Riddly was a plastic surgeon and had just retired from private practice. He had worked during the golden age of medicine and been very successful. There was a time in recent American history when doctors were respected and made good money. Those days were long gone. Now for one to practice medicine, you had to accept the fact that you would probably work for some big clinic and be paid a salary, plus bow to the whims of insurance companies and the government. Dr. Mark Riddly, on the other hand, was still respected and had done most of the boob jobs in Scottsdale. The Riddly touch, they called it. Symmetrical, erect nipple stance and not a hint of skin rippling or adhesion. One of his patients, a stripper, had referred to him as "the doc who does the perfect boob job every time." The young Dr. Riddly had seen his father's handiwork on more than one occasion close up, and did agree he was the best.

Life for the retired Riddlys was at the zenith: lots of disposable money and not enough time to spend it all. Vacations were now the norm and the Paradise Valley estate sat empty much of the time.

The whole Kayenta location was even more devastating because of Dr. Riddly Sr.'s generous offer of the family guesthouse, which looked out on the club's golf course. It would have been Carson's for the two-year stint if he ended up in Phoenix, a real no-brainer of an option. No such luck.

CHAPTER 3

PEP TALK

Arriving at his childhood home, Carson parked his rarely dirty car at the entrance to the long driveway to embrace his old childhood stomping grounds. The mature three-acre parcel of land in the heart of Paradise Valley was dotted with old-growth Sonoran desert terrain now rare in urbanized Arizona. Its presence was calming to Carson Riddly's cluttered mind. He remembered watching Gambel's Quail and the occasional Gila monster making their life in this spot of largely untouched old Phoenix desert. The slow-growing saguaros had barely changed in height in the last decade, but the few century plants on drip watering were gigantic—water, a precious commodity in the desert, the only factor in their prosperity. In the far corner of the lot stood a gnarled, charcoal-colored mesquite tree that Carson remembered all too well.

He had been nine and his best friend from across the wash, Barry Gruever, had brought over a pack of Black Cat firecrackers. Carson was strictly forbidden to play with matches, much less fireworks. But Barry, who had a devilish streak, always managed to convince Carson it was OK or at least no one would get caught. The day was a typically hot June, temperature hovering around 110 degrees. Barry and Carson had made a wooden fort out of old plywood boards in the then green mesquite tree and used it as their home base for operation. Mrs. Riddly had run over to the nearby country club and left the boys to their own devices, a serious mistake, as she would soon find out.

The game was to set up plastic soldiers around the base of the tree, then use the strong gunpowder firecrackers, which were illegal in most states, as grenades to blow up the little units of men. A particularly good hit would be if the plastic men lost body parts and also flew up into the air. It had been an exceptionally fun event until an errant firecracker was tossed into a clump of nearby dry fountain grass and set the whole backyard on fire.

The hot June winds which were kicking up to around 20 miles per hour and the dead old-growth underbrush ignited like a bomb. Quail flew, snakes slithered, and two young boys jumped for safety as the fire engulfed the southwest corner of the property, including their fort, the property that would be forever known by the Riddly family when describing that part of the land as Carson's Folly. Carson preferred Black Cat Ridge.

Today had a very similar feeling to that June day when he was nine. He could still vividly remember panicking at the moment of realization that his house might burn up. At that instance he could imagine not only his house burning, but also the entire neighborhood. Barry vanished, running home to hide in his room. Barry Gruever, his best friend in the world, would deny all involvement to his mom and just hope for the best. After all it wasn't his house that was in jeopardy of annihilation; he had a large dirt wash separating him from the fiasco. Carson responded correctly to the challenge by doing what his mother and father had drilled into his head: calling 911. The fire department was in full response mode when the horrified Mrs. Carson arrived back from her quick errand.

The house and neighborhood were saved by Carson's quick action, but the poor mesquite tree was never quite the same. The hardy wood was permanently burnt black and if not for his father's babying the tree it probably would have not survived. Carson admitted to his entire role in the sordid affair and was grounded for the rest of the summer. No pool, a devastating injury to a nine-year-old in Arizona. Barry Gruever, who would never admit his involvement, enjoyed his summer completely. The last Carson had heard, Barry was doing time at the state prison in Florence, an arson-related crime.

Staring at the tree's branch that had held him as a child caused memories to flood back. Carson remembered playing in the yard for endless hours and throwing a Frisbee repeatedly to his white Labrador, Zachery, up the twisting road every afternoon. Carson felt a strong scene of déjà vu and longed for those days when life was less complicated. No stress, just play, food, and television. No Kayenta looming in the distance.

Finally walking into the house, an old scent immediately challenged his nostrils for recognition, its aroma unchanged for a decade. The permanent hint of his father's Old Spice cologne mixed with a sort of musty carpet flavor that was always present. The unique smell of the Riddly family home. The 1960s brick ranch-style architecture was of typical construction with low ceilings and small windows. Its only distinguishing characteristic was the particularly good western and Indian art that dotted the home's walls and floors. The vibrant blue carpet which had been installed his freshman year in high school was now reaching its breaking point, its color more a gray hue resulting from a mix of Arizona dirt and constant sun exposure. He remembered when it was new, the bright blue color almost blinding and his mother's constant reprimand at wearing dirty shoes inside. "I wonder if she would she still care if I tracked in dirt?" he thought to himself, while staring at the worn-out ply carpet. Suddenly his father's baritone voice broke his inner concentration and Carson's internal stress level eased for the first time that day.

"Carson, why didn't you yell you were here? How long have you been standing there? Better get your shoes off, you know how your mom is." Question answered; no new carpet in the near future.

The delighted voice of Mark Riddly was now almost at a level of shouting. His hearing had decreased dramatically over the last year. The small sensory hairs found in the inner ear had suffered irreparable damage from too many Grateful Dead concerts during the Summer of Love and he was still too vain to consider a hearing aid. Carson knew he too would be hearing impaired in not the too-near future, another casualty of Barry Gruever, his own hearing loss due to a small gunpowder-fired cannon which was ignited too close to Carson's ears. He wondered if like his father he too would be vain and resist a hearing aid. The answer was probably yes.

"Pops, I just got in. I'm hoping Mom made me my favorites—pot roast, browned potatoes, and chocolate cream pie?"

"You're in luck, my boy. It's your graduation meal. Your mother knew you would want just that. It will be ready faster than you can say hepatomegaly," the older doctor said, laughing at his use of a long medical term meaning liver enlargement, a way to bond with his son, the fledgling doctor. "So what's all this about Kayenta? I thought Santa Fe was supposed to be in the bag?"

"Me too," sighed Carson. "It looks like somebody down at the home office just didn't like the Riddly name. Maybe you botched a boob job and now I'm going to the end of the world, Kayenta, Arizona." Carson didn't want to admit to his father it was his own stupidity for putting two extra locations on his wish list form, which was clearly limited to the six blank spaces provided.

"Carson, I know you are disappointed and at your age I probably would have thought it was the worst thing that could every happen, but in reality it might be a blessing in disguise, and you know I never botch a boob job," his father replied, smiling.

"Wow, Pops, I figured I was going to get the old 'I told you so' lecture."

"Nope, you're too old for that now. Besides, I mean it, this could be fun, a once-in-a-lifetime experience. You would never go to this hole-in-the-wall town, so make the most of it and see what comes of it. I wish I had taken some time off and done some more interesting things before I got stuck in the rut of fixing asses and tits for the last 30 years. Now for something more upbeat, I've got a little surprise for you, Doctor Carson Riddly. A graduation present. I was going to wait till later with your mom, but I think you could use a little pick-me-up. Besides, this is really coming from me."

"I'm all for that, Dad. What have you got to show me? That new Mustang I've been hoping for?"

But no. Instead, Dr. Riddly Sr. opened a chest of drawers and pulled out a large, very well made, all-natural color, intricate Navajo rug and handed it to Carson. "This is much better than some old car, Carson. This is one of the finest Two Grey Hills rugs you will ever lay your eyes on. It was made by one of the greatest Navajo weavers who ever lived, Daisy Taugelchee. This particular textile I purchased 30 years ago from the Heard Museum gift shop. I fell in love with it the moment I saw it hanging behind the main counter. It was supposed to be the best example they knew of and a prize winner. They say it's 130 wefts to the inch, which means it's an extremely fine weave. Anyway, it was very valuable when I bought it, and I'm sure it hasn't done anything but appreciate in value since then. I felt since you were going to be in the land of the Navajos, a fine example of their handicraft by one of the best weavers above your office desk might be a nice calling card and break the ice for you."

"Wow," commented Carson. "That's an amazing gift. I can remember as a kid you always warned me not to screw with this rug. I can't believe you're just giving it to me." Carson of course had no clue of value and figured it was probably worth at least a couple thousand dollars by his father's description and his continued enthusiasm for the weaving.

"You're old enough now, Son, to start enjoying such things and besides it would be yours anyway once we're gone so you might as well have it now and who knows maybe it will open some doors. I believe the piece won a first-prize ribbon at the Gallup Intertribal Indian Ceremonial in the 1950s."

"I will hang it up in my office, of course. That assumes I actually have an office, which may be a rather big assumption, I'm afraid."

"Carson, you will be fine," his dad insisted. "Just look at the whole experience as a building block to what will ultimately make you who you are. Besides, there has to be some interesting pathology out there on the reservation. Who knows, maybe you'll see a hantavirus or bubonic plague case. Those are rare and would be interesting as hell, don't you think?"

"Yeah," Carson agreed. "I guess you're right, Dad. I should see some pretty interesting third-world medical cases, and I know it will make me a better doctor in the long run, which is what it's supposed to be all about. Maybe I will start a log of interesting derm cases found among the Northern Arizona Navajo population and get published in a national dermatology magazine."

"Now you're thinking like a real doctor!"

"Thanks, Pops. I feel better already. And I can smell the pot roast. Mom must have taken it out of the oven."

The two men locked arms and headed in for a good home-cooked meal, Carson keeping his right ear to his dad's head, the good ear Barry Gruever's cannon had spared.

CHAPTER 4

KAYENTA CLINIC

Driving to Kayenta the morning of June 30th was a moment of aloneness Carson figured would stay with him for life. He'd packed his polo shirts, jeans, and golf caps, and left the comfort of his boyhood home once again, his room there largely unchanged since the nineties, a mother's memorial to his high-school days. She wanted him to always feel he had a room to come back to. Posters of girls in bikinis and Tiger Woods winning the 2000 U.S. Open still hung in their honored places, only the yellowed edges betraying years gone by.

Carson had spent the morning going through his keepsakes, planning to bring a few with him, a comfort food of sorts for what he knew would be a life-changing and maturing experience: surviving in Kayenta. He selected his old microscope, the one that had helped him win the Arizona State Science Fair as a senior in high school. The winning project was titled: "The Life Habits of the Arizona Gila Monster, *Heloderma suspectum*." He had spent a year following a couple of resident Gila monsters around his family property, picking up their scat, or fecal deposits, and using his microscope to identify the parts of small birds, lizards, and insects therein. Carson learned a tremendous amount about Sonoran wildlife by shadowing the reclusive lizards. His crowning moment was catching a pair of the poisonous lizards mating in the wild—a first for science, and it won him first prize. The two large Gila monsters wiggled for nearly an hour in the dark Arizona night, the male viciously biting the female on the top of the head and she seemed to like it, a fact not lost on Carson. The photos captured were now used in all herpetology books showing the rare event, something Carson was still proud of. He had even briefly considered going into herpetology as a profession, but the constant fieldwork was too much for him. He was more a golf-during-leisure-time kind of person. The doctor track seemed a good fit. He could always catch lizards for fun.

The final inventory of what to take with him was very minimal— his favorite Kathy Ireland swimsuit poster, his bedroom pillow, the Zeist microscope, and an old box of condoms which he had never used and probably never would. Kayenta would be a long, dry spell and Carson should accept that.

Watching the valley of the sun disappear into his rearview mirror now, its smog-filled basin slowly giving way to stands of saguaros and finally hardy junipers, left Carson to wonder how he would perform professionally with few backup doctors and only three years of residency training.

When you leave residency you are supposed to be able to effectively practice medicine, but any doctor will tell you it takes years to really understand the art of medicine and the first few are a continuation of the learning process. Carson fully understood he would be Kayenta's medical doctor for a variety of ailments, including minor surgeries and obstetrics, his least favorite subject. Birthing babies was not something he enjoyed. He found it terrifying, more often than not. It only takes one bad delivery to destroy a doctor's career. Good outcomes are dictated generally by having good prenatal care. Carson could just imagine some 16-year-old coming in at delivery never having been seen before. So much for the derm residency, herpetology might be back on the table. Most places in America use obstetricians, but in rural areas the family doctor is still the go-to person, and that was going to be his new title. Dr. Go-To, until he botched a case. He would get plenty of experience in Kayenta whether he liked it or not.

The two-hour travel time to Flagstaff, the last major city before hitting the reservation, went quickly with Maroon 5 and Adele tunes blasting. Carson concentrated on his immediate challenges. The fourth of July weekend started Friday, and his supervisor had emailed telling him he was low man on the totem pole and would be on-call all weekend. He alone would cover the small hospital/clinic over the holiday break.

Stopping off to enjoy his last Starbucks for what might be months, if not a year, and at a Blake's Lotaburger to refill his energy, made Carson long for medical school where it was all about learning and minimal responsibility. He had never been to an Indian reservation other than to gamble at the large Casino Arizona at Salt River on the east side of Scottsdale. It seemed no different than Las Vegas, and he wasn't sure he had ever noticed Indians in the casino. Carson knew Kayenta was not going to be anything like Casino Arizona. Waiting for the burger to come out, Carson cruised the Internet on his iPhone. He found a site he had never seen and shuddered at what he read. The site was on obscure places to visit. It proclaimed Kayenta, Arizona, to be "the most remote town in the United States." When Carson read this he cursed his recruiter once again. As he bit into his last delicious Green Chile Lotaburger for who knows how long, Carson studied his 1960s vintage road map which his father had given him to help familiarize him with Indian country.

This map represented his new life and he decided he would learn the numerous small villages listed, a way to test his memorization skills which are so important in medicine. This would be fun for Carson. The trip from Flagstaff to Kayenta would be about three hours in length, best he could guess. Carson would leave Flagstaff heading north on Hwy 89, and would enter the Navajo reservation near Cameron. From there, he would repeat each name in order as he drove northeast on Hwy 160 until he got to Kayenta.

Cameron, Tuba City, Moenkopi, Tonalea, Red Lake, Cows Spring, Black Mesa, Shonto, Tsegi, and finally Kayenta. CTCMT RLCS BMSTK. He used the mnemonics to help him learn the 10 villages located on this stretch, his new stomping grounds. Carson was trying to make this part of the world familiar so he would know if his patients lived in Black Mesa, Shonto was not far away. He had learned early in his medical career, the better he could relate to his patients, the more likely he would be able to help them with their problems. Carson wrote the town names on Blake's napkins like flash cards, trying to get ready for his big test. He was going to miss memorization and taking tests. It was something he was good at. He wasn't sure being a doctor would be his calling even though he had just spent seven years learning his trade. Truth be told, he was scared of what awaited him.

The drive up the sparsely traveled road proved beautiful. Carson made mental notes of the topography, which seemed to change at every bend. North of Flagstaff the land opened up into a wide vista, no more trees, just snake weed and miles of open range with the occasional cow or horse. Long lines of the highway's green grass juxtaposed against fields of yellow buffalo grass made for a picture-like setting.

Hitting Tuba City, he was embedded on the Navajo reservation. The environment seemed to change. The city was poor, that was obvious, but there were signs of modern life in the form of a bank, grocery store, and omnipresent fast-food joints. The homes seemed to be all facing the same direction, pointed at a slight angle, almost as if to live here you had to be in sync with each other's architectural aesthetics. Carson, who was very observant, realized this was not by chance and must be something inherent within the Navajo culture. He would ask about it once he was settled in.

The final stretch to Kayenta became rugged, low-riding mesas of red, much more closed-in feeling then around Tuba City. He liked what he saw. Carson knew he was arriving with a negative outlook on his duty station, but now he began feeling that maybe this land of red mesas and poverty could somehow also hold enjoyment for him.

The first few minutes after pulling into Kayenta were exciting and unnerving at the same time. Carson was trying to take it all in, each road-sign name and retail establishment. This was now home, as crazy as it seemed. No big cities for the next two years, except on the occasional holiday furlough, which looked like it would be rare as he had already pulled the 4th of July weekend shift.

It was June 30th and it was his last day of freedom before reporting to duty. He decided to drive around the town and get the lay of the land.

It didn't take long. He was thrilled to see there was some shopping and dining, even if it was of the McDonald's and Burger King variety. It wasn't complete isolation if you could get a Big Mac or a Whopper. There were large tour buses in some parking lots so at least there was the potential to meet someone other than the local inhabitants even if it was for a brief encounter.

The most prominent geographic marker was Agatha's Point, a multimillion-year-old volcanic Huerfano, or butte, which was visible from all advantages. This would be Carson's landmark for north, his orientation beacon.

As much as he didn't want to see the clinic, he couldn't help himself and proceeded on to his new home.

Driving slowly past the entrance sign that read Kayenta Clinic, he saw multiple trailers which were the medical buildings. Seeing the makeshift facilities made Carson's heart rate increase with the classic flight-or-fight response, and he wanted to perform the flight part of the adrenaline rush. The Kayenta Clinic would be his first real job as a physician with no lifeline. He wasn't sure if this would even be his post. He might get the "no photo available" clinic for all he knew. The thought that this antiquated clinic might not even be his actual assignment made Carson want to stop the car and run in and find out immediately what his duty station would be. He fought the urge and decided to return to his self-guided tour of the town. Going into the clinic might risk being put to work immediately. He had learned in medical school to never show up anywhere early as it usually meant more work.

Kayenta was typical small-town America in many ways, with its 5,000 in population. The only difference was it was 98% Navajo, or Diné, as they called themselves, and English was the second language, not to mention the 40% poverty rate. Carson drove his low-riding Mustang convertible down every paved road. There weren't many. He saw the high school, primary school, and the only grocery store, Bashas', which actually looked nice. He then ventured outside the town's perimeter. That's when things got dicey. Trailers. Wooden shacks, most decorated with abandoned cars and ancient appliances surrounding their front doors. There were dogs everywhere. None had collars. All looked like strays and were similar in appearance. Dark brown and black, their origin might have been

Australian Shepherd. Their tails were raccoon-like. They mostly had long noses and many seemed malnourished. He figured that on the reservation there were no rules on dog control so they just bred unmonitored; no such thing as getting your dog fixed. It was an odd thing to see so many sad-looking animals with no apparent owners. He wondered if his patients might have the same type of issues. He hoped not.

After circling about, he decided the town itself was nothing special. Strip malls and fast food. Carson's first official meal in town was at Burger King. It would not be his last there, he was sure. The restaurant had an interesting display on the code talkers of WWII. Reading the story of Navajo men whose language could not be broken by the Japanese and who helped win the war for America made Carson realize he would always be at a disadvantage trying to get medical histories out of patients who would no doubt speak with clicks and lisps in every other word. The world's best interpreters couldn't decipher their language, so how could he hope to? The dinner—a double cheeseburger—didn't match the Lotaburger in Flagstaff, but it did make him feel he was still in America, which helped ease his loneliness.

Carson checked in to the hotel. The front-desk clerk barely looked up from her computer, an ominous sign. His room was booked for a two-week stay. His hotel was nice. It wasn't the Arizona Biltmore Resort & Spa in Phoenix with its million-dollar Maynard Dixon mural, but it was brand new. The Hampton Inn would be his new home for the next couple of weeks.

The views out his eastern-facing window were spectacular. Vistas of red and orange mountains juxtaposed against the McDonald's golden arches made for an almost comic-book image of unreality.

The I.H.S. provided housing, but he had been informed last week his permanent residence would not be ready for two weeks, as it was being treated for a significant bee infestation. The bees had apparently taken up residence in the old trailer which would be his new home. Carson had a serious allergy to bees, and the thought of a potentially deadly outcome to his relocation was disconcerting, even for a man who had seen worse. One sting and if he didn't have an EpiPen he was a goner, or if he got multiple stings, no antidote would help. There was no medical treatment to be had. The medical treatment was just him. He *was* the doctor. He would be happy to stay at the new hotel as long as possible.

He had emailed the head of housing and expressed his deep concern with bees and said he would prefer to stay in the hotel until there was no chance of his being stung. Carson also wanted to hang on to maid service as long as feasibly possible. He had attached a copy of his medical record showing his severe reactivity to bee venom to reinforce the importance of a safe environment. The subtext he tried to communicate: You don't want to kill the golden goose before you have a chance to drain him of his life force first. Carson knew he was valuable property and the I.H.S. would want to protect its investment.

He decided to break out the Kathy Ireland poster so as to have an image communicating home. Carson had had many nice dreams looking at the poster, and at 28 he figured he wasn't too old to have a few more. He lined up his polo shirts in the small closet, his golf caps above them. No ties necessary, at least. He tucked several pairs of slip-on shoes onto the closet floor. Catching a glimpse of himself in the bathroom mirror, he saw short blonde hair and the slightly off-kilter nose he had broken taking a basketball in his face in medical school. It added character.

The next day would start his two-year grind. He would get a good night's sleep and start fresh. He had bought a calendar in Flagstaff along with some food and drink supplies. Each month of the calendar had an Arizona animal. July was the Western diamondback rattlesnake, an auspicious beginning. Carson planned to pass the time by marking off each day of the two-year stint. Tomorrow was day one. Checking into a new environment is difficult for any young professional, but as Carson would soon find out, he was not very welcome here, or at least his name wasn't.

CHAPTER 5

CALL ME DR. DICK INSTEAD

Each trailer at the Kayenta Clinic had a stenciled name on the front. Optometry. Dentistry. Counseling. Clinic. Since the Clinic sign was smack in the middle of the building complex, he figured this must be the place where they were expecting him. Finding the medical complex again had not been hard. It was on one of the few paved roads that wasn't either Highway 163 or Highway 160/64. It was directly across from the elementary school and only a five-minute jaunt from the hotel. Two large water towers marked the spot. It seemed to be humming with activity, which surprised Dr. Riddly as he hadn't expected much of anything. The local police had actually set up and turned on their lights, stopping the minuscule traffic to let the nurses and staff cross the street to begin their day. Carson thought this was odd but in a town so small, how much was there to do? This would be a different kind of existence, it was clear.

Carson was ready to meet his staff, having practiced his introduction line in the mirror a dozen times before leaving the motel. He was surprised how natural it sounded coming out of his mouth at the clinic's check-in desk now. "Hi, I'm your new family practice doctor. Today's my first day," Carson announced to the receptionist, hoping to break the ice. She was obviously Indian. Carson couldn't tell a Hopi from a Navajo at this point, but he assumed she was Navajo as this was Navajo country. Without looking up from her cell phone, on which she was furiously texting, she nodded her head to the right as if to go that way.

"Thanks?" Carson had a bad feeling that his first contact was with a person who couldn't or wouldn't make eye contact and didn't even say hi. He looked down the long linoleum hall lined with medical posters, most of which looked out of date, all in Navajo, and saw what he was looking for: the administration office.

Walking through the door, Carson saw the first positive sign for working in Kayenta. Sitting behind a computer screen was a mid-twenties, dark-complected knockout of an administrator. Her hair looked long enough to touch the ground and her facial features were strong with a perfect nose and high cheekbones. Carson was shocked at how attractive the young Navajo woman was. His heart picked up its pace.

"Hi. I'm Doctor Riddly. I'm reporting for a two-year duty." He announced this like he was a private in the military.

"Oh hi, I'm Brenda Wildhorse. I heard we were getting some fresh meat around here," she replied, laughing as if she really meant it, her smile infectious.

"Great, hope you like white meat?" Carson was surprised by his unprofessional and racially slanted joke.

Brenda fortunately laughed. "Sure, I eat it every once in a while."

Was it his imagination, or was there a hint of lust in her voice? In any case, Carson's own sexuality immediately responded to her voice. It had been a long time since he had felt his face flush.

"So Dr. Riddly, you got a first name or do you want to call me Ms. Wildhorse?"

Carson caught the fact that she had said Ms. and for the first time in a month was starting to feel a little hope about his bleak working environment. "Sorry, my name is Carson. Carson Riddly." Right away, he could tell something changed in her demeanor like an on-off switch had been activated.

"Oh. Carson, huh," Brenda frowned.

This is where Carson Riddly screwed up for the first time as a doctor on the Navajo Nation, and it had only taken five minutes. He had not read his history books and should have, or he would have never made his next fatal joke.

"Yeah, like Kit Carson, the famous frontiersman." He thought that being Indian she would know about Carson and might like a guy who was named after a rugged outdoorsman. The reality was that he was named after Johnny Carson. His dad loved "The Tonight Show" and had paid homage to the man by naming his only child after his favorite celebrity. What the now instantly blackballed Dr. Carson Riddly didn't understand, was Kit Carson in 1864 had rounded up the Diné, burned their peach orchards in Canyon de Chelly just 50 miles from the spot where he was standing, destroyed all their sheep and homes, and starved Brenda's great-great grandparents into submission. Of the 10,000 Navajos sent on the Long Walk, some 1,500 had died en route, and another 1,500 capitulated to disease within their first year in prison. For Brenda Wildhorse, Kit Carson was still recent history and Carson Riddly was now on her shit list for life. He would have been better off being named after Charles Manson.

"So, Kit, I must warn you there are lots of Navajos who don't like whites any more now than they did 150 years ago, and there are lots of them here in Kayenta. The white meat you mentioned earlier could easily be eaten if you let too many people know your namesake, if you get what I'm saying." Brenda then brusquely tossed a packet of paperwork at him to fill out, adding, "Don't leave any blanks, and then go down to the end of the hall and see the head nurse, Cheryl Tsosie. She will orientate you. Two years can be a long time." With that she looked down at her desk and ignored the now red-faced Kit Carson Jr.

Carson had never experienced such an internal transition from sexual excitement to outright fear. He had set her off and it was something to do with Kit Carson. Not a good beginning. She was right. Two years could be a very long time if the staff you depend on hates you.

Determining which nurse was Cheryl was not hard. She was barking orders in Navajo to some young girls and had obviously been in charge for a while.

"Hi Cheryl, I'm Carson." Carson used his first name to try and make a personal appeal to let her know they were equals. Besides, he didn't know how Brenda had pronounced Cheryl's last name Tsosie, and figured he wasn't doing too well with names this morning.

"Carson, well that's an interesting name for a man treating Navajos," Cheryl said, looking him up and down as if he was a dress she was thinking of buying.

"You know Cheryl, I'm afraid there must be something I don't understand about my name. People are not responding very positively when I introduce myself."

"Do you know anything about our Long Walk in the 1860s?"

"Sorry, didn't learn that in school. Sounds like I should have," Carson admitted.

"I'm not surprised. The white schools don't seem to find this part of their American history so compelling." Cheryl spoke eloquently for the next 10 minutes, explaining thoroughly the painful passage of her people, her voice strong yet breaking at certain points that were too personal for a white boy from a rich family to understand. Yet he needed to if he was going to be able to help understand the people his own ancestors had potentially brutalized.

Carson, who was shocked at the story of the Long Walk and his incredible stupidity at joking that he was named after Kit Carson, felt like shit. He wanted to be Bill Murray from *Groundhog Day* and start all over, this time explaining to Brenda he was named after a comedian, Johnny Carson, not a man who led to the death of so many of her people. All he could do was look Cheryl in her eyes and suggest, "Call me Doc Riddly from this point on. I understand and do not want to cause my patients any discomfort." He said this with such compassion it was obvious he felt remorse for all the whites he represented.

"OK, Doc Riddly. You pass the Tsosie test. By the way, I'll talk to Brenda. She already let me know what you said. She's young and didn't understand how an educated man who was going to work with Navajos could not know about such a tragic event in our recent history. She assumed you were just an asshole, rich white guy who didn't like Navajos. I'll let her know you aren't an asshole, just rich and white, or as we call you whites, *bilagaana*, a word you will want to memorize."

Part of Carson's right lip twitched upward in a semi-smile as the social tension broke. His father was right. He would learn a lot. First lesson: don't make jokes about a culture you don't know dick about.

CHAPTER 6

A NEW SANTA FE SPACE

It had been a year and half since Charles Bloom's near-death experience in New York City. The trauma of the ordeal was finally starting to subside. The flashy art world headlines had been like a recurrent nightmare that was now slowly fading from memory. The intense press coverage that followed for the first few months was smothering. Every major art magazine had a feature story, and all went into gory detail. They all called Bloom's Gallery for the inside scoop. An answering machine message said Mr. Bloom was on an extended vacation and they were referred to his website, www.bloomsgallery.com, and to his blog for additional information. Amazingly, for the first time, Bloom's actually made a few Internet sales from those individuals who couldn't get enough of the story.

Googling the words "Bloom's Gallery" now prompted five top listings related to articles on the New York City debacle. The first ranking was a sordid front page *New York Times* article about Bernard Phillips and his bizarre Paint by Numbers theory about the work of dead artists increasing in value, which had ultimately led to

Bernard's own death. Numerous ongoing blogs commented on Charles Bloom's role in the whole affair of tracking down Indian painter Willard Yellowhorse's murderer, and of course how it had affected the art market for Yellowhorse's paintings and his friend Craig Lendskip's sculptures, both skyrocketing in value after their deaths.

Recuperating from the frenetic art scene of Santa Fe and the barrage of questions from art enthusiasts all over the nation became critical for Charles's mental health. Most of his recovery time had been spent living near the Toadlena Trading Post on the Navajo reservation with Rachael Yellowhorse, his now very serious girlfriend, in her prefab aluminum hogan.

Preston Yellowhorse, Rachael's nephew and Willard Yellowhorse's son, was 17 now and would be leaving for college in just a few months. The living arrangements in the hogan were tight to say the least: three adults, two small bedrooms, and a very tiny bathroom with an inadequate water heater. When Preston finally did leave it would be time for a serious reality check for the devout bachelor Charles Bloom. The talk of marriage was coming up more frequently and seriously, none of which was at his behest. He should have been looking forward to having the house and all of Rachael's time to himself, but the marriage issue was a problem for Bloom. Rachael was in her prime childbearing years and the close-knit Navajo community was starting to wonder why she was still living with the *bilagaana* if he wasn't going to marry her and have a family.

Charles Bloom, who was now 48, was convinced he was not the marrying type. Never in his playbook. The old "any woman who would marry me, I wouldn't want to be associated with" rationale.

It wasn't that he was against the institution. His parents had been married for 40 years. For some people, it was great, just not Charles Bloom. It was more the thought of a lifelong commitment that scared the shit out of him. Somewhere in his late thirties Charles had decided if two people really loved each other, then that should be enough to maintain a healthy long relationship. Why bring marriage into the equation? Half the time it spelled disaster, or at least this was Bloom's reasoning, and the marital statistics backed him up.

The other major change in Bloom's life was his gallery staff and location. He had only been back to Santa Fe twice for any extended period of time since he solved the mystery of Willard Yellowhorse's death and had almost been killed himself at the hands of the now dead New York art dealer Bernard Phillips: once in May and again during his busiest time, Indian Market weekend in August. The May trip had set Bloom's new direction in motion, its momentum having begun years earlier.

Three years ago, Charles had been dragged to a lecture at the Santa Fe Community College by his then off-again, on-again girlfriend Patty Doomsday. She was exactly the opposite of her name, an incredibly upbeat person whose shocking red frizzy hair said it all. She was a person who always craved to broaden her intellectual horizons and the horizons of anyone she might have been dating. Her parents had been classic hippies from Taos who raised their only daughter on a commune in northern New Mexico. Bloom often wondered if the name Doomsday was just made up by her wacked-out parents to bring attention to the world's dilemma, and deciding they liked the name they kept it.

Patty's educational attention that week was on shit, literally. The shit lecture was by a retired anthropology professor from Eastern New Mexico University, Dr. John Edwards James, PhD. He was a world expert on early Southwest man, specializing in petroglyphs. Charles Bloom had been mesmerized by Dr. James's voice and enthusiasm for such a crappy subject. The hour-long lecture topic was on desiccated human feces and what they can teach us about our origins. When the old professor came lumbering into Bloom's Gallery one early May morning, Charles knew it had to be more than a coincidence. Living out on the rez and being in intimate contact with Navajos and their culture had opened Bloom's mind to ideas like fate. This allowed him to embrace new ideas easier than before, except of course for the idea of marriage.

Bloom had decided it was time to call it quits in Santa Fe, lock the gallery doors, and return the keys to his cranky landlord. Remove the poorly visible signs (as if anybody would notice) and make his gallery strictly Internet. His www.bloomsgallery.com site had actually developed a nice little community of followers due to his unintentional notoriety, and Charles enjoyed blogging about his life with its oddly refreshing weekly catharses. Fate, however, had intervened in his plans for closing his brick and mortar location when old Dr. James trudged in. Bloom had had no intention of hiring anyone to run his gallery as he was trying desperately to de-leverage and stabilize his fragile financial position.

Dr. James was working his way up Canyon Road, stopping at any gallery that looked of interest to his discerning eye. He was hoping to find some part-time work to help fill his hours of retired boredom. Making money was not the motivation for finding employment. His wife of 45 years had died suddenly two years ago and his gregarious demeanor required human contact. A true teacher and showman doesn't find sitting at home reading textbooks about ancient human symbols in cave walls fulfilling. He needed somebody to talk to.

Bloom found the old professor just as charismatic again, and hired him on the spot. It shocked Bloom that he would do something so impetuous. He never looked up the professor's references or even asked about work experience. He strictly went with his gut. His gut had better be right because there was little extra capital left on the credit line that he expected the bank to call in at any minute.

That had been in early May, and Bloom figured if the old man was willing to work for minimum wage, which was still the highest in the country at $10/hour, Bloom could try him out through August and then make a decision. Full-time work in an intense retail environment like Santa Fe was exhausting, even for Bloom, a regular jogger in good shape at six-foot-one who still had a full head of thick, brown hair. Mostly, it was the fact that every time he started to get into his old rhythm of selling, someone would bring up the New York City Yellowhorse incident, and inevitably the sale was blown and his enthusiasm with it. Bloom's personal touch was just not back yet.

However, years of teaching about Indians and their long-ago past to bored farm kids at a small college had forced Dr. James to develop a skill for weaving interesting tales. Somehow this talent was able to wow his clientele into purchasing the artwork at Bloom's. James's professorial attitude brought a genuine quality to each piece; it was as if he was the interpreter of the past for Bloom's contemporary Native artists.

In Santa Fe, you have a six-month season to sell art. The season starts the last week in June, which coincides with the opening of the Santa Fe Opera season, and ends the week of New Year's Day. If you don't make enough money to cover the other six months, you're kaput. Even despite Professor James's best efforts, it was apparent to the seasoned art dealer Bloom that after August, which accounted for 40 percent of his sales, he would need to make some serious gallery changes or he would be dead in the water, come March. His good friend and fellow dealer Brad Shriver was his answer.

Shriver's Upper Deck Gallery was located overlooking the historic old Santa Fe Plaza. Its real estate was some of the most prized in the city. Unfortunately for Brad Shriver, the longtime owner, his octogenarian landlady, decided she was going to live to be 100 and raised the rent by 25 percent. The hefty increase insured he would only be working for her nursing home payments if he signed on for another five-year stint, or worse, it would put him under.

Charles Bloom, Shriver's best friend, decided a reinvention of sorts was necessary for both gallery owners' survival. So Bloom proposed that he, with his added new employee, and Shriver, with his need for cheaper retail space, should combine resources.

A small 950-foot studio right next door to Bloom's was the answer. The authentic adobe building was owned by the same family that rented Bloom his gallery space. Dangling their willingness to commit to a five-year lease in front of the greedy landlord convinced him to throw in the rent on the adjoining studio space for free, and thus their joint compound of contemporary art was formed. Shriver's Fine Art relocated into the bigger building, and Bloom's into the annex. Removing a coyote fence between the two lots dramatically increased the open space and made the studio seem more spacious. Rachael Yellowhorse consigned four of her early sculptures to the open outdoor space, with any sales proceeds to be equally split between the two galleries. Both men already dealt in contemporary art, with the only difference being that Bloom's only handled Native American artists. Brad Shriver's reputation and the newfound extra cash from a significant rent decrease resulted in funds for added advertising.

As for Bloom's, it was now an almost free space, except for electricity, a small amount of upkeep, Charles's minor contribution to

Brad's rent, and his one employee's marginal salary. If Dr. James could even occasionally sell one small painting, Bloom's could hold on and Charles didn't have to be there often. Charles figured he could come into town in August, stay in Brad Shriver's small guesthouse, and make enough money to keep Bloom's and the old professor around for at least one more year. He had an obligation to try and help his dedicated artists survive during poor economic times even if his heart was now back on the rez.

Ideally, life for Charles Bloom had become a quieter existence among a people he had developed a deep respect for, the Diné. He had arranged to start learning from the old trader who owned the Toadlena Trading Post more about Navajo rugs so he could work on a part-time commission basis there. Little could Charles have known that his bastion of tranquility, the Navajo reservation, could also hold its own hidden excitement, including real danger for the art dealer who had moved there hoping to escape the outer world's turmoil.

CHAPTER 7

LEARNING A TRADE, STEALING A TRADE

There are no university classes or trade schools on how to become an art dealer. A significant number come from the ranks of the collector world. A hobby gone postal, a successful dealer once confessed. "I was only trying to increase the breadth of my collection. Before I knew it, I was out of control," was how he described his de-facto profession. These possessed individuals are often the best in the business. They love everything about art and care more about the aesthetics and joy it brings than any monetary gain. These addicted folks' main goal is to own artwork and they absolutely hate to part with great examples. Selling a stellar piece is only done when it is necessary for financial viability or a better piece becomes available.

The art business is a profession, albeit one that one generally falls into, not a conscious career path. A typical example would be a doctor who avidly collects art and finds out he can buy and sell art and make a decent living while working only eight hours a day. No being on-call nights and weekends. Or a lawyer who collects art for the office and decides he likes the furnishing more than ruining people's lives. Often these individuals are smart and insightful, with well-formed cerebrums of both left and right regions, which allow for critical assessment with a creative bent.

The business skill-set of successful art dealers must be well-honed to navigate the unregulated, imperfect art market which rewards risk takers and punishes mistakes viciously. There are no practical guidelines or agencies to price or regulate art. One can attempt to use auction records or past published sales as objective criteria, but often these are flawed. The records tell nothing about the condition of the piece, its authenticity, or the environment under which it was sold, all critical factors in determining value.

Galleries that publish prices and images on their websites (these are rare) are useful as a gold standard, but these still require investigation of individual pieces to have a realistic understanding of value, which is an art form in itself.

Measurable parameters in evaluating artwork include condition, provenance, location, date, size, signature, media, rarity and especially freshness to the market. Using only objective criteria to evaluate a piece may lead to an inaccurate value, because art is also about visual appeal. The painting has to work on a completely subjective level. Is the piece unique, interesting, challenging, disturbing, revolutionary, or just plain pretty? These right-brained computations take time to digest and regurgitate in a manner the buying public will believe and understand. This is why the best art dealers are collectors. They have already spent 10,000 hours learning why the piece works (or not) before they try to turn their sensibilities into avenues for commerce.

Most beginning dealers learn their trade by working in close association with an experienced dealer. It helps to have a mentor—a gallery owner who will allow you to work and learn from their years of experience. Art is a tricky business because knowledge is a powerful instrument which most dealers don't want to share. Revealing a client list is equally verboten.

The intricate process of becoming a professional art dealer usually takes years, which is why it's a small community. The nature of such a close-knit world also means if you start deceiving other dealers or collectors, word spreads and your days as an art dealer are numbered. Then you move on to a new venture, like real estate.

For Darryl Ridgemount the idea of dealing in art as a profession never crossed his mind until he was 35, and only after years of stumbling and falling through many of life's other choices. His secret dream had been to be a dance instructor, but growing up in poverty had jaded his sense of security. He could only be happy when he had money. His most lucrative work to date had been strong-armed robbery, embezzlement, and as a gigolo for males or females, though females were by far preferred.

The art field would have been Darryl's last choice as a career if it weren't for Melinda J. Hughes, a recent divorcee from one of Texas's best-known oil tycoons. Melinda was the current lover of Darryl Ridgemount. Dealing in art seemed a feminine career choice to Darryl, which was odd considering he did not think the same of teaching dance professionally. But the fact was that art dealers seemed to live well, plus the work was not illegal and therefore not highly risky. These two factors sealed his selection process. He became an art dealer.

His good fortune to find Ms. Hughes came through his dancing prowess. Darryl competed weekly at dancing events. He danced to win money, but truly enjoyed the athleticism it required. On the dance floor he felt joy and it showed. The odd couple had met late one night in an Austin bar, the Lazy X, known for its high-quality patrons and expensive liquor. Ridgemount often used the bar as a home base to seduce woman and then extract money from them. The usual method was through sex, but blackmail was not out of the question. Whatever worked for the greatest gain and the least amount of work.

The night they met, he was at the top of his game: a titillating tango performed in front of Melinda with a young attractive professional from the nearby Dell headquarters was his calling card. Gyrating hips and quick turns, plus occasional eye contact with the nearby Melinda Hughes, seduced her before a single word was ever spoken. Darryl had known who she was and his dance performance was partially for her benefit.

Unfortunately for the vulnerable Ms. Hughes (and her old husband's bank account), she fell hard for the tall Texan with the thick western drawl. Money for Melinda Hughes would never be a problem in the community property state of Texas, as her now ex paid up big time for a failed 20-year second marriage. There wouldn't be a third.

Mr. Hughes was Bill "Gusher" Hughes, a fifth-generation Texan who earned his nickname Gusher after his first and most important oil find. The Permian Basin, a geographical formation, runs the length of west Texas. Deep land structures know no state borders. Its precious dark fluids seep deep underground throughout oil-rich west Texas, and in a few spots into the barren landscape of economically challenged eastern New Mexico's *Llano Estacado*. You could always tell when you crossed over the New Mexico state line from Texas as the spacious two-lane highway became a bumpy one lane and went from black top to a worn-out gray.

Bill was as Texas as they come, but thought his fellow Texas brethren were missing the boat by not looking beyond the state border, their Texas roots obscuring their business sense. Looking along the horizon just north of Artesia, New Mexico, Bill could tell the topography was identical to Lubbock's, just a bit flatter, with fewer trees and more antelope. Bill figured, "Hell, the people around these parts sound like they're from Texas, anyway. There's got to be oil under this here earth, and lots of it," and he was very right, even if his deductive reasoning was a bit flawed. The Hughes field was such a major and unexpected mother lode, the oil community could only describe his first well in terms of "a true gusher." The expression rubbed off, and he became Bill "Gusher" Hughes.

All Bill's money now gave his ex, Melinda, plenty of time for the "finer and funner things in life," as they say in Texas, and Melinda indulged in them all. Melinda loved dancing and pictured herself as the young Dell executive in Darryl's arms, even if she was five-foot-four and pushing 175 pounds. Dancing with the much younger, still-virile Ridgemount made her feel 20 years younger, and the bonus was she relished the turnabout as fair play when thinking of her secretary-chasing, infidel ex-husband who she had recently unloaded. It was her turn for fun, and lots of it, and not while she was married.

Melinda's true passion was the arts. She decided she would waste money on art and Darryl, and not in that order. Both were things you didn't need, but craved anyway. Melinda and Darryl spent their evenings visiting art galleries and museum openings. Darryl's day required visiting Melinda's bed, a prerequisite for his boyfriend status.

Shopping for Melinda was also a daily exercise and she spent voraciously, not unlike her sex drive. Nothing was lost on Darryl. Her favorite art purchases were masters of the early west, like Frederic Remington and Maynard Dixon. "Painters who had stones," she told dealers. It's unusual for a woman to be the primary art buyer of large-ticket works, especially in the western genre, but Melinda loved the attention and manipulating the male art dealers at their own game. She would hammer some viciously (the less charismatic ones), while others, who were to her liking, she never bargained with, even for a cent. "A woman's prerogative. My money, and I'll spend it how I like—art or men," she liked to brag to her rich divorced girlfriends.

In the divorce settlement, Melinda was awarded their magnificent art collection, which both Hugheses had carefully assembled. During the marriage, Melinda focused on acquiring the paintings and Bill the western memorabilia and Indian art. They had always planned to donate it to some Texas institution. He wanted U.T., she Baylor. Their names would be etched in perpetuity. When Gusher left his long-term spouse for his new young secretary Tiffany, all Melinda's lofty plans flew out the proverbial window and she decided to make him pay. She'd take all of the art collection. The only etched name would be hers, and it would be most likely at Baylor, though she was an ardent U.T. football fan.

The art collection was a nonnegotiable point for Melinda. She wanted the entire collection, including Bill's prized Navajo blanket and rug collection. She didn't particularly care about "these Indian things," as she called them at the final hearing. She was a flat-art kind of girl. But because he cared so deeply about the blankets, she demanded them in spite. "If he wants that big-titted Tiffany instead of me, he's going to have to start from scratch on his precious blanket collection," she told her lawyer at their first meeting, making clear her intention to deprive Gusher of his Navajo textiles.

The Navajo blanket collection that Bill gave up was deep in quality, but still had a few glaring holes he hadn't been able to fill. Because he still hadn't found those key blankets, Bill figured he could replace the collection over time, albeit at a much higher cost basis. He had become emotionally attached to many of the weavings. Watching them go was hard for a man who was used to getting his way. Grudgingly he gave in to Melinda's demands, for at that point in time he still liked Tiffany's ass better than the blankets she used to lie on.

CHAPTER 8

NAVAJO BLANKETS

Those with real wealth in America and those who seriously collect art usually have one common denominator: they maintain in their employment a personal curator for whatever they might collect. This person is in charge of cataloging, authenticating, and advising, most importantly to keep up with the Joneses. You never know when you might need to express your curator's viewpoint at some important social event, as in, "Our art curator thinks our collection should be featured at the Met, as it's now at that level."

Generally these private curators are smart, interesting, over-educated individuals who for some reason didn't mesh well in the museum world. In some cases, the money is more lucrative working for the very rich. Many of these personal guiders of artistic taste have side businesses appraising or selling art, although retail is a disdain of most academic types. A large majority of curators think of themselves strictly as educators, not sales people.

art curator to the rich

Trevor Middleman was the quintessential personal curator, Melinda's trusted dictator of taste for 10 years. "Ms. Hughes" was his first priority and he put her needs always above his own. During the divorce settlement, Middleman and the family dog Rosie got equal billing. Bill wanted and got the black lab, Rosie; Melinda got Trevor. Gusher figured you could always find another textile curator, but a good hunting dog is much harder to come by.

Trevor's training was outstanding, having a bachelor in fine arts degree from U.C.L.A. and a master's in fiber composition. An impeccable résumé. His primary love was for all types of textiles.

Educated in dye and yarn composition, Trevor had grown into a respected expert in the field. His interest in Navajo weavings was piqued while watching an episode of the "Antiques Roadshow" in 2002 and seeing an early Navajo chief's blanket being discovered in Tucson, Arizona. A clearly excited appraiser claimed the blanket to be "a national treasure." Trevor couldn't have agreed more. The 150-year-old blanket with its simple lines of blue, brown, and white wool was mesmerizing. Trevor decided the Hugheses must begin in earnest building their fledgling Navajo blanket collection to include the best examples. Bill, who had also seen the show, was as excited by Trevor's planned collection expansion and decided he too would start seriously learning the intricacies of these Indian blankets.

Like most academically inclined curators, Trevor Middleman didn't understand or care much about market pricing. But when it came to the nuances of what made a weaving rare, nobody was better at evaluating than Trevor. In time this made the Hughes collection special, as it now contained a large number of early rare examples, all in excellent condition with outstanding provenance on each piece.

To truly appreciate Navajo blankets, you first have to understand the people who wove them. The Navajo were a nomadic people living in northeastern Arizona and northwestern New Mexico. Their life was spent raising sheep and raiding those who ventured too close to their land: first the Spanish, then the Mexicans, and later the Americans. The raiding stopped permanently after Kit Carson rounded up the Navajos at the behest of the United States Government, and starved them into submission. In 1864 the Navajos were sent on a 400-mile forced march to imprisonment at Fort Sumner in the *Llano Estacado* (Bosque Redondo) of eastern New

Mexico. This march became known as The Long Walk. The great blankets made before, during, and slightly after their imprisonment are referred to as classic period blankets. They are the most sought-after of all the Navajo textiles. Early chief's blankets, like the one on the television show, fall into this classic period. So do other chief's blankets referred to as second phase and third phase, along with dresses, mantas, serapes, and ponchos.

The wool used during the classic period was from the Churro sheep. It had a long staple fiber and was not too greasy. The Spanish Churros originated from the Spanish conquistador Coronado who arrived in New Mexico in the 16th century bringing them with him. These were hardy animals much like the Navajos themselves. The name "chief's blanket" was a misnomer, as the Navajos have clan leaders but no real chiefs. The chief's blankets, which were prized by other tribes of Native people too, were often draped on the shoulders of Plains Indian chiefs, as evidenced by historical photographs. These blankets, woven wider than long, are classified stylistically and chronologically. The first-phase type is the simplest in design and the earliest. Their production was from around 1800 until 1865.

First-phase chief's blankets are exceptionally rare today. There are maybe 50 still in existence. Pristine examples can be worth over a million dollars. Navajo textile collectors covet these over all other pieces, and Bill "Gusher" Hughes had never been able to acquire a quality example. He was glad he hadn't, as "giving it over to the bitch," as he now referred to Melinda, might have been too much. So he told his lawyer as he signed the final documents giving away his prized blanket collection.

Once he had come very close to buying a first phase when he underbid on a marginal example at Christie's auction house. Trevor Middleman had decided that a better blanket could be found, one in more pristine condition that had a better provenance, and so he had not been aggressive in his encouragement of Bill's bidding. It was the only time Bill wondered why he listened to his supposed fiber expert (although now of course he was glad he had). No other examples had come up since and it had been several years. He had been kicking himself ever since, up until the divorce. A simple blue, brown, and white first phase was now number one on Bill's wish list. He was planning to reacquire a significant Navajo blanket collection, and he wouldn't let money or Trevor's stupid opinion get in the way of the next opportunity he had (if ever).

The classic second-phase chief's blanket was the next development in Navajo aesthetics. It's basically a first-phase design with twelve carefully placed red bayeta rectangles laid on top. A great example might bring a quarter of a million dollars or more if it were early, in great condition, and well woven with good provenance. Bill (now Melinda) had two of these in the important Hughes collection.

The third-phase chief's blanket is the next evolution. These blankets' backgrounds are also in the banded first- and second-phase tradition, but with nine diamonds, triangles, crosses, or rectangles laid over the indigo blue, natural white, and brown bands. Third-phase chief's blankets came in a variety of prices depending on age, quality, materials, and history, with the top end somewhat less than a second phase in value, and the low end still valued in tens of thousands of dollars.

Bill decided he had plenty of money, a hot girlfriend, and the only thing missing was a way to spend his ever-growing oil revenues. Putting together a world-class Navajo textile collection and donating it to his alma mater, the University of Texas at Austin, with only his name etched on the entrance of a building, would finally give him the sense of accomplishment he'd never gotten from drilling oil wells.

Gusher decided the fastest way to acquire major blankets was to go back to the source he knew had great ones: his ex-wife. Bill would embrace the enemy and make friends with Melinda's new boyfriend, the quasi-art dealer Darryl Ridgemount. Darryl seemed like the kind of man Bill could do business with. Bill knew to keep his friends close and his enemies closer.

Talking into the mirror looking at his sparse graying beard, he planned, "Yes, now that's using my noggin. Just screw her like she screwed me. We'll see who the better businessman is. I'll get old Ridgemount on my payroll too, a kind of double agent." As he said this, Gusher's face lit up. He loved the idea of fucking his ex-wife with her own boy toy and getting back his treasured blankets at the same time.

CHAPTER 9

MAKING A DEALER

Watching the drama of money and artwork changing hands hooked Darryl as much as he had hooked Melinda. Darryl particularly liked it when she bought Navajo textiles. It was clear she didn't have any real appreciation and was doing it more to compete with her ex than anything else. She didn't spend any time really looking at the pieces. She told Trevor, "If you think it makes the collection more complete, then get it. You know this isn't my thing." For Darryl, it was definitely his thing. He had always pictured himself in one of those early shoot-up westerns and the Indians always had beautiful blankets. When his mom used to bring home dates (as she called them) she always would stick him back in the den and tell him to watch a good cowboy and Indian movie. "I love the Indians, Darryl. You be a good boy while mommy works and go put a blanket on your shoulders and tell 'em 'How' for me." Darryl loved his mom and wished she had not given him away to the decrepit boys' home. He had always been a good child till then.

Darryl decided his new career would be as an art dealer focusing on Indian art, specifically Navajo textiles. He would drain Trevor's professional brain to learn his trade, easier then reading. Once he had enough knowledge he would go out on his own and use all of Melinda's contacts as clients. It seemed like a great scam, especially specializing in blankets. Melinda's girl friends would decorate with them and price comparison was nearly impossible, which allowed him to be aggressive on pricing and no one would know or care. A couple of clients like the Hugheses and he could retire, especially if they were as cavalier as Melinda was when it came to purchasing.

than

Darryl had vowed never to be a collector of anything himself, to sell everything. Don't get attached and cash was king. He was a piranha looking for meat—strictly for the money and he could give a shit about the beauty. That was Darryl's mantra. Convert all pieces quickly to cold, hard cash. Money was the object, not the art. He would make a great art dealer.

CHAPTER 10

THE CALL

Screwing someone's wife, even an ex-wife, can be a treacherous road especially if that someone is paying all your bills indirectly. If he had thought about it more, Darryl might've hesitated longer. But he didn't know what was coming when he answered his phone, offering his standard greeting, "Hello, this here's Darryl. How can I hep you?"

"Darryl Ridgemount?"

"Yep, that's me. How can I hep you?"

"Darryl, this here is Bill Hughes, I believe you know my wife rather well?"

Darryl's silence at his end of the conversation was deadening to his own ears, as he usually knew just what to say.

"You still with me there, Darryl?"

"Yes sir, I still am. Not exactly a call I was expecting. What can I hep you with?" This was where Darryl expected Mr. Hughes to tell him to get the hell off his hind tit and find a real job, and quit living high on the hog with his nightmare of an ex-wife. But pleasantly he got just the opposite.

"Well, it's like this, Darryl. You have direct access to something I would like very much and I'm hopin' you can help me out."

"Yes, I'm listening, Bill." At this point Darryl Ridgemount was all ears. He knew Bill wasn't calling for a friendly chat about a wife screwing. This call involved money and that was Darryl's true love.

Bill explained, "I need your help and you seem to be in an ideal position, so to speak. I love those damn Injun blankets my wife rooked me out of, and if I read you right I believe you could be my guy. I want you to wrangle a few back my way, at a handsome profit of course."

Darryl Ridgemount could be cautious, especially when it was potentially going to ruin his newly acquired golden calf, Melinda. "Nothing personal, Bill, but you at work?" Darryl inquired.

"Yeah, why?"

"I'd feel more comfortable if I called you back," Darryl suggested. "Let it go through your office system, make sure we are all on the same page, if you know what I mean."

"I understand completely, afraid somebody from Melinda's camp might be testing your loyalty or I'm doing some taping? I might not be who I say I am. That's smart boy, I like that. Sure, here's my number. I'll let Tiffany transfer the call through. She's the little filly that cost me all my pretty little blankets to begin with," Gusher chuckled at the irony of Darryl wanting to go through Tiffany first.

Darryl Ridgemount was rightfully afraid of Melinda doing some detective work. She had been getting closer to Darryl of late. An unsolicited test of loyalty was possible. Melinda might be in love but she was no fool. She might seem like one by wearing her neckline low and her eyelashes long, but she realized her best days were behind her. Good-looking men like Darryl were usually only after one thing: money.

Darryl was tall, with thick black hair, graying around the edges, a striking face in a rough kind of way, and he was very, very smooth. A man who could talk out of both sides of his mouth at the same time, his pearl-white teeth glowing. Truth and fiction blended together as one in a smooth lie tonic you never even knew you were swallowing. People liked and trusted him. Ridgemount played his part well with a strong Texas drawl, a west Texas variety. His accent said Amarillo panhandle, though he claimed origins in all cities in Texas depending who he was charming at the time. Everything was always described as "purtee." "Yes sir, this one here is quite purtee, the Amon Carter down in Ft. Worth doesn't even have something this nice," he'd assure, or, "Melinda, you're the most purtee thing my eyes have ever set on."

Using his folksy demeanor to lure the unexpected victim close, Darryl disarmed any hesitation one might have. He used this technique most effectively when he started practicing his true calling, art dealer. He was already running ads in small newspapers reading, "Good Christian collector now purchasing Indian and Western Art. Highest prices always paid, guaranteed!" The key words of deception were Christian, highest, and guaranteed. These three words should have translated to: "criminal, lowest, seller beware."

By running these ads in church, school, and retirement papers, he got his most lucrative pigeons. Old trusting widows were his favorites as they were the easiest to take advantage of, always falling for his hometown boy approach. They never knew he had just screwed them royally out of a prized family heirloom for pennies on the dollar. Time was spent talking about the family and dead husband, and how much he would love the piece for his own home, then wham, he offered a ridiculously low fee which he insisted he really shouldn't as it was overpaying.

Unfortunately for Melinda, she hadn't set up the loyalty check. It really was Bill Hughes. Darryl Googled the number Bill gave him and it was a match for Bill Hughes's office. When he called it, Tiffany answered, "Bill Hughes's office. This is Tiffany, how may I help you?"

"This is Darryl Ridgemount. I'm returning Mr. Hughes's call."

"Yes Mr. Ridgemount, he is expecting your call."

The background noise was the typical office chatter with distant phones ringing. The call was genuine. Darryl had an image of a blonde, big-breasted woman with a headset doing her nails at the other end. He wasn't far off. She had flaming orange hair, Gusher's favorite color.

"OK, Darryl, you convinced it's me?" Bill said.

Darryl decided to cut to the chase and find out what kind of man Bill Hughes was. He had heard Melinda's rants, but that was jealous wife crap. Darryl figured he could read Bill even if couldn't see the man's eyes. "Yes, I'm on the same page now. What kind of opportunity we looking at here, Bill, or should I call you Gusher?"

"Man who does his homework. I like that, means you're even smarter than I figured good you for. Tell you what: if you get some of my

Injun blankets back, you can feel free to call me Gusher. Till then, it's Bill. Here's the deal, Darryl, if I can call you that?"

"Sure, it's my God-given name, feel free," Darryl responded, although no one was actually sure of this, including Darryl.

"First of all, Darryl, let's get one thing straight. I could give a rat's ass that you're screwing old Melinda. You can do it till the cows come home for all I care. All I want are my blankets, and best I can figure, she's adding to the damn collection just to piss me off. I want her to stop buying and I want you to talk her into selling some, if not all, back to me. Now if she finds out it's me doing the buying, you'll be toast and we're both done. If you and I can play ball, I'll cut you a 20% finder's fee on top of what it cost me to buy them back, and just to sweeten the deal, that money can be cash and we're talking some fairly serious money. I will send you a copy of the original invoices of what each weaving cost so you will have a basis for buying them back. Remember this is between you and me, no one else will know. I want to build a world-class Indian blanket collection and I want it to be the Bill Hughes Collection not the Melinda Hughes Collection. This was my baby from the start, and I plan to keep it that way, even if I have to overpay a bit to do it."

Bill continued, "The gravy train doesn't have to end with Melinda, either. You can help me find lots of other great rugs and make a bundle of commissions off my fat wallet. Business with this Hughes means you can sleep in your own bed at night. So what do you say, my boy, care to screw my wife in a new sort of way? Could be fun, it's got to be better than what you got now."

Darryl liked what he was hearing. "I tell you Bill, what you're saying makes a lot of good horse sense. I think Melinda got you all wrong. I know she doesn't give a hoot about those damn rugs. This way she can make a nice profit on her investment and you get what you really love. The way I see it, everyone wins. I'll take care of everything. When you send the list, mark the ones you really want and I'll work on those first. This is going to take some tact, as I'm sure you know. If I can, I'll try to get the whole kit and caboodle. Since we're talking straight, Bill, I'm putting my neck on the line. I would think a little good faith advance would be a nice way to start off our budding relationship." Darryl never missed an opportunity to take advantage of the situation.

"Son, I'm happy to oblige you," Bill agreed. "Slip by my office in a couple of days, and there will be an envelope with copies of my receipts and $10K in cash. Good luck my boy, you've got your work cut out for you. She'll cut your balls off if she finds out you're working with me, you can trust me on that."

"I like my balls just where they're at. I'll get you your weavings. Start rounding up the cash."

Both men laughed as they hung up their phones.

CHAPTER 11

A NEW CURATOR

The plan was simple enough. Learn everything about Navajo weavings, then get rid of Trevor and step into his slot. The process by which it happened was a bit more complex. Darryl had picked up quite a lot listening to Trevor talk about the collection, but for him to become an expert would require books and reading, not favorite pursuits for a boy who grew up in an orphanage.

His mother had read to him before she dumped him off permanently, but at the Reed Baptist Christian Home for Boys, academia came to a halt and hard labor began. You worked, went to school, worked some more, and if time allowed, did homework. Feeding calves and bailing hay trumped schoolwork and no one cared about your grades, just how strong your back was. All the boys had the same look—poor haircuts, sunburnt skin, and strong physiques. Somehow the weak, sick kids never ended up at this home.

A faltering academic background left Darryl feeling dumb when it came to reading. He dreaded opening technical books about Navajo blankets. Luckily when he finally opened the thick textbooks, most had lots of colorful illustrations that allowed him to muddle through. Darryl enjoyed educational accomplishment for the first time in his life. He was now able to ask Trevor an art professional's intelligent questions.

Trevor was delighted to have someone who was interested in the Navajo textiles. Bill Hughes used to spend time with Trevor discussing the finer points of the collection. Trevor loved sharing his knowledge, pulling out each of the blankets, which were arranged chronologically, and having lengthy discussions about their history and yarn composition. Unbeknownst to Trevor, Darryl knew the costs and would quiz Trevor on these points to see if he would share what he knew, a tricky subject for many personal curators.

Surprisingly, Trevor would reveal price and current value. Cost was of little interest to Trevor, but was simply an annoyance he had to put up with as part of his job description. You didn't want to have something horrible like a flood or theft and not have a good accounting of what the collection was worth.

There were 40 textiles in the collection. Their current values ran from $10,000 to $350,000. Most seemed to be in the $50,000 range. Every time Trevor would announce a value, Darryl would do the math as to how much he would make on that piece or something similar to it if he couldn't get Melinda to sell. Bill was not kidding when he had said it was a nice chunk of change. If he could somehow get the collection as a whole, Darryl was looking at a bonus of nearly a half a million in cash.

The thought of so much money excited him tremendously. Darryl would use the imagery of a money pile as a visualization tool when he was having sex with the ever-growing Melinda as it helped him concentrate on his real mission, which was getting the damn blankets.

The daily lessons on blanket style, yarn composition, and dye analysis began to sink in. Darryl broke it down into his own terms.

Blankets which were made before the Navajos were imprisoned by Kit Carson were the most expensive and desirable and were thus hardest to find. The Hughes collection had about 20 of these, all early classic blankets including second and third phase examples, but no first phase.

The dyes in these early classic blankets were all natural, which could be confirmed through testing with a spectrophotometer. Darryl didn't understand dick about what this instrument was, but knew without it you couldn't determine age, and the blanket value would go down. Trevor explained in great detail the process, and who were the noted authorities in the field (he was also one but didn't share this with Darryl as he didn't like to brag). Darryl took down the names and number of these experts, lesson learned, and moved on except for one final question. "Could one ever use modern dyes that were the same kind as the old dyes and fool the experts?"

Trevor had never really thought about that possibility. He dealt with professional dealers who wouldn't consider such a travesty. Trevor mused, "One could have yarn that had the same dye and the spectrophotometer would read identical to the old dye. It would be hard to do for any blanket that was using the early yarn types like bayeta, as this can be either Cochineal or Lac dyed and the yarn has a very specific look. But for, say, a first phase—which is all handspun yarn and only indigo dye—it could be possible. These blankets rarely come on the market and usually have long family histories and are tremendous examples of workmanship so it would seem highly unlikely, but possible."

Darryl made a note with a little exclamation mark next to his scribble.

The bayeta Trevor referred to was primarily red yarn found only in expensive early blankets. It came from a commercial trade cloth that the Navajos would barter for. The many sources of cloth were meticulously raveled by the weavers, who were almost always women, and then re-spun or bundled together to make their own red wool yarn. Bayeta was the buzzword the Navajo rug dealers used to say "important and pricey." First-phase blankets generally didn't use bayeta; they were just blue and brown.

It took Darryl a month before he could recognize the weavings with bayeta, but like mastering a hard dance step, once he finally learned the moves it stuck. All the great blankets and rugs had the same thing in common: their wool was expertly spun and very fine and tight. Darryl would play a game with Trevor. He would have Trevor pick out 10 weavings and then Darryl would try and arrange them from tightest to loosest weave. Darryl always got it right. For Darryl, this was like rating a woman at a bikini contest. The big-boobed girls went to the front, and the flat-chested ones, the end.

Darryl had Trevor evaluate the weaknesses and strengths of the Melinda Hughes collection. Trevor was happy with what had been accomplished, but there were a couple of glaring holes. The most important weaving in any Navajo blanket collection is always a first phase. It's like Spiderman: #1 to the comic world. Trevor remembered Bill's tirades. "Trevor, goddamn it, why haven't we gotten one of those phase ones? I knew I should have bought that one at Christie's." Trevor explained how he had looked exhaustedly for a piece and even tracked down the "Roadshow" blanket, but it had gotten sold long ago to a museum in Detroit, so he had to be patient. Now that Ms. Hughes owned the collection, the pressure was off, as Trevor was pretty sure she wasn't even aware of what a first-phase blanket was. Chances were good that that part of the collection would just go unfilled.

The other blankets missing were by a couple of long-gone Toadlena/Two Grey Hills weavers, and should be able to be found in time. The saddle blankets were also not up to standard; they had to compete with some doctor in Tucson who kept buying all the good examples when they hit the market. Saddle blankets were more common, with the best examples coming from the 1890-1920 period. Trevor was looking forward to filling in this part of the collection as good examples could still be found at fairly reasonable prices. Little did Trevor know Darryl planned to fill these holes himself. Lots of church ladies' late husbands had owned saddle blankets, and there were great margins to be made there.

The receipts Darryl had gotten had helped him understand value and he spent endless hours on the Internet filling in any gaps. A website called www.navajotextiles.com had lots of examples and information, and most listed prices except for on the classic pieces. On these he emailed asking for prices, and they were good about giving the list price.

Six months into his self-taught course, Darryl finally felt he had the knowledge to work on prying loose the blanket collection from Melinda's liver-spotted grip. Bill was becoming impatient. It was time for Trevor's position to be filled with a new curator, Darryl Ridgemount.

CHAPTER 12

BIG BUGS!

To sabotage a 10-year fruitful relationship would be hard for most, but not Darryl. He had broken up many marriages in his career and this was nothing different, except Melinda wasn't sleeping with Trevor. In some ways it was easier. He knew Trevor would end up on his feet, and Darryl had a hell of a lot to gain by the destruction.

Blankets and moths don't mix. Moths like wool. In fact, they can destroy a great blanket in months if gone unchecked. Trevor had told Darryl a story of how a museum collection's first phase had been ruined in less than a year by poor entomology control. The Hughes collection was stored in a large humidity-controlled room, with all the blankets rolled on acid-free paper and left in complete darkness most of the time. Trevor's job was to check on the pieces and make sure they were taken care of properly. Trevor's annual two-week vacation was nearly over. He had gone to France to examine the Louvre's fifteenth-century tapestries.

Growing up in Texas, you learn a lot about where bugs hang out, especially if you're poor and live with them a good part of the time. Darryl's plan was simple: to spend a couple of nights collecting as many moths as possible and let them loose in the textile room. He also took a small c.1860 saddle blanket, a choice example that Trevor had commented was a favorite of Ms. Hughes's, and relocated it from the textile storage area to Trevor's closet. Ms. Hughes had given Trevor the guesthouse, and access was not hard for a resourceful man like Darryl.

Timing was everything. Darryl planned it perfectly. He used the movie *My Big Fat Greek Wedding* as a template. Let Melinda come up with the idea of firing Trevor.

Darryl asked if Melinda might give him a personal tour of the weaving collection since he thought her insight would give him a deeper understanding of what she liked about them. When she opened the door to the textile room—which Darryl had sabotaged by turning the heat up to its maximum—it was almost unbearable to enter. A large blast of hot air and numerous moths escaped simultaneously as Melinda released the locked door.

"My god, what in the world is going on in here!" Melinda screamed as the first wave of moths flew by. "It must be nearly 90 degrees in here. Where did those creatures come from? Moths are horrible on wool. I know those are moths. God, I wonder what kind of damage has been done. I can't believe Trevor would be so irresponsible, especially before leaving on vacation."

Darryl nudged, "I didn't want to say anything, Melinda. I know you care for him so much and I like him too, but he has been acting quite weird lately. I think there may be something else going on in his life, probably drugs. I've seen it before. For that many moths to have gotten in, he must have left the door open for some period of time. I hope all the rugs are here. Do you know how many rugs are in the collection?"

"About 40 I think. I got 36 in the settlement and I've added four since. You really think some could be missing?"

"Melinda, I hope not, but if you're drugged out, you often need money, and it doesn't seem like he gave a shit about the pieces with the heat on so hot. These moths must have been here for a while for there to be so many. I wonder when he checked on this room last. Any idea?"

"No," Melinda wailed. "Trevor has not said a word about the collection in months. You know it was really Bill's thing. I just kept the rugs to piss him off."

Darryl knew exactly how to play this: "Bill was a fool to throw away a woman of your quality and beauty. His loss, my gain. I'm with you, the blankets are fun in a tribal kind of way, but real art is what you should focus on. It can't be eaten. We better do a quick head count and make sure none of the pieces have disappeared or been ruined by moths."

Darryl had carefully set aside a weaving which Trevor had pointed out in one of his extensive tours, a great child's blanket that unfortunately had suffered fairly extensive moth-grazing in its camel colors on one side. He planned to upgrade to a better piece as soon as a replacement was located. Darryl had sprinkled most of the moths (which were not even wool moths but larger, more impressive-looking specimens) all over this piece, hoping at least one would stay around till the "unveiling."

"Melinda, I'm afraid you better take a look at this," Darryl motioned, pointing to two large moths sitting on the damaged portion of the child's blanket. "I'm afraid this one has already been damaged. Look, I'm sure moths did that." He pointed to the old moth grazing under a large, harmless moth.

"Goddamn that Trevor! How could he allow such a thing! And I fought to get him in the settlement. I wish I had taken Rosie instead. I can't believe he would betray my trust." Tears started to stream from Melinda's face, Darryl stepping over and hugging her tightly.

"Honey, don't worry. Trevor is not the person you thought he was. You're just a very trusting person and he took advantage of your generosity. We better make sure nothing's missing. This may even be worse than we think." A count of the pieces showed one was missing, a piece Melinda knew well. It was one of her favorites.

"Darryl, I think we have to search Trevor's room. I know damn well which blanket is missing, and if it's gone and he had anything to do with it, he's finished in this family."

"It takes a strong woman to realize what has to be done. If he stole from you, then he has left you no choice," Darryl agreed.

The master key to the guesthouse was used, and with a little prodding like a parent does on an Easter egg hunt, the blanket in question was discovered by Melinda under a large group of gay porno magazines. Darryl had thrown these in along with the last of his marijuana stash. "Nothing like a pile of gay men's magazines and a bag of dope to piss off a good Baptist woman," Darryl thought to himself as he watched Melinda's reaction, trying not to laugh.

"Well the nerve of that man! He's sick, Darryl. He needs counseling and fast. I can't have someone like that in my home, he might be dangerous," Melinda decided.

"I agree. I would never let him in this home again. Can you imagine—he's up here using drugs with who knows who, all under your roof. What if one of your friends found out? The word on the street would not be good."

"My god, can you imagine if that nosey Mary Beth got wind of his moral corruption? I would never hear the last of it. What should I do?"

This was what Darryl had been waiting for, the final kill of Trevor. "Follow your instincts and fire him, but do it in a very smart, ladylike Melinda Hughes fashion. Running him through the ringer won't help. A desperate man will make all sorts of accusations to try and tarnish your social standing in Austin. People like Trevor don't leave town. He will find another job and the bad mouthing will begin. As much as it will bother you I would simply give him a six-month severance package and tell him his services are no longer needed. You're going in a different direction. We will take your blanket back and confiscate his filthy magazines and drugs so he will know we are on to him. He won't say a word. He'll disappear and pop back up later and since you let him have his dignity he will only say nice things."

"Thank you so, so much Darryl. I don't know what I would do without your guidance and companionship," Melinda sighed.

"Don't worry about anything, my dear. I'll dispose of those illegal drugs and pornography, and I'll personally go through the rugs and make sure nothing is damaged. I do think you should think about disposing of the entire collection. Transfer the money you can make off them into an important oil painting, something that bugs can't eat. I have a connection to a collector in Japan who loves everything Indian and he would probably buy the whole damn thing, at a premium. Can you imagine if Bill found out his prized collection was in Japan? He would go ape."

"I like the sound of that," Melinda admitted. "Bill's dad was in World War II. He was a very angry man, much like his son, I might add. The Japs shot him down over the Philippines. He never forgave them. Gusher would just go nuts if his precious rugs left the country. Let's do it. Get Trevor out of my life and free up a room and plenty of money for my new purse collection, which I'm about to begin storing in the new purse storage area."

Later that evening while relaxing in his small apartment on the poor side of town, Darryl lit up a big fatty, the last of his stash, as he reviewed some good male porn. "Never hurts to see what the competition has to offer," he thought, as he compared his own tool to those of the professionals'.

CHAPTER 13

BEANIE BABIES

The exit of Trevor went as planned. His bags and walking papers were waiting when he arrived home from his French vacation. Melinda couldn't face the traitor. Darryl was more than happy to handle the unpleasant deed.

"Trevor, my friend, I've got some good news and bad news. Which you want first?"

"OK, I guess the good news?"

"You get another six months of vacation time." Darryl loved seeing Trevor's mind spin as he awaited door number two. He knew it wasn't going to be good.

"And the bad?"

"I'm afraid Melinda won't be needing your services any longer. She's going in a different direction and decided she no longer needs a personal curator. Trevor, with this poor economy she felt it just didn't look right to have an art curator on the staff. Besides, she isn't planning to add on to the existing collection. Here's six months of salary as severance pay and a nice letter of recommendation signed by Ms. Hughes." The letter was a form letter that Darryl had taken off the Internet under the chapter about covering your butt with a disgruntled employee.

Trevor's mouth was completely open, a YouTube kind of moment. He was speechless. After 10 years of dedicated service, to be summarily let go and not by his boss but by some fly-by-night lover? It was incomprehensible. All he could think was Ms. Hughes's finances must be in very poor shape to let him go. He took the envelope from Darryl, his hand slightly shaking, staring at it like it was kryptonite, unsure of its powers.

"Well, it's been nice knowing you buddy, wish you the best of luck," wrapped up Darryl. "I would tell you to go try the old Mr. Hughes, but I hear his new squeeze is more into collecting beanie babies. Probably not your field."

CHAPTER 14

WINNING THE LOTTO

The look on Bill Hughes's face when Darryl told him about his progress with Melinda was going to be priceless. They met for drinks.

"Darryl, you got any good news for me? It's been seven months and I'm damn ready to get a few of my blankets back," Bill launched in.

"As a matter of fact, Gusher, I do." The fact that Darryl called him by his special nickname meant good news, and Bill got a shit-eating grin on his face.

"I have gotten Melinda to agree to sell the entire collection of 36 pieces," Darryl announced, skimming off the four rugs Melinda had added since the divorce. "She will want a 25 percent profit over what she has into them. We rounded up to make it an even number, $3 million. This seems fair, Gusher, as some of those weavings you've had for a very long time and prices have gone way up since then," negotiated Darryl. The bumped-up price would also cover the four soon-to-be missing rugs.

Darryl added, "Also, Gusher, I told her a Japanese buyer was going to acquire the collection, so I need for the funds to come out of a Japanese bank account."

"She's a real pistol, that one is," Bill reacted, "selling my damn rugs off to the Japs. She knows how I feel about our treasures leaving this country, especially to the Japs. You do not want to cross this lady, my friend."

"I'm very careful, Gusher, when it comes to the female gender. Their brains work differently than ours."

Gusher nodded his head as if he understood completely how unpredictable women could be. "Darryl, my boy, I got to tell you that's a shitload of *dinero* for a bunch of old wool blankets, but I'm dead set on building the best blanket collection there is and this will get me most of the way. I'll get an account set up by tomorrow. Get me the transfer information. We'll have this puppy in the bag before the weekend. I'll need a name for a holding company to make the receipt. Any suggestions?"

"Hell, I don't know Gusher, it's your baby."

"I'd like to call it Fuck You Melinda Corporation, but she might catch on, so let's just go with FYM Inc., a nice international- sounding organization."

"FYM it is," Darryl seconded.

"Darryl, once I have the pieces in my possession, you and I will settle up. I will go ahead and give you an advance of $50K in appreciation of all you've done so far. If you don't want everything in cash, I can set up an overseas account."

"I'm still just an old-fashioned country boy," Darryl demurred. "I like cash, something I can handle. Besides, I've got plans for how to spend it, and cash is always king in my world. Our next big deal, we can do the overseas stuff." Darryl's world was one of no taxes ever. He was off the financial grid and planned to stay that way. Nearly middle aged and still no S.S.N. Never needed a bank account. Always paid in cash. The deals were much sweeter when Benjamin Franklin's face was waving, and Darryl planned to reinvest some of his money into Navajo weavings. Safer than drugs and just as profitable. He had found his niche and it was perfect for the man with no real identity or home.

Coming up with $600,000 in cash was not an easy feat, even for Bill Hughes. Banking institutions start asking questions and forms need to be submitted. In the fast, furious early days of wildcatting most deals involved cash and Bill had put a sizable amount away for just such a day. The rest he brought in from his Caribbean account, boated over to Miami a la drug-deal style.

Darryl envisioned a dozen duffel bags stuffed with cash but was surprised when all $600,000 came neatly packed in a medium-sized, cobalt-blue Tumi suitcase hand delivered to his house by Gusher's limo driver Jake. The bag was rolled in as if every day luggage, not something special that a private jet had just picked up in South Florida four hours earlier. Jake had Darryl sign a receipt acknowledging he received the delivery, then left. No big deal.

Opening the bag was a magical experience for Darryl, a man who craved money. The smell of new leather with a hint of human sweat whiffed through the tiny living room, an aroma Darryl instantly loved. The cash was neatly stacked in large bundles of $100 bills, each with a professional looking paper wrapper. Whoever had prepared the case knew what they were doing when it came to large sums of cash. Darryl kept his .45 Magnum close at hand in case someone got wind of his newfound fortune. He knew the man who had dropped off the case had worked for Gusher for years but one could never be too careful when it came to this kind of payload.

The entire afternoon Darryl spent arranging the money, he was like a kid with a new set of building blocks. He counted the money twice; a man of his limited means needed every dollar. Amazingly, he had gotten exactly what was due, less the $60K.

Darryl carefully divided the money into stacks of $20,000. Then he separated $200,000 from the pile. This would be turned into gold bars. Darryl might have been a man without a FICA score but he understood gold was his best bet against inflation. It was his retirement strategy. The remaining $340,000, in $20K bundles, was placed in individual double-strength Ziploc bags. Each was stuffed into a different-colored metal paint can. Each can was a Ridgemount safety-deposit box, which he would distribute to numerous hidey-holes around Austin, always in close proximity to his favorite drinking haunts, never to be far from money. He carefully drew a map to each of the planned locations and color coded it just in case he forgot where he had placed the cans. The gold bars would be in their own cans and mapped for added diversification, one you don't read about in the economic books. The thought of having monetary security for the rest of his life was very satisfying for Darryl. He felt rich and important for the first time in his life.

His only splurge was on a custom-made brown leather jacket outfitted with a second hidden lining for money and his gun. A specialty jacket was required in case he needed to move cash quickly through an airport or do a clandestine art deal. He didn't know if those existed, but he liked thinking about being some big-shot dealer making huge plays for stolen art.

The well-fitting, quality jacket was plain in appearance except for a small orange longhorn logo. He wanted no doubts as to where his loyalties lay when it came to his favorite university team. Darryl might have been a lifelong criminal and morally bankrupt, but he was still a native Texan and supported his team when and how he could. Bill Hughes, also a rabid University of Texas fan, respected Darryl for his good taste in football teams. The hook-um horns attitude helped bond the two men even more than screwing his ex-wife had.

With the cash safely deposited in his First Dirt Bank of Austin account, Darryl put his energy into disposing of his now useless relationship with Melinda. She was an ends to a means, one which provided food, nice digs, and some finical support, all of which he no longer needed thanks to Mr. Hughes. Darryl didn't want to cut off Melinda completely, because one never knows when you might need a drink from the old well, but for now that water tasted bad and he wasn't that thirsty.

Women love a man who takes care of his mother and this was Darryl's out. He told Melinda his mother needed his attention. She was very ill and he had no idea if she would be well enough to function by herself anytime soon. Darryl had not seen his mother since age 10, but now she came to his rescue when he needed her even if it was just in name. Melinda understood his desire to help family and said to let her know if she could help in any way.

For the first time in his life, Darryl had money to invest and a career. His goal was to take the wish list he had gotten from Trevor regarding blankets, fill in the holes, and buy for the Bill Hughes collection. The most glaring piece missing was the first-phase chief's blanket. He didn't know how hard it would be to locate, but if found it could be the big hit he had always dreamed of, a million-dollar score. For now, he would focus on rugs by known weavers who were deceased. These would be easier to locate than a first phase and still make a nice commission. A trip to Santa Fe might be a good place to start the hunt.

CHAPTER 15

BLOOM'S GOES TRADITIONAL

It had been over a year since Rachael Yellowhorse had returned to her Diné roots, weaving again. She had quickly finished her late Grandmother Ethel's rug that had been languishing on the loom for 10 months. It flowed like she had always woven, and turned out wonderfully. She kept this piece for herself, as it was one of the few things in her life that had deep meaning. She believed Ethel's hand was helping her complete the rug and set her own life back on track.

If you ask almost any Navajo grandmother why they weave they will almost invariably answer the same way: "For the money." It seems hard to believe with all the important religious connotations and the family bonding which weaving holds for the Diné, that it's only for money. What Anglos don't understand is women weave to help their families. It provides extra clothes, food, basketballs, and new tires for the pickup. The gift of Spiderwoman has always allowed Navajos to have warmth. In the old days it was a blanket and now it's to buy the propane. For Rachael not to sell the rug was unusual, but she was that way. Too many years near the whites at the trading post, she would complain to Bloom, when she felt a need to keep an object. The blanket was placed over Rachael and Bloom's bed right across from Bloom's small Yellowhorse painting and Preston's Craig Lendskip sculpture. Three extraordinary works of art worth a great deal of money, the rug being the least valuable by far, but Rachael's favorite, all hanging in an $18,000 prefab metal hogan.

Rachael's first rug by herself took twice as long as planned. Envisioning the intricate pattern in her head and translating it onto the loom's canvas was harder than she remembered. She'd grown more used to sculpting. She understood she was talented at both sculpting and weaving equally, but weaving currently controlled her creative juices. She could make more money as a sculptor, but her motivation barometer nowadays read: weaving. Her nights were filled with dreams of the loom and its pull on her life. Spiderwoman ruled the subconscious. Rachael had forgotten weaving could be such hard work, starting with the mechanics. A loom is needed, and simple tools to make a piece. Rachael preferred her grandmother's weaving tools—three battens and two weaving combs. The wooden battens that help separate the warps were so old and well-used that there were ¼-inch grooves permanently etched into the otherwise smooth oak sticks. The smaller sticks were used for stirring the dyes and finishing a rug, which was rare since she wove in the natural Toadlena/Two Grey Hills style. The battens with their slick feel and sculptural qualities were beautiful objects.

Bloom was amazed some entrepreneurial dealer had not gone around and bought up all the old sticks and then mounted them individually as works of art, making 1000X on the investment. He considered doing this himself, but thought offering grandmothers money for battens they should hand down to their daughters and grand-daughters was ethically wrong, even if they would sell them.

The best weavings still used homespun yarn. Spinning and carding to prepare the wool took 40% of the total construction time, unless you were Rachael and it took 60%. Wool preparation was not her strong suit yet, so she had to grin and bear through the process. She wished she had spent more time helping her mother and grandmother. They had laughed at the little girl who only wanted to weave. They told her she was starting the rug by spinning the wool, she just didn't know it. Rachael understood her matriarchal mentors all too well now.

Rachael's first piece finally came off the loom, six months in the making. Bloom was amazed to see such a delicate yet powerful piece of art come to life, one strand of yarn at a time. He too had developed a deep appreciation for the medium of wool manipulated in an expert's hands, and Rachael was an expert even if she wouldn't admit to such a title yet.

The Toadlena Post's rough old owner, Sal Lito, had finally hired Bloom to work three days a week and was teaching him the ropes. The selling part wasn't hard for Bloom, a man who had sold $70K paintings. But understanding the intricacies of what was good, bad, or fake in the textile world was something else altogether. Even in the heart of Navajo Country, some good-for-nothing would try and pawn off a copy of a piece calling it Navajo. The real tip-off to a fraud was if the piece was described as "Navajo style." Bloom was well aware of the so-called "Indian style" anything, having lived and worked in the art field in Santa Fe.

It was very common for vendors around the fringe edges of the Santa Fe Plaza to sell knock-offs to the tourists, emphasizing the word *Indian* or *Navajo* and barely mentioning (if at all) the word that came after, *style*. This was code for copy. It was also a way to stay one step ahead of the law, as in New Mexico, faking Indian art is considered a big no-no and by saying *style* the crooks were protected.

Slowly the subtleties of the older rugs vs. brand new pieces were understood through seeing so many weavings. Sal was unusual. Most trading posts only dealt in new rugs, as great old blankets were hard to come by. The grandmothers always sold their pieces so these weavings had left the reservation long ago. It was very rare for a Navajo family to actually have an old piece as these were always sold to help pay the bills and feed the family. Sal obtained his antique pieces through tourists visiting the post. They would come in and say, "Oh, my family has some old rugs, would you be interested?" Once the word had gotten out that Sal would buy the older rugs, dealers would also stop by the post to see what he had and show him their latest finds. Over the last 20 years he had been able to get a very good collection of quality old rugs and blankets that Bloom now used as his teaching guide.

Sal saw himself much like Herman Switzer, one of the first traders to come to the rez and work for the Fred Harvey Company. Switzer would search for old examples of blankets to purchase and sell to individuals. His favorite was William Randolph Hearst. In the early 1900s, Hearst would pay $1,500 dollars for a great first-phase chief's blanket. They were expensive even in their day.

What struck Bloom after seeing numerous great rugs was how good Rachael's weaving skills were for having not seriously worked on them for over a decade. Seeing her gift made the juices in Bloom's creative retail gut start to churn. He still thought of his gallery often. Even if he wasn't in Santa Fe, retail was in his blood. It was a part of him for over 20 years and a great new artist or idea was not easily tossed aside. Bloom still wanted to add a new artist to his dwindling stable and it just so happened his newest discovery slept next to him at night. It wasn't her sculpture he was so interested in, which surprised him, but it was her other art form that got him excited now. Adding a traditional weaver to the mix! For Bloom to be able to sell he needed to believe in the piece and the artist.

Bloom felt true enthusiasm when it came to Rachael's weavings. The daily interaction with weavers and sheep, and the sound of the loom's beating comb, had permeated his soul. No longer was he a purist of the abstract. He now saw the beauty in traditional works. Juxtaposing them with the abstract seemed apropos. Bloom's was the perfect place, in fact the only place. He felt it must have been the Diné gods making him wait so long before he could appreciate a traditional artist, the weaver Rachael Yellowhorse.

Charles was waiting for Rachael at their house door with great anticipation to share this epiphany of his new gallery concept, in which he would feature textile artists, specifically her weavings. He had placed a small sign on her half-finished rug, which simply said, SOLD.

Rachael's day had been tough, teaching art to ninth graders who are only interested in how their bodies are changing and what second base is. She wished her day were spent weaving, manipulating wool, not teenagers. The wool was easier.

The smile on Charles's face told the entire story. He had something important to tell her. She hoped it might be an engagement proposal. It was obvious by the way he kept fidgeting, waiting for her to settle in for the night, that he had something to say.

"OK, Charles Bloom, what up? I know you are excited about something?"

"I don't know why, Rachael Yellowhorse, you would say such a thing."

"Is this about making our commitment more, shall I say, permanent?" Rachael hinted, looking anxiously into Bloom's eyes.

"Well I guess you could say it's about a growing relationship, kind of like a rug that grows to be a masterpiece from just little balls of yarn," he responded.

With his rug coaching she began looking around the room. Rachael finally spotted what he hoped she would see, his little orange sign reading SOLD. "Hmm, what's this, sold? How can it be sold? You don't even know what I'm going to ask for it. Hasn't old Sal down at the post taught you anything? You have to negotiate with me. You could start by taking me to bed! The fact is if you want price pre-bedding, I want $50K for this first Yellowhorse masterpiece. Is it still sold?" Rachael flashed a seductive smile, putting the idea of marriage out of her expectations for the time being.

"Well, I guess we will just have to work out the fine details, but I would first like to see how it does in my gallery in Santa Fe. The new Bloom's, which includes only the best in Navajo textile art."

"What! Charles, I'm not ready to show my work. Hell, I'll be lucky to sell this to old Sal out of pity. I'm not ready for Santa Fe, even a little-known gallery like yours." She laughed like a kid at her dissing of Bloom's pride and joy, her sexual interest still very much intact.

"I have to strongly disagree, my little sheep-herder maiden." Bloom emphasized *maiden,* as he knew she was wanting to get engaged and he was smarting from the gallery diss, not realizing his jab stung more than he could imagine. "You are most definitely ready for the big time, and of course there is no place bigger than Bloom's on Canyon Road." Charles deepened his voice at the end to sound a radio announcer's voice promoting Bloom's on an advertising spot.

"Listen honey, I love you, and I know you want to help me, but I'm not that good. You need to see a couple of my grandmother Ethel's works if you want to understand what a great weaver can be. Maybe I'll be that good someday, but not yet," Rachael turned serious.

"Rachael, I see rugs all day long," Charles countered. "I touch them, I hold them, shit, sometimes I even caress the damn things. You are in the upper pantheons of weaving and if you will let me, I would love to showcase your weavings in Santa Fe during my busiest weekend, Indian Market."

Rachael was shocked by his passion with regards to her weavings. They were good, she knew it in her heart, but this was something altogether different. He believed wholeheartedly in her talents.

"Let me think about it," Rachael hedged. "I'm not sure, maybe if you could get some other great Diné weaver to show with me I wouldn't feel so much pressure. I want you to be able to sell the damn things if I do this and I'm not sure you will recoup your money—our money—

on my name alone. I'm Rachael Yellowhorse, not my brother, remember."

"I know you're not Willard," Charles said, flashing the underside of his right wrist that still bore the scar of his near-death encounter with Willard's other art dealer, the now-dead big-time New Yorker.

Rachael's face turned red, embarrassed she had brought up Willard's name and the incident that had nearly killed Charles last year.

"How about I see if I can get Randal Begay to show with you, a kind of his-and-her show," Charles suggested. "He's not from Toadlena, so Sal won't care, and from the couple of rugs I've had the pleasure of examining, he is an exceptional artist who could make anything. It can be Begay and Yellowhorse, Modern Master Weavers of the Diné."

"Wow," Rachael responded. "How did you just come up with the title? It actually sounds important, a show I would want to see. Though does it sound better, Yellowhorse and Begay?" Rachael giggled at her joke of self-importance, a very un-Navajo characteristic.

Bloom ignored her silliness, trying to keep her focused on committing to the show, his dealer mentality kicking in. "So my dear, is it a go if I can get Begay on board?"

"OK," she agreed. "If Randal commits, I will too. I'll warn you he won't have a clue who I am, so good luck getting him to exhibit in a two-person show where one of the persons is a total unknown. Also, if by some miracle he does commit, I can't make but a couple of rugs by the time the show opens. You won't make much off me, I'm afraid."

"You Yellowhorses are known for your slow production, but you always make each one count. It will be a great show. There will be so much interest I'll have clients waiting in line to get a chance to buy one of your rugs. I'm back, baby!"

Bloom's excitement was contagious. Rachael believed maybe they would wait in line for one of her weavings. Charles locked arms with her and led her over to her loom, where she immediately started working, the bed now an afterthought. Charles sat down next to her and watched in awe.

CHAPTER 16

RANDAL BEGAY FINDS A GALLERY

The word on the rez was that Randal Begay was guided directly by Spiderwoman when it came to his abilities as a weaver. His yarn was perfectly spun, thin and hard like the old grandmother masters who made the greatest blankets. It has always been exceptionally rare for men to weave; this is generally done by women. It isn't considered a bad thing for a man to weave, it just rarely happens. The boys usually learn about herding sheep and if interested in the old ways, sand painting. The women learn from their mothers the art of weaving.

Randal's father was an alcoholic who had died on a back alley in Winslow when Randal was three, freezing to death while in an alcoholic haze. Cirrhosis of the liver would have gotten him shortly but Mother Earth saved his body the trouble. He was only 38, a tough life. Randal's mother vowed not to let the same fate happen to her only son, so she kept him close at all times and this meant he spent a lot of time next to her on the loom. Like a musical protégé, Randal could play effortlessly the song of the loom. Its voice spoke to him. His mother did not discourage or encourage her son; it just was. He wove next to her and soon he was making little tapestry weavings better than his mother's. He was so adept at spinning that she would have him spin all her yarn, which allowed her more time to weave and thus more money for the family. Her weavings became noticeably improved due to her son's talent at spinning wool, and she began to receive notice from local trading posts. None knew her 13-year-old son was the true genius.

The partnership continued till Randal's 25th birthday when he decided to make a copy of an old third-phase blanket using Spiderwoman crosses in the field in a very Randal sort of way. Oversized for the field and not really resembling the old blankets, but it worked. He won 1st prize at the annual Gallup Inter-Tribal Indian Ceremonial for his traditional style weaving. From that point on, his star continued to rise. He could always take his rug into Goulding's Lodge north of Kayenta and sell it for top dollar. The word on the street was he really loved money and would sell his rugs to anyone if he could get his price.

Most Navajo weavers sell through trading posts or dealers near the rez. These individuals, like Sal Lito at the Toadlena Post, act as their de facto agents. No written contract, but you knew if you lived in that area the trader for that post would get the first crack at buying the rug. For someone in Randal's category it would be a big deal to have first right of refusal. A good, big weaving by him would bring nearly $10K, an astounding price for such a young weaver.

Bloom knew Randal's background and understood that sniping another post's artist was very bad form. Stealing artists was a part of the art world he hated. But he wanted Rachael to show with him this summer in Santa Fe, so he felt he would have to let the chips fall where they may. It wasn't like he was setting up a store in Kayenta; he only wanted Randal for a show during Indian Market, two rugs max. Besides, no one really represented Randal exclusively. Highest price won, when it came to Randal. At least that was the word on the street.

So Bloom made the two-and-a-half hour trip west from Toadlena to Kayenta to track down Randal, who didn't own a phone. Randal Begay lived in a traditional hogan that was hard to find. It would have been impossible without a good map from Sal, who had once worked in Kayenta and knew the back roads well. For Navajos, maps are not necessary. They know the land and everyone's home. The directions to Randal's hogan required four different dirt roads, each more treacherous than the last when driving in a low-to-the-ground car like Bloom's. Finally crossing a cattle fence, a structure appeared on the horizon. Randal's hogan was 15 miles outside of Kayenta, but it took 35 minutes to reach. It was on a small stretch of barren earth, nestled underneath a large red butte, a stone's throw away from the Utah border. It was a magnificent setting. Large tiers of red rock stuck out in all directions. Their weather-beaten edges allowed veins of the rock composition to show through in areas. It was no wonder a weaver could be inspired to create, looking up at what the gods had already produced.

The hogan itself was much less impressive. In fact, it was verging on being a dump. There were two old vehicles in stages of disintegration. The old 1948 trailer behind Rachael's home, Charles's first rez home, was a castle in comparison to these heaps. There appeared to be one greenish Ford pickup that was maybe capable of running, though it was doubtful it did so more than just periodically. It had to be Randal's vehicle. Piles of crushed Schlitz cans formed an odd mound behind the house. Half the cans had bullet holes piercing their surfaces. The heap as a whole took on a sculptural effect, something Bloom was sure the original owner had not intended. The beer cans were probably remnants of Randal's late father's addiction. Bloom pulled up and wondered if he might have gotten the wrong location. Maybe he had missed a turn and this was some drunken lunatic's house. With the amount of money Randal made on his weavings, it was hard to believe this was his home. Bloom was seriously considering turning around when a handsome young Navajo in cowboy boots, jeans, and a black Stetson hat with an ingot silver hat band emerged from the 19th-century hogan door.

"Yá át ééh," Bloom yelled out from his car window, trying to sound as friendly as possible. The Navajo with the black hat and ponytail was closing in quickly on Bloom, who felt vulnerable sitting in his car. The Indian was looking somewhat menacing as he got closer to Bloom, who was still strapped in by his seatbelt. It was a disconcerting feeling for Bloom to come unannounced to an isolated location to see someone he had never met, a complete stranger. In the back of his mind, Bloom could picture a crazy person walking to the car and firing a gun into his face and then dragging him out and tossing his body out back with the disintegrating beer cans. The car cut up for parts, no one would know.

"*Yá át ééh*. Can I help you? Are you lost or something?" Randal said, wondering what the *bilagaana* in the beat-up Mercedes was looking for and feeling a bit apprehensive himself.

"No, I'm not lost if you're Randal Begay, the great Navajo weaver." Bloom knew it never hurt to stroke the ego of an artist, even an unpretentious Navajo one.

"Thanks for the compliment. You here looking to buy one of my rugs? I got one on the loom."

Relieved, Bloom emerged from his car. Even though the cowboy boots and Stetson added height to Randal, now that he was on even ground Bloom stood inches taller. Still, this was Randal's territory. "Yes, I guess I am. My name is Charles Bloom. I own a Native American gallery in Santa Fe on Canyon Road, Bloom's. I'm organizing an August show in my gallery over Indian Market weekend featuring outstanding contemporary Navajo weavers, and I was hoping you might be one of the two invited guest artists. My girlfriend is a weaver, Rachael Yellowhorse. She will be sharing the stage with you if you're up for it. She is Ethel Sherman's granddaughter."

"I recently read about a Yellowhorse, it was in the *Navajo Times*. Sounded like a very interesting artist, he was a painter. Same guy?" Randal was avoiding saying Willard's name, following the traditional Navajo way of avoiding voicing the name of the dead.

Charles had no such hesitation. "Yes, Willard was Rachael's older brother. I also used to represent him in my gallery. Rachael is just as talented, but in weaving. She was born to the Bear Clan and born for the Towering House Clan." By giving the two lineages, Charles let Randal know both Rachael's maternal and parental clans, and made it clear that he was not oblivious to Diné ways, even if he would speak a dead man's name.

"I know some Bear Clan Diné, near Toadlena?"

"Yes, that's Rachael's family."

"Good people. I would love to see Rachael's work. Does she only sell to old Sal? He won't look at my rugs 'cause I don't weave in the

Toadlena/Two Grey Hills style. He only wants the Grey ones or the old blankets," commented Randal.

"No, she only shows at my gallery in Santa Fe, and she wants you to show with her. We're both fans of yours."

"How many rugs we talking about? You know I usually don't do consignment, but outright sales. My big stuff can bring close to $10K."

"Yes, I saw a great piece online. A revival pictorial with trains. The Tucson gallery had it at $12K."

"Yeah, that was my piece. I sell to that guy sometimes. He really only likes the old Navajo blankets like Sal, but he sometimes shows up-and-comers, which I guess is me. Occasionally I will do these old-style weavings. My mom wove only traditional pieces, so I kind of like to take it back a couple of generations, but I always try to put my own personal touch in the rug."

"Here's what I can do, Randal," Bloom suggested. "If you can do two major works, I will buy one outright at wholesale and the other one I will only take a third from if you can give it to me on consignment. I will do a big press release and pay for one national advertisement. I don't expect to make a whole lot this year, but if it goes well, next year's market could be big for us both. What do you say, want a great gallery in Santa Fe for the summer?"

"OK, you got it. I'll do two weavings. Maybe one very traditional and the other piece more my own style. Each one will be around $7,500 to $10,000 retail, depending on how long it takes."

"Great. I thought the title could be 'Yellowhorse and Begay, Modern Master Weavers of the Diné.' What you think?" Bloom figured he would put Rachael's name first even though she was only kidding when she suggested it.

"Pretty good, but it would be better if the B came first, alphabetical and all." Randal wasn't kidding. He wanted the additional press. It might help him get a better premium on future rugs.

"No problem. Has a nice ring to it. I'll need at least one weaving by June so I can use it in the ad and press release." Charles hadn't taken so much as a step away from his car, and he was already closing the deal.

"I don't have no phone, but will get you word when it's done. Any chance I can get an advance? I've got a lot of bills around here. If I do these rugs for you, means I can't knock out any little ones to pay for gas and food," Randal reasoned.

"Sure, how about $1,000? I can spare that now."

"OK," Randal agreed. "Don't tell anyone I'm doing these rugs for you. I don't want any one at Goulding's to know yet. The trader over there won't be happy, so I need to bring him in something to ease his pain."

"I understand," assured Bloom. "Mum's the word."

CHAPTER 17

THE MEDICINE MAN

Week one for Carson Riddly was about learning the ropes of the Kayenta main clinic. His real assignment was a week away. He had been selected to head the clinic he had dreaded, the one that had no picture on the Internet. It was called simply the North Clinic, as it was the farthest north Indian clinic on the Navajo Nation, barely in Arizona, a stone's throw away from Utah. He would have one nurse and be responsible for all medical duties of the Navajo people on the border of Utah and Arizona, a 50-square mile radius.

Time flew by, and soon it was time to assume his duty station at the North Clinic. It took more than 30 minutes from Kayenta on washboard red-sand roads to reach the little aluminum-trailer clinic that was positioned on a parched, almost treeless patch of earth. The drive was brutal on his Mustang, avoiding ruts and deep sand impossible. He could say goodbye to ever using the car as it was intended, as a convertible. Sand particles got into everything. It would require a cleaning of dust channels which would accumulate at every place there was a joint. There was a small wooden sign at the clinic. The black lettering burned in the plank appeared to have been made at a high school vo-tech class. It said "Kayenta North

Clinic." The deep burn marks engraved in the old juniper board reminded Carson of his own burnt mesquite tree from childhood. Maybe he was here for a reason, he told himself as he experienced déjà vu looking at the sign.

And yet the location of the new clinic was beyond beautiful, he had to admit. Tall 300-foot red cliffs lined with black sediment formed the backdrop. It was hard not to be impressed by one of the most unique clinic settings in the United States. The clinic trailer itself was divided into five tiny areas: reception, patient examination room, doctor's office, kitchen, and indoor restroom. The last two amenities were unusual for such a remote place as almost none of the hogans in this part of the reservation had such luxuries. Water for most residences near the clinic was trucked in weekly, and kerosene lamps provided light.

Surprisingly, Carson adapted to his new clinic digs fairly quickly. He found the high vistas of the desert with their crimson spires of rock relaxing to the mind. Wildlife was everywhere. Walks in the area gave him a sense of freedom he had never felt before. No longer was he afraid of his new position as the head doctor of Kayenta North (and also the only doctor).

His assignment was to run Kayenta North with an older Navajo nurse named Dotty who looked a lot like Cheryl. Maybe she was her mom? He wouldn't pry. Dotty spoke English but it was obviously not her first language. It was broken and oddly paced. She often had to think what the English translation for some word was. She wore a white nurse's uniform from the sixties with buckskin moccasins underneath. The skin on her arms was barely visible, hidden under an ocean of cluster turquoise bracelets. Over her chest were multiple turquoise necklaces plus was a long string of turquoise *heishe* with a clamshell hung from its end. Dotty's stethoscope was covered in its own decoration of beads. Carson was amazed the apparatus didn't ever seem to get tangled up with the hundreds of beads and turquoise stones. So far, Dotty's eye contact and emotion was nonexistent when she talked with Doc Riddly. Needless to say, he never told her his first name.

"Just call me Doc Riddly or Doc, that's what I like to go by," he suggested.

She didn't question his motives. Her Navajo sensibilities didn't need an answer.

Clinic life here was similar to that in the main Kayenta clinic. Carson's work revolved around seeing between four and nine patients a day. Now and then the occasional sick goat or sheep became a patient as well. Most of the human exams involved simple things like a school physical for sports or a cut hand.

Occasionally though, something serious walked in. With no ER within a 40-minute drive, the North Clinic needed to be a life-saving outpost when necessary. These moments were few but when they occurred, the trepidation Carson had initially worried about filled him up and the North Clinic became a frightening place to be the only doctor on staff. One such event occurred in the form of a scene out of an old western movie.

An elderly Navajo rode in on a horse and collapsed in front of the clinic. With Navajos, age is often difficult to judge. The old grandmothers in their 80s can have black hair and require no glasses to weave their intricate rugs. Living to 100 is commonplace. The man who had collapsed on the front porch of Carson's clinic had silver hair, so he was probably at least 80 or more likely pushing 90. He was semi-comatose when they dragged him in to the patient examination office, and even Carson's nurse who had seen it all was flustered. The old man was in clear distress. His heart rate was thready and his breathing shallow. His eyes were responsive but dilated. He appeared to be in some sort of delirium, speaking in Navajo and occasionally chanting like some Gregorian monk. Carson didn't understand a single word. It wasn't clear if Dotty did either.

Carson placed an I.V. in the old man's arm, which was a miracle in itself as his veins were nearly nonexistent. Then he hooked him up for an EKG using a 1950s machine which came with paper matched in vintage that was cracking and disintegrating to the human touch. The man's heart rate was fast but with normal rhythm so it was probably not a heart attack. Stroke was possible, as he was not making sense, though no paralysis of his face or extremities was visible. His abdomen was soft and subtle and he didn't seem to have a fever. As a doctor, you use everything at your disposal during an evaluation. If you are good at certain areas you key in on these. Carson liked dermatology, so he figured maybe he could find something in a skin diagnosis. He stripped the old man's clothes off and started looking for anything that would help him with a diagnosis of what appeared to be someone about to die.

A good dermatologist looks at the entire body and in the nude. Any area of skin, including the anus, can give you an idea of what the problem could be. At first glance, there was nothing that indicated the skin was even involved with this problem, but it was his last resort for trying to help the man who was dying in front of his eyes. Typically, you start at the bottom and work your way up. Carson got lucky. The great toe of the old man's foot was starting to swell and had a hint of a bluish coloration. The tip looked like it had two puncture wounds. Carson decided it had to be a rattlesnake bite, and guessed which species would be involved in the area, his love of herpetology paying off.

However, to administer rattlesnake anti-venom to a severely sick person who turns out not to have been bitten is asking for a serious lawsuit. No way to defend against it. "So Dr. Riddly, you gave anti-venom to a 90-year-old man whose toe had been stuck by a cactus. This is what you're telling me?" Carson could hear the lawyer's voice in his head as he pushed the first dose, holding his own breath, waiting for some sort of reaction. He was thankful the clinic actually had anti-venom, unless he got the diagnosis wrong that is, then it would be the last time they would ever carry the drug. The old man reacted like a heroin addict given Narcan. He suddenly popped up and said something in Navajo to the very excited nurse.

"What did he say? It was a rattlesnake bite, wasn't it? Is there something else?" Carson asked Dotty, relief simultaneously flowing through his own body.

"He said that you are a great medicine man and must understand snakes be able to convince the snake's venom to leave him. He thanks you."

A little more time passed. The elderly man began to sit up and drink small sips of water. Again he said something and the nurse translated.

"He wants you to know the snake that bit him was not a bad spirit and not to worry. He had been doing a curing chant when he accidentally stepped on the little fellow. 'He didn't mean to hurt me; his bite was pure and only venom not meant to kill,' he says. There will be no bad spirit to worry about."

She added, "Hastiin Johnson—that's your patient's name—wants to thank you for your great medicine and would like to invite you to his home for dinner. He says he will need to leave soon if he wants to get home by nightfall."

"Dotty, tell Hastiin Johnson he needs much more of my medicine and has to go to the Flagstaff hospital and spend the night for probably quite a few nights. We can have someone get him back home afterwards. Do you know where he lives and can someone help with the horse?"

"Yeah, he lives about 10 miles from here next to the state line, near Buck Wilson's ranch. They're good friends. Buck's a *bilagaana* like you and he's got a phone. I'll call, see if he can get the old man's grandson to come trailer the horse home."

✹ ✹ ✹ ✹

Buck Wilson was the third generation of ranchers to take care of the extensive Wilson ranch. The spread was nearly 1,000 acres of some of the most beautiful yet barren land in the United States. Buck's family had been traders and ranchers in the area since it first opened up to whites. His grandfather had negotiated rights at the turn of the 19th century with the Navajos to put up a trading post. The original homestead had been near the Wetherill's trading post of Oljeto, an old natural stone building outside of Goulding's. Wilson was white, though his skin looked more like his Navajo neighbors' and he spoke perfect Navajo. His rancher buddies thought he acted more Diné than white. Dotty explained Wilson understood much of what was meant to be Diné though he was still a *bilagaana* in her eyes. None of the Wilson bloodline had ever been diluted with Diné blood, which is surprising since they had lived together for so long. His only son, who was not the smartest of cookies, was the fourth generation of Wilson ranchers and was next in line to take over the family farm. The main income for the Wilson ranch in recent years was pigs and sheep, as the old trading post had closed 25 years ago. The pig business had fallen on very hard times after the swine flu outbreak, which had devastated the pig growers of the United States. Especially hard hit had been those near Kayenta.

Wilson was the one affected the hardest. He had the unfortunate luck to have his pigs infected with swine flu. Ironically, it had been transmitted from a sick human to his pig farm. The entire operation had been put into quarantine for two months. The big pork buyers would not touch his hogs even after the FDA had given him the thumbs up after the pigs recovered. No pigs were lost to disease, yet no one would buy his livestock. The word on the rez was Wilson could lose his homestead if the crisis didn't turn around soon and people didn't start buying Wilson pork again. His sheep income was not large enough to cover the mounting losses from his pork business. He did have some family Indian art that he apparently had started selling off through Goulding's. The truth was he was in trouble and his second mortgage on the farm would come due in about eight months. Unless a miracle occurred, he was running out of options and starting to consider desperate methods to hold on to the family property.

CHAPTER 18

PICKUP TRUCKS AND NAVAJO RUGS

Dotty got through to Buck Wilson, explained what had happened to his neighbor, and asked if he or one of Hastiin Johnson's family members could come get the mare, which was currently tethered to Carson's own horse, his Mustang convertible, unbeknownst to the good doctor.

"I'll send down his grandson Randal, he's the only one still lives around here. All his other relatives work as guides out at the park and are ferrying tourists around. Randal's usually working on a rug so he can come down and get Lightning. That's the horse. How's my old friend doing? He's getting up there in age. Can't handle too many more snake bites." Wilson had a 1960s vintage phone, but it still worked.

"Has he been bitten before, Mr. Wilson?" Dotty asked, already suspecting the answer.

"Twice that I know of, not counting this one. The last one should have killed him. It got him in the shoulder, but that was nearly 10 years ago and he was still was strong as an ox then. Tell him *yá át ééh* and not to worry. I'll check on his place for him, and give his horse some water. I've known his family all my life and they are good people. Randal is a bit of a rebel, likes to spend money and is a slow weaver. He's great at his craft, but doesn't make enough money for his lifestyle. If you don't produce a lot of rugs, no matter how good you are you will be in trouble, especially if you like Indian casinos."

Dotty affirmed her disdain for those in her community that wasted money on gambling, while Carson arranged for the transportation to bring Hastiin Johnson into Flagstaff.

Eventually, Randal Begay showed up pulling an old horse trailer whose tires looked in danger of coming off behind a broken-down green Ford truck also on its last legs.

"Hey, I'm here to get my grandfather's horse. Is he doing OK? Can I talk to him?" Randal asked Dotty, who made up the entire front staff of the North Clinic.

"I'm afraid he has already been transferred to Flagstaff," she answered. "We had a helicopter come in and life-line him out of here. That was a first. Your grandfather was smiling the whole time. He said if he had known he would get to see his home from a helicopter he would have come in the last time he got bit."

"Yeah, that's my grandfather, not afraid of anything. We come from a long line of strong people—Bitterwater Clan."

Dotty nodded her head, understanding what he meant and knowing Randal's clan without his explanation. "Let me have you speak to Doc Riddly. He can tell you what he knows about your grandfather's condition." Dotty ushered Randal, who was dripping with sweat from the hot summer day's near-record temperature, in to what was referred to as Dr. Riddly's office. It was more like a closet.

The Navajo rug Carson's father had given him took up the entire wall space and then some. Riddly's little metal desk was dwarfed by the magnificent weaving's presence. There was no room for his diplomas, which were tucked in a drawer. Carson thought it just as well as this would keep his first name out of sight of his patients. The window was wide open and a strong breeze was flapping one end of the weaving as if saying hello to Randal. Carson was typing on his laptop, but stopped when Randal walked in.

Carson told him, "We had quite a scare with your grandfather. He tried to die on us. How old is he?"

"Not sure anyone knows, but I would guess nearly 90, give or take five years. He still remembers his grandmother telling him about the Long Walk. You know about that, right?"

By now, Carson knew all too well. "Yes, I'm aware of your people's mistreatment at the hands of the government."

"I don't think about it much, but for the older Diné it's still very real and not a happy topic. Even some of us young Navajo have heard enough about it to get angry."

Carson knew this too.

"I got to ask you, Doc. That is the best weaving I have ever seen. It looks like a Daisy. Is it?"

"Yes, it was done in the fifties. Pretty good one, huh?" Carson couldn't wait to tell his dad about this conversation.

"Good is not the word. It's a masterpiece. You mind if I touch it? I never got to touch one of her pieces before. She's kind of a legend."

"Sure," Carson encouraged. "Take your time. I hear you're a weaver, too."

Randal picked up the free corner and gently began rubbing the wool to feel the tightness of the weave. "Yeah, I'm trying, but she was the best. Her spinning was so good. I'm known as a great spinner, but I don't think I can do what she could. Just amazing how her yarn was so even and tight. I hope someday people remember me by my first name like they do her."

"I'd love to see your weavings some time," Carson said, surprising himself with real interest in something he had not heretofore cared about, Navajo textiles. His father's gift had affected him, and until that moment he didn't realize how much. Being in close contact with the rug and numerous weavers had made him appreciate the abilities of these Navajo artists. A really great weaver might only be able to make five or six rugs in the same time period it takes someone to become a doctor. It took great patience to be a weaver, and Carson appreciated a person who could focus for so long on a single task.

7 yrs.

"If you want Doc," Randal offered, "since it's after five and if you're getting off soon, you can follow me home and I'll drop off Lighting and you can see my latest piece. I'm making this weaving for a show in Santa Fe, and it's almost finished. It's a very good one. I think you'll like it. If you want to bring your Daisy, we can drop by Buck's house and show it to him. He will flip. Buck knew Daisy well. He used to own a couple of her great weavings in the old days. He may be able to tell you something about it you don't even know. Wouldn't surprise me if he even owned it once."

Carson made a snap decision. "Fine, you get the horse and I'll finish up here. I'll make a call to Flagstaff Medical and check on your grandfather's condition before we go."

❋ ❋ ❋ ❋

The ride over to Hastiin Johnson's was 10 miles of pure hell, with bumps, ruts, and the occasional rattlesnake crossing the dirt road. Thank goodness Carson had his golf cap to cut the sun's glare. Carson's Mustang almost bottomed out a couple of times even going as slow as possible and still keeping in visual contact with the ever-fading horse trailer. Finally they arrived at Hastiin Johnson's hogan —a traditional log home that was as old as the man. Surrounding it, just a few scraggly junipers and the usual accoutrement of nonfunctioning vehicles. It was no wonder there were lots of rattlesnakes. This was the perfect habitat for them, Carson thought to himself upon seeing the family land. Hastiin Johnson lived alone, his wife of 60 years having died two years ago.

The Wilson ranch was only a mile away, just over the Arizona border into Utah. Once they crossed over the Utah state line the dirt road seemed smoother and better maintained. Carson figured it was a state thing, like California and Arizona used to be before the recession brought California to its knees.

The Wilson property, which was just outside the Navajo reservation, was the opposite of Johnson's land. Numerous large elms and cottonwoods lined the Wilson entry, leading into an incongruent grass lawn which lately had also been used as a sheep-grazing area. The house was an old Victorian-looking white two-story, with paint that was starting to peel badly. It was apparent the house had lost some of its charm in the last few years. A few obligatory abandoned vehicles did grace the property, but were in the back, out of sight of the main home. Buck Wilson was sitting on the front porch-swing drinking what appeared to be a mint julep and chewing on the butt of a cigar. His face was invisible under the overlarge brim of his very old, stained gray Stetson hat.

"Hey Mr. Wilson, I brought our new doc from over at the North Clinic. He took care of Grandfather. He's got something you will find very interesting," Randal said.

"Hi Mr. Wilson. I'm Carson Riddly, but everyone just calls me Doc Riddly."

Buck chuckled, "I understand. I wouldn't go by Carson around these parts, either. How's my old friend Johnson doing? I may need a blessing way ceremony soon and I'm counting on him as my medicine man."

"We flew him into Flagstaff and I'm expecting he will do OK. He's lucky we had the correct antivenin on hand, otherwise he would have died for sure."

Buck nodded, "That sounds right. That old man has cheated death more times than I can count. Must be something the gods are keeping him around for. So what do you want to show me?"

Randal, who had stashed the Daisy in a black trash sack for its transportation, pulled the work of art out as if he were delivering a baby. "How about this…."

Old-man Wilson's cataract-filled eyes lit up like they hadn't in years. "Well, well you do have something to show an old man. I remember this beauty. 1954, if memory serves me, same year my son Elmer was born. Expensive year. Daisy worked hard all winter long and I had to give her extra money because her truck broke down. She said she would make it worth my time and money, she had a good one on the loom. Boy, was she right. That lady was quite the professional. Finished it just in time for the Gallup Ceremonial. It took first prize! I thought about keeping it as I figured it might be one of the last great weavings she would ever complete, but like they say out here, I needed the money. It changed hands twice until it got sold at the Heard Museum gift shop around 1980. To some doctor, I heard. You're too young to be the person who bought it?"

"My dad gave it to me," Carson said.

"He was the doctor in Phoenix?"

"Yep, he was the one who bought it from the Heard."

"I always hoped it might turn up again and I would have another shot at owning it. Still gives me goose bumps just seeing it. Too bad I'm hurting for cash these days. You're not interested in trading a shit load of hogs for her are you? Give you enough to set you up in the pig business?"

"Sorry," Carson replied, "can't ever sell her. My dad gave this to me as a gift, so I would really have to be in trouble to let it go."

"Well anytime you want me to baby-sit her, just let me know. I'd take good care of her."

Carson surprised himself by replying, "I'm glad to know the history. It makes it just that much more special. How about I leave it with you tonight and you can enjoy it? Just bring it back to the clinic tomorrow."

The old man's eyes, which had been so large a moment ago, started to fill with tears. Buck could only nod his head in accord.

CHAPTER 19

CONNECTING WITH RANDAL BEGAY

Figuring friendships were forged differently in remote terrain, Carson followed Randal's truck off Buck's ranch as they drove away, leaving Buck to enjoy his old friend for the night. They headed over to Randal's place.

At this point, Randal was hoping Carson might be a great rug collector, considering he already owned one of the best weavings Randal had ever seen. Sure, Randal was working on an important piece for Bloom's August show, but it wasn't out of the realm of possibility for him to sell it today if the money was right. He knew it would be wrong, but if he could make a retail sale he would. Stocking up at Bashas' with a full wad of cash in his jeans would be sweet. So would a trip to the casino.

Randal's hogan was in moderate disrepair. It was an older family hogan of juniper logs packed with mud. The door opened to the east to greet the sun each morning. Randal was raised partially by his grandfather the medicine man, and was traditional in many ways. He tried to be a good Navajo, but had a serious problem with gambling that had gotten him in trouble on more than one occasion. The demons of obsessive behavior haunted him, as they had his late father.

There was no indoor plumbing or electricity, no computer, and only occasional spotty cell service. It was remote living but excellent for weaving. Excluding Mr. Wilson and his grandfather, the closest neighbor was four miles away. You had to like isolation to live in Randal's world. The inside of the hogan, which was one room, had a central wood-burning stove, a hard-packed dirt floor, a couple of museum posters tacked to the walls, and a small cot near the stove. The weaving dominated the room. It was on two massive metal poles and appeared to be almost completed to Carson's untrained eye. The only other noticeable objects were some skeins of white and brown wool hanging from a couple of hooks behind the rug. Looking around at the hogan's ultra-sparse décor, Carson, who was still residing at the Hampton Inn, had the horrible feeling that his home to be (once rid of bees) would be similar.

"Doc," said Randal, "I wanted you to see my newest creation. It's an old-style weaving with a kind of modern look."

Carson, who knew very little about weavings, nodded his head in approval. "When is your show in Santa Fe?"

"It's Indian Market weekend. That's the third weekend in August every year."

"Will you have more than one rug?"

"I wish I had more, Doc, but this is all I could manage. This piece has taken five months to weave and that's fast for me. I could let it go for around $15K if you are interested? I'm supposed to save it for my Santa Fe show, but seeing how much you like rugs and all, I thought you might like it?" Randal knew Bloom would be devastated, especially since he had paid money upfront and was advertising the show, but Randal was broke and couldn't count on his grandfather for money, in fact he would need to help the old man while he recovered from his snakebite. He thought if he could get the $15K he could take part of it and double it at the casino, then he could pay Bloom back. Randal's greatest concern was Bloom's girlfriend

Rachael. She was Diné and sharing the Santa Fe show with him. She would not be pleased and it could have ramifications he cared not to think about. As Randal contemplated all the scenarios, Carson answered all his questions with one statement.

"Wow, I had no idea rugs were so expensive. You must be a great weaver. Maybe one day I can afford a little weaving of yours."

This is when Randal knew Doc was not ever going to be a buyer for his weavings. He obviously wasn't aware of the price structure for a great Navajo weavings. Bloom's show was safe; the gods had made their intention clear. "Yeah, I guess I would be considered one of the better weavers. My show is being held at an important painting gallery in Santa Fe, Bloom's. The gallery owner actually lives part time on the rez near the Toadlena Trading Post."

Trying to impress Randal with his knowledge of reservation geography, Carson said, "Oh I know where Tonalea is. It's between Moenkopi and Red Lake, pretty small place."

"Doc, that's Tonalea. This is Toadlena and it's in western New Mexico. It's an old-time trading post a couple of hours from here. It's where your Daisy rug was made. She lived right by the post and she's buried not far from there." Randal now knew for sure the doctor didn't know shit about rugs, the rez, or weavers, for that matter.

"That's right, it is Tonalea. I got my Navajo names mixed up. I'm better with medical terms, I assure you," Carson sheepishly said, trying to ease Randal's mind that the man who just took care of his grandfather's emergency was not an idiot. "I bet you can hardly wait for Santa Fe. That's a lot of money coming in once you sell your rug. You'll make what I do as a doctor for four months of work. Guess our educations are worth about the same."

Carson thought his comment would make Randal feel good about his worth as a weaver, but in reality it only made him depressed, thinking, "If doctors can't afford my rugs, who can?"

Changing subjects, realizing his rugs would never be in the budget for the North Clinic doctor, Randal remarked, "So you got a girl, Doc? Not a lot available around here, especially *bilagaana* girls."

Carson remembered Nurse Tsosie's Navajo language lesson and knew whites were *bilagaanas*. His vocabulary was improving even if his geography was not. "Nobody yet, and I'm afraid the pickings look slim."

"Yeah, you have to do like Charles Bloom, my *bilagaana* art dealer. He's hooked up with a very fine Navajo weaver, Rachael Yellowhorse. They live at Toadlena. Find one like her and your time out here with us Indians could be a lot more fun." Randal's grin was the universal man's code for having great sex.

Carson immediately thought of the receptionist Brenda who was very fine but unfortunately had dismissed him as Kit Carson's relative. What a screw-up on his part. "Bloom's a white guy, huh? Why's he living here and not Santa Fe? Nothing personal Randal, but I would think Santa Fe would be preferable for an art guy, girl or no girl."

"You would think so, but his girl keeps him in line. Some guys go Indian and don't want to leave the rez. I get the feeling he's one of those. He works part time now at the Toadlena Trading Post. I expect he would love to see that Daisy of yours. It's done in the Toadlena/Two Grey Hills style."

This was a jab at Carson's lack of any knowledge when it came to rugs, though Carson did realize it was a Two Grey Hills, he just didn't know where it was located, the answer being around Toadlena.

"Randal, when you see Bloom in Santa Fe, let him know about me and my Daisy. Tell him I'd like to meet the only other *bilagaana* around these parts. Maybe he can share his trade secret regarding finding a girl on the Navajo reservation. I know I could use one," Carson said, getting ready to leave. It was best that he drive back to Kayenta before total darkness.

"OK, I'll tell him. You probably do need some help with our girls. I'll give you one tip: get rid of your hat when you're outside. You need some color. That pasty-white face is blinding to us Navajos." Both men laughed and Carson for the first time felt like he might be fitting in.

CHAPTER 20

AUGUST COMETH

July came without the promised rug from Randal, though Bloom did send an additional $2,000 as Randal called him from the Kayenta McDonald's and said he was desperate and couldn't finish the piece without it.

The full-page ad in the local Indian Market guide was going to feature two rugs, one Randal's and the other Rachael's. Without Randal's rug it seemed weird to have just hers since it was a two-person show. So Bloom took the photo of Rachael's bigger Navajo rug and made a ghost image for the background where you could tell it was a Navajo weaving but not clearly identify the artist. The ad read in big bold red letters BEGAY and underneath that YELLOWHORSE, then below their names in yellow, MODERN MASTER WEAVERS OF THE DINÉ.

Bloom began thinking there was no way Randal was going to show up with two rugs. He was now hoping for at least one weaving so as to not look like a complete fool for having a flake be part of his first major weaving show. Worse yet, poor Rachael would be left hanging alone.

It was Rachael who assured him Randal would come through, maybe not for both pieces but he would be there. Bloom just had to have faith. She advised, "Send him another $1,000. Remind him of the opening day, and I will write a note too. He'll be there." To love someone is to have faith. Charles believed in Rachael and hoped she was right.

Santa Fe in summer is usually heaven for retailers. The final snow melts on the upper reaches of the Sangre de Cristo Mountains simultaneously as cash starts flowing from Texans depositing their oil revenues at the doorsteps of Canyon Road.

This year the normal river was more an intermittent creek. Oil prices were down from the year before. As oil goes, so goes the Texas economy and subsequently New Mexico art dealers. Santa Fe watches not only the price at the pump, but also what a barrel of Texas sweet crude sells for. It was hovering around $80/barrel, a minimum for a decent season.

Bloom had decided to come in and work the months of July and August through Indian Market. His rent was nothing, thanks to the Shriver deal. His main expense was his one cheap but very good employee, Dr. James. If all went well, he could leave Santa Fe just before September's Fiesta and head back to Rachael's place, which would be very quiet by then with Preston off to the U of A. Bloom rationalized, "If this retail season sucks, it's telling me I better stay here in Santa Fe and avoid the marriage pressure with Rachael. Let the retail gods decide. Hope Mr. Begay shows up, or I'm out $4K and probably out of the weaving business." Since living on the rez, Bloom was more willing to let things play out how they would. Unknown forces would exert their own influences, he now realized.

July was bumpy. It seemed as if it was going to be great, then nothing for two days. The smaller gallery digs didn't seem to hurt business as far as Bloom could tell. During the day, Bloom would set up easels in the shared garden so as to increase his gallery wall space by 30%. Shriver was a good sport and allowed the overkill to his space. He wanted Bloom to make it, and he enjoyed having him nearby to share complaints about tourists and their inane questions. This summer they amused themselves with a joint project using an erasable board in Shriver's kitchen: a David Letterman-type Top 10.

The board's header read, "The most inane questions asked this summer season." So far the top 10 were:

1) I love your front sign. Is it for sale?

2) How much are the plants?

3) What kind of dog is that? Oh, that's a pig sculpture.

4) Did you make everything?

5) What's the area code for Mexico?

6) Can I park in your private parking for a couple of weeks?

7) Can I eat your patio apples? I love them green.

8) Your artwork is too expensive—you should look at mine.

9) You don't mind if I take photos of what I like to make copies for my friends since I can't afford your stuff?

10) What do you have for a buck?

Not a lot of changes on the board were expected before Labor Day, though there was still Indian Market to go and that was always good for a couple of idiotic sayings.

Santa Fe in August is a frenetic place no matter the economy. Tourists from all over the world arrive, wanting to see Indians and the second-oldest city in America. Santa Fe has had strict architectural zoning. Starting in 1957, every building had to meet a certain level of "Santa Fe style," which meant an adobe façade or something very close. The only homes and businesses that were immune were those built before 1957. Those early establishments were regulated by the historical preservation society, also called the "hysterical society" for its often extreme-seeming regulations. Bloom's old space fell under some of the regulations, but he never had the money to attempt to change things so he was fine with the status quo. Bloom loved the consistent look the city maintained and was grateful there was a historical committee, no matter how difficult they made the process. Because of the city's fathers, both Wal-Mart and McDonald's were adobe-style buildings as were all the retail businesses. The look helped avoid the cookie-cutter mall effect which is so endemic to most of America.

Santa Fe had a charm Bloom never tired of. The rez also had an old-world feeling with its hand-hewn hogans and Anasazi ruins. The rez had no historical committee. It was a mixture of ancient history with modern poverty. The dilapidated double-wides and shacks of found metal melded into the magnificent environment. Bloom loved Santa Fe and the rez equally.

Getting back into the rhythm of white man's time was surprisingly difficult though. The stress of making sales made Bloom aware of the burden of maintaining a certain lifestyle for the first time in months. Life without money, while hard, has its benefits. You sleep well at night and concentrate on what's truly important—family, health, and happiness, not how big your home is or what model Mercedes you drive.

By August, Bloom had his watch back on and a constant sense of urgency had returned to his life. There was a definite need to make as many sales as possible before the Texans returned to their ancestral grounds. Bloom missed Rachael and the sound of her loom at work. She had come to visit, but just for a short stay. Sheep need tending and Preston still was not a man. He was a tweener of sorts, a man-boy. She wanted to make sure his last few months at home were fulfilling, as she knew college in a primarily Anglo world would be a challenge. It was a time to let him know all the problems she had encountered in her own education with whites, and to arrange connections with other Native Americans, especially Diné.

Kids from the reservation who go to college often have a difficult time adjusting to the whites' world of timelines and stress. It is not a Diné characteristic to worry about having something done at a particular time. The kids can lose their *hozho*, or sense of balance and harmony, and feel trapped in a foreign environment. No Diné is spoken at a white person's college, except by the few Navajos at school. Having been through the process herself, Rachael wanted to make sure Preston had all the tools to succeed.

The week of Indian Market is a blur for retailers in Santa Fe. It's like the Christmas season, but on steroids. The lines are long for everything, work hours dictated by the clients' needs, not by those stated on your gallery door. Bloom had done it for 20 years and like an old hand going out to sea during crabbing season he could see the stress was building on his one 70-year-old employee. Dr. James was not used to the constant mill of people in and out of the gallery, which was a small space when just two people were in it. Bloom found the new space claustrophobic at times but loved the thought that he basically only had to pay the utility bills. He could live with the claustrophobia. He advised Dr. James, "Just open the doors to the outside and all your space problems disappear."

Being in business for yourself you learn to recheck all things twice, especially when you're in the thick of retail war. Bloom caught two mistakes in one day on Dr. James's invoices. They were small in the big picture, but they counted more when you're making a living on a shoestring. Bloom blew up one time and he could tell the old man felt horrible. He had forgotten to charge tax on an in-state transaction. The approximately 8% tax, which Bloom would eat, could have paid his light bill for the month and he let Dr. James know his concerns in no uncertain terms. He felt terrible afterwards and wished he could have retracted his words of anger but it was Indian Market and the stress was building on him as well. He was the captain of the ship and there were only a few crabbing days left in the short season and there were lots of boats competing for fewer crabs this year.

Wednesday was the lightest day of the festival-packed week. It was when he planned to hang his textile show. Rachael had come in to help him focus and bring in her last creation. The 3 X 5-foot weaving was almost as fine as a silk scarf, an amazing feat for someone who had been weaving seriously for such a short time. It was the most compelling piece of art Bloom had ever seen. Bloom wondered if his love for Rachael was affecting his ability to remain impartial. He had watched the majority of the rug being made. He could visualize vividly the first few strands of the yarn on the loom. Rachael's voice was part of the textile, from the excitement when she had finished half the weaving to the exhaustion during the last two weeks calling him nightly, trying to finish in time for Indian Market. Bloom wanted to mark it SOLD and put it away. In retail this was impossible. It could only be a consignment from Rachael who was old school

Navajo. You did it for the money. They both realized this was their current reality.

Rachael and Charles discussed the price for the textile given the amount of time it had taken to weave. On an hourly basis, it was around $1.25 an hour, but that was weaving. It was important to get her first major textile priced correctly as it would be the basis for all the subsequent weavings. Everyone knew the weavings of her grandmother, Ethel Sherman, but Rachael's own following was nonexistent. Being Ethel's granddaughter would help. After all, she had taught her most of what she knew. But this rug would set the precedent for price structure in the future; her bench mark to judge all others. Bloom had confidence in his selling ability, but this was a new venue for the man whose clients knew him for contemporary art. Both Charles and Rachael decided they would rather starve this fall than sell it too cheaply. Lately decisions were being made as a couple not individually, a first for Charles Bloom. If Randal showed up, his higher prices would help sell her work. They decided on a retail price of $10K. Rachael had invested almost all her time in the one textile and had produced only one other rug, a small 1.5 X 1.5-foot sampler. The mat-sized rug was priced at $975, making sure to keep it below the magic $1,000 mark. They wanted at least one piece to sell.

It is well known in retail circles that there are certain break points that clients have to think about before they will buy. It is strictly an emotional response and has nothing to do with reason. Those points fall in quarter increments. It doesn't matter if it's hundreds or thousands of dollars. A price that ends at 25, 50, 75, or 100 might as well be marketed at a higher level in the minds of the retail buyer.

Bloom marked Rachael's small rug at $975 because it avoided a four-figure number, the thousand-dollar barrier. He could have priced it anywhere between $800-900 dollars and it wouldn't matter. Clients hesitate to spend a $1,000 but will plunk down $25 dollars less for the more-than-fair $975; that was the psychology of pricing. By placing Rachael's big rug at $10K, they took a big chance. It was that next digit up the retail food chain and mentally it would make a difference for some buyers, but a statement was being made. Rachael Yellowhorse's larger weavings would always demand five-figure sums.

A large sandwich sign had been made for the occasion. It read in red letters BEGAY/YELLOWHORSE on one side, and on the other in yellow letters MODERN MASTER WEAVERS OF THE DINÉ. The Santa Fe historical society had strict rules for signage on Canyon Road. A semi-permanent banner was forbidden, but a sandwich sign that could be taken in each day was OK if it had the word OPEN on it. All the Canyon Road stores took advantage of this idiosyncratic rule so in August the road looked as if a giant had put his dominos up and down Canyon Road just waiting to knock them down the street which was littered with OPEN signs.

Having a traditional show at such a prominent time seemed odd for Bloom, who was known in the business as specializing in contemporary artwork. At least the sign had the word MODERN on it. Bloom figured his competition would be making lots of derogatory remarks, like: "He's no longer a purist, sold out to the Santa Fe crowd. He must be struggling. Next he will have cheap Indian jewelry." Some of the Native American galleries might be carping how, "He doesn't know anything about Navajo rugs; his girlfriend is a weaver so he now thinks he's a big expert in the field. He should stick to what he understands."

The good dealers would never stoop to this kind of petty behavior, but since the art recession was into its third year there weren't many of those galleries left. It was more of an "every dog for himself" mentality. The truth lay somewhere in the middle for Bloom. He loved the art form of weavings, but he was also taking advantage of his position working at Toadlena part time and living with a Navajo weaver. His standing in the art-world hierarchy might become a moot point if Randal stood him up. With the prominent signage and lettering on the wall all proclaiming Randal Begay's talent, a no-show by Randal would damn Bloom as a nonentity in the world of Navajo weaving. It would also be an exceptionally bad start for Rachael's career which Bloom felt a great deal of pressure to help. He could hear it now: "His girlfriend's Navajo and he couldn't even get the other Navajo artist to show. That can't be good."

Wednesday came and went. No Randal Begay. The main room's best wall was painfully blank, with only the words RANDAL BEGAY sticking to its architectural white surface and a sheet of paper in the middle saying "coming soon." The letters were looking more like symbols of disgrace. Bloom felt like scraping off Begay's name and hanging a painting so as to not look like a complete fool during Rachael's opening, which was less than 48 hours away and the busiest day of the year at his gallery. He had decided if Begay were a no show by Friday morning, he would place a large vertical painting over the lettering to hide his fuck-up of a show. It would be incongruent with Rachael's textile, which was on the opposite wall. The fill-in for Begay was a pink-and-blue abstraction that didn't work well with her natural Two Grey Hills-designed weaving, but there were no other good choices at such a late date.

Closing the store on Thursday three hours later than normal, a miracle occurred. A beat-up green Ford pickup honked outside the front of Bloom's annex, and Randal Begay plunked his body out, adjusting his Stetson.

"Yá át ééh, Bloom. I got my piece here early. I know the show isn't till tomorrow, but I figured you wouldn't mind if I brought it in a day early. Maybe get someone interested beforehand?"

"No, I don't mind at all. In fact I thought you might have had some trouble. I haven't heard from you in months," Bloom pointed out.

"Nah, it's an Indian thing. We forget about stuff sometimes. Besides, your girlfriend's note said if I didn't show up she would cut my balls off."

"She said that?"

"Well not in so many words. It was more about me being true to Spiderwoman and if I didn't follow our beliefs I wouldn't be a man weaver anymore, just a girl like all the other weavers."

Understanding the implication full well, Bloom chuckled, "Well, she is a very strong woman, and also a great weaver. So I can hardly wait to see the weavings you brought me, Randal."

"Yeah, 'bout that. I only had time for one rug, so if you could I'd like you to buy it. I don't have nothing for consignment. I just didn't have time. But the one I made is a very good rug."

Charles wasn't surprised. He had dealt in Native art for 20 years. Some of the artists just couldn't afford to consign work even though it is standard practice for most of the art world. At least the wall reading BEGAY would have a textile. His reputation was saved. Begay pulled out a 4 X 6-foot, wider-than-long revival third-phase chief's blanket. It was obviously new, but Begay had caught the essence of the old weavings. For what would have been indigo blue in an old original chief's blanket, Begay had used a dark plum color. The nine-spots pattern in the old blanket he transposed into boxes inside of boxes of varying shades of crimson and light purple/pink. The most amazing part was the weaving's quality of spinning. The handspun wool was incredibly tight and as fine as any classic Navajo blanket woven 150 years ago. The weaving felt like a blanket, even though it was really more of an art piece. It was magnificent and it was clear he was a better weaver than Rachael, at least at this point. Bloom hoped she didn't ask him his opinion.

"Randal, I'm stunned, it's amazing. The wool is perfect and so tight."

"My mom taught me the old way to spin and I'm pretty good with the spindle. It helps being a man. I've got strong fingers and can get the wool very small and tight which really helps the rug. So Charles, I was thinking you could put it at $15K retail? You could give me $7,500. What do you think?"

"Well, tell me Randal, what's the most one of your rugs has sold for?"

"Ummm, about $12K retail."

"Is this rug $3K better?"

"I don't know. I guess I could use the money, so I want to get as much as I can."

"How about this, Randal," Bloom proposed. "I'll pay half of $12K, which is $6K. I've already given you $4K, so I'll owe you $2K more now. If I actually get the $15,000, then I will pay you an additional $2,000. This will give $500 more if your piece does sell, and I'm not on the hook for the extra money if it doesn't."

Randal thought about the proposition and realized it was the best deal he would get. He knew he was pushing the price because he had already been paid upfront money which he had spent. He would have to hope it sold.

"OK," Randal agreed, "it's a deal. But if it sells, Bloom, I need to get the extra money right away. I've got a bunch of bills to pay and my truck is barely working."

"Deal. Now let's go hang the rug and get it up on my website. I've got people who check my site hourly this time of year. They have been waiting for your rug."

CHAPTER 21

SHOWTIME

Randal's and Rachael's rugs were put up on Bloom's home page of his website with the heading MODERN MASTER WEAVERS OF THE DINÉ. The pictures of the weavings couldn't show the depth of the browns in Rachael's weavings, but Randal's was an excellent representation.

The images were good enough to catch the attention of Darryl Ridgemount, who just happened to be searching the web under the heading "Two Grey Hills, Daisy Taugelchee, Ethel Sherman weavings." These were specific weavers Trevor had thought Gusher needed in his collection. They were dead now and highly sought after. Both had always woven in the Toadlena/Two Grey Hills style of natural rugs. Older women weavers known as grandmothers generally wove their rugs stylistically with color palettes in accordance with the trading post owner's taste. Daisy and Ethel, who both grew up near Toadlena, specialized in rugs woven of natural-colored brown, black, and white wool, a longstanding style of that area. Both women had major works in important museums and there was almost nothing for sale. One small Ethel Sherman rug was available in a Santa Fe gallery that specialized in antique Navajo rugs. The piece was expensive and not important enough for Gusher's collection. A website that Ridgemount did find however, www.bloomsgallery.com, had something exciting: an exceptional textile by her granddaughter, Rachael Yellowhorse. There was an opening of her work the very next day, Friday, during Indian Market weekend. Ridgemount couldn't believe his good fortune. A possible weaving to show Gusher.

You don't live in Texas all your life and not know about Indian Market in Santa Fe. Darryl had never gone, but was more interested now with his new title as Gusher's textile consultant. This is what he called himself currently and his Kinko's business card proved it. The other person at the show he had vaguely heard of too, Randal Begay. Randal's work was very skilled and it looked very similar to one of Gusher's old chief's blankets, but the colors were different. The website said "Price on request," and that the pieces could not be put on hold during Indian Market.

Ridgemount called the gallery. "What's the ticket on those two major Navajo blankets you got down there?"

"Hi, I'm Bloom, the owner, and they are both terrific rugs. I just hung them today. At this point they are still available. The opening is tonight at 6 pm. The Yellowhorse is $10K and the Begay is $15K." Bloom had technically hung them the night before when the gallery was closed, but it sounded better to say he just hung the pieces to make the potential buyer feel pressure like Bloom was.

"I know you aren't supposed to hold them," Darryl said, "but I work for a man who I will advise to buy the pieces and if you could make an exception for, say, one hour, I'll get right back to you."

Bloom knew this could be a mistake as his window for selling one or both was today and someone could easily walk in and want one. If they're on hold, potential buyers get pissed or lose interest and spend their money at some other gallery.

"How sure are you your guy would want them both?" Bloom asked. "I hate to hold anything during our busiest day of the year, even for an hour. I'm sure you can understand."

"Damn sure," Darryl responded. "I just need to show him the photos. I'm going to tell him to do the deal. If we get both, can you come off some?"

"OK, I'll hold them for one hour," Bloom agreed. "If you get them both, I'll knock off 5%. I'll need a number I can reach you at just in case I get a call on them."

Ridgemount agreed and gave him his cell, then tracked down Gusher.

"Gusher, I've got two great rugs on hold for you in Santa Fe, both by Navajo artists. They are the best I've seen by any living artist. They are $25K for the pair, and each probably took six months to make. Pretty good size as well. Nice fit for your collection, if you want my opinion. They're being exhibited in a good gallery in Santa Fe. They're the gallery's Indian Market show pieces."

"Well you haven't fucked me yet. I'll give you your usual 20%, and you can go ahead and close the deal. Any chance the guy might come down if we get them both?"

"No, already tried. It's his biggest weekend and he's not budging," Darryl lied. "Can't blame him, it is Indian Market weekend."

"I'll have Harold fly you over in my jet," Bill decided. "Go pick 'em up. No sense somebody making him a better offer and we lose the damn things. I need to fill in those holes. No luck on that Daisy or finding a first-phase blanket?"

"No, I'm afraid nothing on either. But the Yellowhorse weaver is Ethel Sherman's granddaughter. She might have one of grandma's rugs hanging around the hogan that I could break loose," Darryl speculated.

"Hot damn. Get going, boy. See if we can get a big one. Maybe she knows some Indian that has an old first-phase hanging around, tell 'em I can change their life. Come by and I can cut you a check for the $25K."

"Not necessary, Gusher. I'll pay in cash and you can reimburse me when I bring them to you. I don't want to take the time to go across town and get caught in traffic. The guy said he would hold them, but I figure if someone walks in with cash he will sell them out from under us."

"Good thinking. I'll pay you in cash plus your commission when you get back. Harold will be waiting for you at the airport. Give me a call once you got 'em safe in hand."

Harold was Gusher's pilot of 10 years. He was overpaid for exactly this sort of situation: to be on-call at a moment's notice. This eliminated any normal life, including alcohol consumption or a social agenda. Too risky, since Gusher could get an urge to go somewhere and call him at 10 at night saying, "Let's go, see you in 20."

The small jet could seat eight comfortably and had a full bathroom, a nice luxury in any private plane. Gusher had decorated the seats with embroidered longhorn cattle heads and outfitted the entire interior in his favorite color, neon orange, the University of Texas colors. It hurt the eyes upon entering the interior for the first time, but Darryl appreciated it.

There were three co-pilots on staff who rotated call, their only requirement being that they had to be UT fans. No one but Harold was willing to have no life for a job. Harold was ready by the time Darryl arrived, having made a quick paint-can stop to pick up a zip-locked bag of cash. He had called Bloom's from the road and emphasized, "Sold! I'm heading over in my private plane and will be there in a few hours. Do not sell them. I will be there with cash in hand." He gave Bloom the tail number of Gusher's plane in case he wanted to check to make sure it was real since he had no credit card to secure the pieces to. Bloom had to have some faith and this was tough as he had been screwed before on his biggest retail day by an art dealer and didn't care for it one bit. He called the private jet port. The number checked out. The plane was en route.

Darryl had only flown commercial and was not expecting how different it was flying private. He pulled into the private airport in Austin, gave his tail number, and was let through the chain-length fence. No searching for a parking place, just drive up to the plane. Harold and the copilot were waiting, anticipating Darryl's arrival.

"Mr. Ridgemount, I'm Harold, Mr. Hughes's pilot, and this is Don your copilot. Can we get you anything before we take off, coffee or a soft drink?" Don took Darryl's brand new Tumi suitcase, which was packed with a few cloths, two pairs of boots, and plenty of hats, his cash safely tucked into his leather jacket. Darryl was liking this VIP service. Maybe there would be additional jet perks. He hoped Gusher had a masseuse waiting, something he would really remember.

"Sure, I'll have a Dr. Pepper if you got one." In Texas the favorite drink is Dr. Pepper, and it was a given that Harold was well stocked.

"You got it, Mr. Ridgemount. Diet or regular?"

"Diet would be great. When we leaving?" Darryl was new to the private jet world and didn't realize it was really more up to him than the pilot when it came to shoving off.

"As soon as you like, Mr. Ridgemount. It's a little less than a two-hour flight. We've got a pretty good head wind today. Do you need a driver when you get there?"

Darryl hadn't even thought about transportation past the plane and he also had never had a driver, but this was Gusher's money so his response was, "Yes, I will need a driver. If you can have him waiting when we arrive, that would be dandy." Darryl liked the life as a big-time curator. No wonder Trevor cherished his job so damn much. Too bad about the porn and dope.

Flying into Santa Fe is always bumpy, but on a hot August afternoon filled with thunderheads threatening to explode at any moment, it is plain miserable. Indian Market weekend is notorious for being rained on. Too many Indians doing rain dances, one Native exhibitor complained. The skies said this would be a typical Market weekend. The little jet scurried around the huge cumulonimbus clouds that were already 30,000 feet high by mid-afternoon. Darryl was in awe and scared as the pilots guided the aircraft through Mother Nature's obstacle course. He was feeling nauseated from the bumps, and hoped he didn't throw up like some novice flier on his first private excursion.

The final approach coming in over the 13,000-foot-high Sangre de Cristo Mountain range from Texas is exhilarating for the first time, especially in a small private jet. The plane practically clips the mountains, then turns sharply to swoop down into the tiny jet strip on the far west side of Santa Fe. Today the airport was like an L.A. freeway: hundreds of private jets from all over were coming in to Santa Fe for Market. Harold had to circle the airport twice before he was given the go-ahead to land, each circle increasing Darryl's nausea. Every Texan with money and a love of Indian art was in Santa Fe for the weekend.

"Mr. Ridgemount, we've been given clearance to land if you want to get your seatbelt on. We'll be on ground in less than five."

With that, the plane banked hard, leaving the last of Darryl's stomach in his mouth. He had tried hard not to throw up. Harold was ex-military and had never quite broken the habit of sharp precise turns.

Once on the ground, Darryl's face returned to its rich tan color. He bid Harold goodbye and took his first limousine to Bloom's. The plan was to spend the night and be ready to depart at 1 pm tomorrow. Darryl didn't take long to become the surrogate VIP and take charge. He might as well have some fun at the big Indian festival that opened at 7 am on Saturday. But first, to Bloom's to finish the deal and make his money.

※ ※ ※ ※

Charles Bloom was pacing. His opening was less than two hours away. Rachael was getting cleaned up at Shriver's guest home and Randal said he would be there on time. Both big rugs were on hold, supposedly sold, but Bloom didn't know the Texas client and he was a no-show so far. The early clients would arrive in about an hour and half, and Bloom couldn't hold the rugs much longer. Bloom considered calling the number the Texan had given him but bit his lip and waited. At 4 pm he would release the rugs, and take his chances with pissing off the mysterious Ridgemount.

Dealers hate these situations. A possible sale by an unknown entity that makes big promises but often won't follow through. It was looking like a classic example. The Texan would make a big entrance and then a bogus excuse once he saw the pieces as to why he didn't want them, if he showed at all.

Bloom had had a prior experience where a client flew in, looked at a piece, and said he just wanted to make sure it worked in his house. Bloom sent it out even though it was during a show for the artist;

after all, the client had flown in and it was a done deal. Two weeks passed and Bloom called asking what the scoop was. The supposed client told him his wife had been out of town but she would be back soon, and he was still sure they would purchase the piece but needed to get the little woman's OK.

Two days later he had gotten an email from a dealer who offered him his own piece back at a greatly increased price. Turned out the supposed client was nothing more than a private quasi-dealer who had been offering the piece all over, trying to make a buck. As Bloom started to pressure the client to get the piece back, he had sent e-mail blasts to other dealers, who then offered it to Bloom. Bloom had flipped. His painting, which at this point was who knows where, had been overexposed and worse yet, when he chastised the swindler for his extremely unethical behavior, the fellow simply said, "Sorry, it wasn't quite right for the place I had hoped and my wife hated it." The guy explained the e-mails as his trying to help Bloom out by helping him sell the painting. Individuals like this are the scourge of the art business. They will do anything for a buck and don't care who they screw or what piece they destroy. They go from dealer to dealer taking advantage until they get caught.

"They're all the same, only concerned with how much it cost, how fast it can sell, and how much will be made," Bloom thought now. Since cost, not artistic merit, is the deciding factor, these so-called dealers never develop an eye. All they care about is what Benjamin Franklin looks like. These Judah's of the art world have no filter other than price. Relationships mean nothing. Everything revolves around the deal. If money can be skimmed off the top from either the buyer's or seller's end, they're in. These so-called art dealers believe stealing is only frowned upon if you're caught. Selling fakes, frauds, or simply damaged goods is acceptable as long as one is careful. Taking advantage of little old ladies is a sport and fucking a dealer both figuratively and literally is a given.

Bloom's past experiences were all playing out in his mind as he paced the floor, worrying about his unknown sure thing. Was Ridgemount just another guy who didn't have the balls to open up his own gallery and would take sport in ruining him on his most important retail day?

CHAPTER 22

LET'S MAKE A DEAL

Bloom recognized Ridgemount instantaneously by the way he strutted through the gallery entrance. He didn't need to see the limo that Ridgemount had pulled up in... the same limo that was now taking up most of Bloom's precious parking space on his biggest retail day of the year. Bloom had seen the type many times. They know everything and you must cater to their demanding needs. You can spot them every time. Something about their air of superiority. Bloom wished Ridgemount would say something ridiculous so he could add him to the kitchen wall of shame.

"I'm looking for the owner, Bloom. You him?" Darryl said, already knowing the answer, having seen his image on the www.bloomsgallery.com website when he discovered the rugs.

"Yes, are you Mr. Ridgemount?"

"Call me Darryl. Sorry I'm late. Our jet had some nasty headwinds coming into Santa Fe and the airport's packed." Darryl wanted to remind Bloom he had traveled in privately at great cost. The gas was as much as the weavings, but money was not the object for Gusher, who was filling holes in his collection.

"You still have *my* rugs on hold, right?" Darryl asked, emphasizing *my* as if to pick a fight. Darryl was letting Bloom know they were his unless he said otherwise.

"Yes, I've had a lot of interest in both textiles." This was not exactly the truth. One couple had asked about them, then scoffed when they realized the prices, not having a clue what masterpiece textiles cost. "I rarely hold anything right before an opening, especially Indian Market weekend. Our busiest day of the year is today."

"I appreciate it, Bloom. So let's see these bad boys, find out if I need to spend some cash today," Ridgemount offered, already knowing he would definitely be buying them as he had a guaranteed payday waiting. He strolled over to the sign that said BEGAY, and inspected the weaving, running his hand on the smooth blanket.

"Purtee nice. Boy's got good wool sense. Hard to believe it's new. It has an old feel and look," Darryl remarked.

"Yes," Bloom agreed. "Randal's amazing. He weaves like one of the great blanket weavers of long ago, a master at his craft."

"Now the Begay is $15K," Darryl clarified, "and if I remember correctly, you going to give me 5% off for both?" He announced his discount loudly as if no one was around, not caring if other potential clients heard his backroom deal. Bloom hated when people did this as he tried to be consistent and not discount prices. This is not easy in Santa Fe, which is known for its permanent 50% off signs, but times were tough and he wanted to prove to Begay he could sell Navajo rugs, and he and Rachael could use the money. Bloom was not yet known as a textile dealer and it was a market he still felt uncomfortable with, even after 20 years as an art dealer.

In almost a whisper, Bloom replied, "Yes, that was what we discussed."

"Couldn't hear ya, 5% off, right?" Darryl was almost yelling to the red-faced, flustered Bloom, his voice clearly being heard by anyone in the claustrophobic building.

"Yes, if you get both," Bloom said back, whispering more clearly this time.

"OK, well, I like this here Begay rug. Let's look at the Yellowhorse, never heard of her. She's as good as her Grandma Ethel?"

"I think in some ways she's better," replied Bloom. "Already her weavings are as fine, yet her designs are much more complex and she hasn't been weaving that long."

Both men stared intently at the large dark brown and tan rug hanging on the white architectural wall below the words "YELLOWHORSE."

"Hmm, yeah. Good work. I must admit, this one surprises me. I like it." Ridgemount stroked his hand over the wool, purring as he finished. He simultaneously picked up a biography that was under the textile, featuring a color image of Rachael Yellowhorse.

Still purring as he had done while caressing Rachael's rug, Darryl added, "Damn she's too good-looking to be weaving rugs, should be partying over in Austin making real money." Darryl laughed at the perverse thought he had just let Bloom in on. Bloom smiled weakly, trying not let on that she was his girlfriend. He wanted his art relationship to be strictly professional and he didn't want to screw the deal. He also now hated selling the rug to the Texan and wished he wouldn't touch either rug any more.

"OK here's the deal, Bloom. I'm interested in getting both. I have cash and figured you could do a least another 5% better for cash. Your artists won't be the wiser. I don't need any fancy receipts."

There it was for Bloom: instant recognition of a scumbag dealer. Any dealer who can skim off the top from his artists and feels it's business as usual is a crook. He still hoped to close the deal, but was afraid now of what kind of person Darryl Ridgemount was.

"Darryl, I wish cash made a difference, but it doesn't. What I will do is knock off another 1.5% for the cash as I would have to pay this if it were a credit card, so you get the savings and I will give you a complete receipt."

To Darryl, this meant Bloom was honest and a fool. A guy who would actually declare almost $25K of cash? Darryl, who only dealt in cash and never had participated in paying taxes, saw this as a terrible flaw in Bloom's character. Bloom became a man Darryl couldn't trust. Bloom would always do the right thing.

"OK," Darryl sighed, "it's your cash. Seems to me like you're just giving Uncle Sam more than he deserves, but I'll take them both. Wrap 'em up. I'll take them with me."

Bloom's heart started to race at the thought of this obviously clueless Texan who wanted to wreck his show opening by leaving two blank walls with only letters. Ridgemount would make the Top 10 list after all.

"Well," Bloom explained, "I can't really give them to you right now. My show opens in an hour and lots of folks will be coming to see these great works. The artists want to show them. I'm sure you can understand?"

Darryl, who had never been to an opening before, much less participated in one, hadn't even thought about the consequences of his doing a grab-and-run. He tried to backtrack. "Of course, I knew that was a given. It's not like I'm going to pull 'em off the wall right this second. I just need to have them by the time I leave tomorrow afternoon. Hey, when's the girl coming? I'd like to meet her." He raised his eyebrows to imply he would like to sleep with her. After all, he had just bought her prized rug. Maybe she came with the rug, a bonus of sorts.

"Ms. Yellowhorse will be here shortly. If you like maybe you want to stroll up Canyon Road and take in the sights. It's great people-watching tonight. Come back in an hour or so, and both artists will be here."

"You got it, Pard. I'll take a hike. How about we settle up now, so I can take off when I'm ready. You got a rest room I can use?" All galleries have a restroom in Santa Fe but if you ask every gallery on Canyon Road it will be nonexistent. Unless you buy, you don't pee.

"It's right through that back room I call an office. I'll meet you in there after you're done," said Bloom.

As Ridgemount went to the restroom, Bloom finished his favorite part of any show, placing small red dots on the wall tags next to each weaving to proudly proclaim the show's success. Red dots are the universal sign of a great opening. They represent SOLD in the art world. Everyone loves lots of red dots.

Darryl didn't need to pee, but he did want to retrieve his stash of cash and didn't want to show his hidden jacket lining. He also wanted to look for any extra gallery stationary stored in the restroom, as he wanted to make his own receipt to keep the extra 6.5% he had skimmed. He found a box in a high set of drawers and helped himself.

After Darryl counted the money twice, Bloom gave him an invoice that clearly stated cash. Bloom was a stickler for accuracy when it came to declaring cash. No sense getting put in jail over a small-time tax dodge. He slept well at night.

"Bloom, if you would please put the original retail prices on your website and print me off a couple of copies of the rugs with their information, this would be helpful for my paperwork. I like a nice paper trail," Ridgemount requested, planning to make his own invoice and show Gusher copies of the weavings with their non-discounted prices.

"Not a problem, Mr. Ridgemount. In fact I will also make you certificates for your insurance."

"Peachy. While you're doing that I'll take my stroll and be back soon. Looking forward to meeting Ms. Yellowhorse," Ridgemount grinned and winked at Bloom as he outstretched his hand in a Texan gesture. The deal was officially complete.

Bloom half-heartedly shook his hand as Ridgemount walked out the door, his tall frame with his black cowboy hat just barely clearing the entrance of the small 19th-century doorjamb. Bloom felt relief at selling the two pieces, even if it was at a discount, but his inner voice was warning, "Don't trust that guy ever." He went immediately to wash his hands. If he had only bothered to look up he would have noticed his box of gallery stationary was slightly ajar, thanks to Darryl Ridgemount's handiwork.

CHAPTER 23

SLIME BALL

The look on Rachael's face when she saw the red sticker was one of surprise and great joy. This was extra college money for Preston's freshman year, a couple of great dinners on the town, a pair of new shoes from Goler which was the best shoe store in Santa Fe.

"I can't believe it, you sold my big rug! You are the great *bilagaana* art dealer!"

"Yes, my Navajo princess, I am god of the rug merchants. See me, I am able to sell something I still don't know shit about."

Both were laughing at their good fortune to sell her first major weaving for so much and in a terrible retail economy, to boot.

"So how much? Did you get close?"

"$9,350 cash," replied Bloom.

"Oh my God, we are rich, or at least I am. Who is the big spender?"

"Well that's the part that isn't as good. He seems pretty much like a slime ball kind of guy. I feel bad your first great rug is going to someone I don't like who seems only concerned about money. He also was making comments about how good you looked in your biography, and not in such a proper way if you get my drift. He's looking forward to meeting you."

"That sucks. I wish he was a nice guy, but he does have good taste in women," she giggled at her jab at Bloom for showing jealousy. She was too happy about the sale to worry that he was a jerky person.

"I sent him up Canyon Road. I figured you would want to know before he came strolling in asking you out for dinner," Bloom said.

"Wow, you don't like this guy at all. OK, I get the picture, not the kind of guy I would take home to the family."

"You could say that."

A loud blast of hard-rock music came through the front door as Randal Begay rolled up in his fading green truck, taking the last parking spot in front of Bloom's. Charles wanted to scream, "Move the damn truck. We might have a real paying customer come through the door." But he was happy there was actually money in his pocket for the first time in a while. Most importantly, he would get back the money he had fronted Begay, which until yesterday Bloom thought was gone forever.

"*Yá át ééh*, the star of the show has arrived!" Randal was only partly kidding. He knew he was great at his craft and he looked the part. Under his Stetson, his jet-black hair was pulled back in a tight braid. His eyes were hidden behind dark Kmart sunglasses and his tee shirt read KICK ASS INJUN in bright red letters.

"*Yá át ééh*, Randal. My *bilagaana* boyfriend sold our rugs, if you can believe it. C-A-S-H," said Rachael, taking her time to emphasize their good fortune.

"I'm sure glad you wrote me that note, my Toadlena sister. I can use some money bad. Bloom, can I get paid now?"

"Randal, the guy who bought them is going to pick them up tomorrow afternoon. I'll pay you after he has them in his possession.

Sometimes people back out and I want to make sure he has left with the rugs first," Bloom replied.

"OK, I guess I can wait, but how about $100 in advance? I'd like to go celebrate tonight."

Bloom pulled out a $100 bill and handed it to Randal. Bloom knew Randal was not planning to pay this back; it was a thank you for showing up. Randal caressed the bill, looking closely at its texture like it was his sheep's wool. Then a big grin came over his face. It had been a long time since he had spending money.

Artists have a reputation for being bad business people. For many it is well-deserved. Creating art hardly teaches them the art of business. Clients back out of deals for no good reason. It's part of the game. If an artist's work is paid directly after the sale and the deal falls through, the art dealer is caught holding the bag. Bloom's had a seven-day return policy, shorter than many, and Ridgemount had a receipt stating that fact. If for some reason he or his client got cold feet, he could ask for his money back. The chances were extremely small considering he had paid in cash, but stranger things had happened. Bloom had negotiated the deal with Randal that if he got $15K he would pay Begay an additional $2K. He had actually gotten closer to $14K, but knew Begay wouldn't understand. If he discounted, that was on his end. Bloom cringed at the thought of the deal going south and him loosing another $2K. If Ridgemount backed out and Begay was paid, Bloom would be the proud owner of a very expensive weaving. As much as he loved Begay's work, he couldn't afford to be a collector at this point in his life. He hated paying artists early and they would never understand why.

At the stroke of 5 pm, the gallery filled as the tourists who had seen Bloom's sandwich sign and advertisements came to see the famous Indian weavers. Bloom handed out the obligatory cheese and salami trays, which he had bought at Albertsons grocery store that morning. The regulars used the Friday night Canyon Road walk for a free dinner and cheap buzz. Bloom recognized many of the free-food crowd by face after 20 years. They knew better than to make eye contact. They simply came in, loaded up, and removed themselves to the porch to devour, drink, and move on. Art was not on the agenda, just finger food and screw-top wine.

A Scottsdale plastic surgeon that had seen the rugs on the Internet came in to purchase one of the pieces. He was disappointed that the two major works were already gone. For some reason retail buyers feel that nothing should be sold before they have had the chance to preview the show, and are amazed and peeved when it's not waiting for them. Bloom luckily had the little rug of Rachael's, which he offered at a slight discount to placate him for not getting her big rug and promised when she finished her next piece, the surgeon would get first shot. Rachael, who was charming, made the sale and Bloom got out of her way. He could see her training at the side of her late grandmother at Toadlena had been well learned. She was a pro and Bloom realized watching her, she didn't need his gallery. She was one of those rare persons who could make and sell the art equally well. He was lucky and he knew it. Marriage once again entered his mind, this time with positive thoughts.

The night was going well. A few contemporary paintings sold, and a large number of Navajo artists came by to visit Begay and Yellowhorse. All were in town for the big shindig tomorrow, Indian Market. Word spread quickly among the other Navajo weavers that all three rugs at Bloom's had sold, and they came by to see how good the pieces really were. Navajos are not competitive by nature, but it still didn't hurt to see what was possible with the loom.

Ridgemount finally came back to the opening after having drunk his own share of cheap wine along the street. He was tipsy and didn't care as his driver was waiting patiently for him to finish, still taking up two of Bloom's precious parking spaces.

"Hi Bloom, where's Yellowhorse? Like to see her in the flesh," Darryl slurred. Bloom found Rachael and made the obligatory introductions. The process sickened him, as he truly disliked the braggadocio of the all-cash Texan.

"Nice to meet you, Mr. Ridgemount," Rachael said, putting out the typically limp Indian handshake which Darryl squeezed aggressively in his Texan way. He obviously hurt her fingers, which were not dainty from years of sculpting metal. She disliked him immediately as well.

"Damn, girl, you sure can weave. I hear you're Ethel's granddaughter. You got any of your grandmom's rugs hanging around?"

His lack of decorum in mentioning her dead grandmother's name and trying to get rugs in the first words out of his mouth really did make Rachael wish the Scottsdale doctor could have gotten her rug.

"No, nothing for sale, I'm afraid. Hard to get grandma's rugs these days, but at least you got my big one," Rachael said.

"Yeah, true enough. But if you do get one, or decide to let one of your own go, I'll pay you good money. Cash."

Again, Bloom thought. Darryl was trying to use cash as if it was the elixir of selling. Mention the word and everyone will drop their drawers. In Darryl's world, this was true.

"OK. I hope I don't ever have to sell mine," Rachael replied, immediately regretting that she had let out the fact that she had one of Ethel's rugs, even if it was one she had finished. She didn't trust this guy and couldn't wait to wash her aching fingers.

"Great, I'll hold you to that," Darryl said, winking at her as if he had made a mental note and she was now fully committed to the future deal. "I'm free for dinner, and I've got a limo waiting outside if you're interested?" He slurred his words just a bit.

"No, I'm afraid Mr. Bloom has already made plans with me," Rachael said, taking Bloom's hand. She wanted the tall, inebriated Texan to know to fuck off. He got her rug and that's all the Yellowhorse he would ever get.

"Gotcha, I didn't know. Bloom, you're a good businessman. Where's old Begay? Like to talk with that boy."

"Sure, he's over under the sign that says BEGAY," the peeved Bloom retorted to the man who was too drunk to catch his sarcasm.

"Great, introduce me."

Walking over to a crowd of people all of whom seemed to be Indian, Bloom slipped through to make the obligatory introduction, then Bloom exited the conversation, not wanting to listen to Ridgemount any more than he had to. Bloom figured Begay knew all about drunks and could handle his inebriated patron. Bloom innately knew the more time he spent around Darryl the more his dislike would grow.

He needed to keep business his first priority, something all good salesmen understand.

The night was a huge success by anyone's standards. Weavings and paintings sold, a great turnout, and all the food and wine had disappeared, so he didn't have to worry about eating it for the next few days. Ridgemount left around 7 pm and seemed to have a great conversation with Begay. In fact, they left together, apparently to get a bite.

The sight of Ridgemount leaving with his best Navajo weaver bothered Bloom, as he knew the kind of man Ridgemount was: a shark who couldn't be trusted. He would warn Begay tomorrow when he showed up to get his $2,000. Bloom hoped Begay had enough common sense not to do anything he would regret with the tall man from Texas.

CHAPTER 24

AUSTIN'S GOSSIP TRAIL

Trevor Middleman's sudden release from the Hughes family's inner circle was not only shocking, it was also disconcerting as far as the manner in which it had been handled. He was never given the opportunity to talk with Ms. Hughes. He was basically summarily dismissed by her hick boyfriend, Mr. Hook-Um Horns Ridgemount. The excuse of going in a different direction seemed lame to the logical Trevor. Something else was at play, and if he had to guess it was Ridgemount trying to manipulate Ms. Hughes and he didn't want Trevor raining on his party.

It had been nearly six months since the sad event and Trevor had found a new job as a curator at a small private museum that specialized in textiles and pre-Columbian artifacts. It was a good fit for Trevor's interests. He was glad to be away from the private curator scene after it had left such a bad taste in his mouth. The museum world allowed for plenty of time for research and they had a spectrophotometer for dye analysis along with an electron microscope for yarn evaluation. The Navajo collection was only so-so, leaning more towards Incan textiles, but he planned on improving that.

The first hint of the real reason he had been fired occurred when Trevor overheard a docent talking about how Ms. Hughes wouldn't visit the museum because she didn't want to run into Trevor. Apparently he had left on bad terms and she was still upset.

Hearing the outrageous accusation he wanted to run over and scream at the two old nosey busybodies, but that was not Trevor's style. He was a man of taste, culture, and manners. He would get to the bottom of what was going on and do it in Trevor fashion. "A man who has patience is also virtuous," he had told one of his lovers and he wasn't talking about ethics, but it still applied.

Trevor figured the answer lay literally between Ms. Hughes and Ridgemount. He decided to put out some feelers and see what fish he reeled in (although he hated fishing).

Anonymously Trevor contacted a few of the large Indian art dealers and told them he had a very important blanket, a first- phase chief's, and wanted to know if anybody in the Austin area would be interested in buying it. Trevor was only interested in showing it to someone locally as he didn't like shipping such a valuable piece and wanted to keep the piece very private. The calls were made, and it took less than 24 hours before he was contacted by a man looking for such an item: Darryl Ridgemount.

Working through an intermediary to keep his name confidential, Trevor asked what Darryl would be willing to pay. The answer was $300K, all cash if the piece was in excellent condition and had a reliable history.

Trevor knew something had changed upon hearing the amount he would pay and that it would be in cash. Melinda Hughes would have been interested in a first-phase blanket, as she knew this was something Bill would have wanted for his collection, but she would not offer so much thinking it would be a waste of money, and she would never want to pay in cash. All her purchases were by check or credit card. Ridgemount was working for someone besides Ms. Hughes or for himself; both were disconcerting if he was still the acting curator for Ms. Hughes's collection.

Reluctantly, a call to Bill Hughes was in order.

"Mr. Hughes, this is Trevor Middleman. I was wondering, are you buying Navajo rugs again?"

"As a matter of fact I am. You got a lead on something I might want?

"No, not exactly, but I heard there could be a great first phase coming on the market and I knew you always wanted one and didn't know if you still did, since you don't have the collection anymore?"

"Trevor, I've always liked you so I'm going to be straight with you. But you cannot tell Ms. Hughes. I know you don't work for her any more but I figure you're still close. I ended up buying back all Ms. Hughes's rugs for myself. She doesn't know it's me and I would like to keep it that way for now. I paid her a very handsome profit, but she wouldn't ever have sold them if she knew I was the buyer. She's still pretty pissed about the Tiffany thing. You know those damn blankets were my interest and she took them to make me mad and of course it did."

"I understand completely and will respect your wishes. Ms. Hughes and I aren't on the best of terms either, right now."

"Trevor, I'm still trying to fill in those gaps in the collection, so if you come up with something you think the collection needs, let me know. I'm especially interested in a first-phase chief's blanket."

"Is anyone currently helping you to curate the collection or are you doing it yourself?"

"I'm too busy to devote much time so I hired my ex-wife's ex-boyfriend, Darryl Ridgemount. Real nice guy. I see why she liked him. He's found a couple of great pieces so far, but frankly I don't care who brings me things as long as I get what I need."

"Mr. Ridgemount. I didn't know he was knowledgeable about textiles. And he's no longer with Ms. Hughes?"

"Yeah, they're on the outs for now, lucky him. As far as the blankets go, he seems like an expert to me or he's a quick study. He knows his shit better than I do and I like to think I know quite a bit. Seems he liked them even before he met Melinda and has taken the time and effort to learn the subject in depth. He also has a good understanding of the business end, which is rare for you curators."

This entire statement made Trevor livid, but he never changed his tone even though he knew Ridgemount's knowledge all came from his tutorials. "Interesting. Well, Mr. Hughes, I'll let you know if I can locate the supposedly fresh first-phase blanket. I know you have always wanted one."

"Trevor, if you get one, I sure would be grateful. My collection will never be completed until I have that damn first phase, but I guess you already knew that."

"Yes, Mr. Hughes, I did." Trevor now knew his dismissal and the selling of the blanket collection were related and he was somehow caught in the middle. He hated confrontation, so he had let things lay. The recommendation and severance pay had eased the pain. But now it was clear something fishy had happened. Trevor's mom had always told him: "The truth always comes out and bad people get their just reward when they lie." Trevor had a feeling about Ridgemount. He was a bad man and the truth would come out.

CHAPTER 25

WHO'S ON FIRST

Gusher's first call after talking with Trevor was to Darryl Ridgemount.

"Darryl, I've got some good news. Trevor Middleman called and he says he might have located a first-phase blanket. I figured you should know in case you want to use your powers of persuasion to determine what the scoop is. I know in my business when someone is ready to sell, it generally happens quickly."

"I'm already on top of it, Gusher. Got wind of it the other day. I made kind of a lowball offer, $400K cash. I figured it was a good starting point."

"Sounds fine. I expected it would cost me half a mil at least. I might even pay a million if that's what it takes. Hopefully this lead's got legs. Remember, it has to have a good history on the piece. Gonna spend that kind of money, I better know it's the real thing."

"Don't worry, Gusher. You're paying me to make sure you're getting the good stuff and I will."

"Keep me updated." Gusher hung up.

Trevor Middleman calling Gusher out of the blue had to be more than a coincidence. He was up to something. Ridgemount planned to get to the bottom of it. If he did have a first phase, why would he be brokering it? Didn't seem like something an academic would take part in. "He was too good to stoop to the level of a rug merchant," Darryl said out loud as he figured out how to handle the situation. Trevor must know about Gusher buying his collection back, so Melinda would find out soon. No big deal, that gravy train had already played out. Darryl figured the most Trevor could do would be to try and cut him out on the first-phase deal if he really had one, and if he didn't then he was just fishing to find out why he was axed.

Darryl was a businessman and crook. The combination could be a powerful tool if you were good at both professions and he was. Time to make a visit to Trevor's house and find out what he knew. Finding Trevor turned out to be very easy for Ridgemount, who in his younger days was a rogue bounty hunter. He liked hunting people, what with the thrill of the chase. Hurting his prey would be a nice bonus, but he wasn't getting paid to do that and too many cops would get involved. An Internet search found Trevor's new job. He also had just purchased a house near the U.T. campus. Real-estate records gave Ridgemount all he needed.

The small brick home was painfully tiny in comparison to the massive estates on the hills directly above it, a throwback to days of old. The upper ridges were now comprised of rows of magnificent Texas rock homes, each of them 7,000 to 10,000 square feet in size and employing their own crews of Mexican workers. These were products of Austin's productive high-tech industry, behemoths with the required views of the state capitol, city vista, and Ladybird Lake. By comparison, Trevor's home—hidden away on a mature cul-de-sac—was a classic teardown sandwiched between other soon-to-be teardowns. He had acquired it from an older gay man who sold it under its true value for a fee a curator's salary could afford. The seller saw himself in Trevor: a person who appreciated the home's intrinsic beauty. They were saving a piece of Austin's past. Normally homes the size of Trevor's were bulldozed within hours of the deal being completed. Darryl laughed at the tiny house, realizing that the misguided curator could make a bundle simply by selling out. Once he did, the other small surrounding homes would have to follow. Darryl despised this kind of weakness.

Trevor worked from eight to five at his museum job so Darryl scheduled the B-and-E during business hours. Having worked successfully as a robber in his twenties meant undetected entry would be no problem. This was a very simple job. The house wasn't alarmed and no dog. Cats were more Trevor's style.

Once inside the home, Ridgemount went about his mission like the professional he was. Gloves, dark clothes, and good tennis shoes in case he needed a hasty exit, his loaded .45 available for unexpected problems. Trevor's office was filled with file drawers, all extremely well organized. It was easy to find the file marked "First-Phase Chief's." It was a card catalog of all the known specimens including a few examples of historic photos of Indians and early wearing blankets. It was in one of these photos that he realized he had stumbled on a potentially very valuable item.

No leads to any owners of private blankets for sale were found. All the remaining file information was for museum holdings. Not a single individual person even owned a first phase, as far as Ridgemount could tell. But the photo gave him a different idea.

Ridgemount carefully removed the old worn photograph, and placed it in one of his jacket's hidden pockets, then put everything back as he had found it and exited. Trevor would never be the wiser.

A follow-up conversation with Trevor that evening confirmed what Ridgemount had thought. Trevor was full of shit and he had no first phase. He'd been fishing for information as to why he got sacked.

Trevor was taken off guard by Ridgemount's call. He hadn't expected Mr. Hughes to alert Ridgemount, at least not right away. It told Trevor that Hughes trusted this man and he better be careful if dealing with him, as all information would flow directly back to Ridgemount, who he was sure had prematurely ended his career as the Hughes curator.

Ridgemount decided to let Trevor slide for right now. If he had any more problems with his little friend in the neat house he would be back to rearrange his life for him. Ridgemount had memorized the house floor plan in case he visited again. Trevor never knew his house and inner sanctum had been violated and his life might be in grave danger.

CHAPTER 26

INDIAN MARKET'S AFTERMATHS

Bloom's entry into the world of traditional Navajo rugs was a huge success. In a single Friday night he had developed a whole new group of collectors who had never been in his gallery before. Having Brad Shriver in his old space was also working out well. Shriver made sure Bloom's clients knew he was still in business, just one door down, and a few of Shriver's clients found him as well. Without Brad's help he would never have made it another year in Santa Fe, but his summer so far had been better than expected. He had at least two very serious new clients who wanted both Begay and Yellowhorse rugs, and expensive ones at that.

Filling the Yellowhorse order would be no problem but the Begay might be another story. Randal had left with the man from Texas last night. Bloom figured the Texas dealer would be trying to get more material directly from his artist. This is not atypical in the art world. Dealers and collectors often try to go around the dealer who sells the work so as to cut out the middleman. Most artists will let their dealer know or even send them a check if the sale is a result of the gallery's initial efforts. In the case of Begay, Bloom could tell he would never get a check from him, if he actually owned a bank account. Bloom was lucky to even get the rug he had prepaid for. Ridgemount was obviously dirty. Bloom could tell by the way he worked only in cash and was looking for angles to get money off. Ridgemount would screw him at any opportune moment. Bloom realized this and all he could do was be careful about any dealings he had with the man from Texas.

Darryl was one of the Black Hat dealers, as Bloom called them. Bloom divided all art dealers into thirds. The top third were the White Hats. They were great people, ethical individuals you enjoyed doing business with. The middle third were the Grey Hats. They were generally trustworthy but could also screw you if the circumstances were in their favor. You watched them closely but still did business with them. Then there were the Black Hats, the Darryl Ridgemounts of the world. They would always be looking for the edge. Every deal with them was potentially hazardous. You only dealt with them knowing that they probably were screwing you but you just didn't know it yet.

On Saturday morning Bloom allowed himself free time to visit Indian Market's opening, viewing all the Native artists set up around the Plaza. Usually he would only visit the painters, as this had been his main area of interest and where he had discovered Rachael's brother Willard over 20 years ago. Nobody in Bloom's eyes today seemed like a breakout artist. What did surprise him was how much time he spent looking at other Navajo weavers' work, something he had never done before. Neither Randal nor Rachael had entered Market, but many other fine weavers had. The quality of work was very high and some were frankly as good as Rachael, whose work was terrific by any standards. Bloom picked up cards from two weavers and explained who he was and about his show. They were both very interested in talking with him about potentially showing work at Bloom's new textile wing. To be in retail over 20 years and to find something new you could really sink your teeth into was exhilarating. Little more than a year ago Bloom was looking at getting out of business altogether. Now he was considering a whole new direction and adding artists to his gallery. Bloom couldn't count on Randal, so to find potential additions to the mix was a necessity if he wanted this part of his business to thrive.

When Bloom arrived to open his gallery late Saturday morning he was not surprised to find Begay sitting on the door steps to pick up his two grand he had been promised from last night's sale. Begay was in a hurry. He had a lot to do and needed his cash so he could get back to the rez. Their conversation was short but quickly put a damper on what had been a great morning.

"Hi Randal. Thought you would be down on the Plaza buying fresh fry bread," Bloom said.

"Yeah, I love that shit but I've got to get back, start working on a new piece. Two grand don't go far in my world these days."

"What you going to do, another revival?"

"Well you could say that. I promised an old collector friend I would do them a big piece so I've got to start it. You know how that is."

Bloom did know. He also knew that the old collector was probably Ridgemount, who had wined and dined Randal last night and most likely stolen his weaver. "I noticed you and Mr. Ridgemount left together last night. You do dinner?"

Bloom watched Begay's body language. A quarter century in retail, and you learn to read people. Begay immediately looked at his feet, which answered the question.

"Yeah, he took me out for dinner. Nice guy. Hope I run into him again. Maybe he will come here next year when I do my show."

Bloom knew he was sunk. The fucker had got to him. The way Begay never made eye contact and was promising things for next year, he knew Ridgemount had stolen his artist. There would be no second Begay show. Bloom was glad he had taken the time to get the other weavers' information. "Hmm. Well you'll probably see Mr. Ridgemount sooner than you think."

Randal looked at Bloom who was looking right at him, and then Randal looked away. Randal knew he knew.

"Yeah, maybe. Well I got to go." Randal Begay would see Ridgemount again, and there would not be another Santa Fe show.

CHAPTER 27

AGAINST THE CLOCK

When a collector is ready to buy, you fill their needs or they will fill them elsewhere. Ridgemount knew the clock was ticking. Gusher wanted his blanket collection finished. He only lacked a few key pieces for a world-class display. The best-known artist missing was Daisy Taugelchee, a Toadlena/Two Grey Hills weaver. The collection had one very small piece by her, which Gusher referred to as a dinner napkin because it was the same size as one, but he wanted a major piece. Almost all of her bigger pieces were in museum collections, with only a few scragglier ones still out there. Ridgemount knew the chances were good he could find one. A great rug by Daisy would be worth around $100,000.

The other glaring hole was a lot harder to fill, a first-phase chief's blanket. This seemed to be impossible. They only came on the market every half-dozen years or so, and when they did materialize it was never to the masses; a quiet sale was held privately and quickly. Ridgemount figured he might have to actually steal one from a museum to fill Gusher's order. After all, they were very simple looking, just white, brown, and blue stripes. It would be hard to identify which piece came out of what museum. The more he thought about how simple these incredibly valuable blankets looked, the more he realized he didn't have to take the risk and steal one.

He'd make one instead. The trick was to find someone talented enough to pull it off who would never let on they had made the forgery.

Randal Begay was such a person. The piece he had made for Bloom's show had all the elements of a great early blanket. The piece was tight and made from old sheep stock that originally had roamed the land 150 years ago. The design was different, but there really wasn't any pattern in a first phase other than simple lines of brown, white, and blue. The blue was made from indigo, a dark cobalt color that occurred naturally but was rarely used in the 20th century. You could never quite achieve the same exact color with synthetic aniline dyes. Under close scrutiny of a spectrophotometer the synthetic blue would give away its secret, but indigo whether old or new would register the same element value.

To successfully pull off a first-phase forgery required exceptional spinning ability, stealth, and obtaining indigo dye, all doable.

Once a piece showed up out of nowhere on the market it would need two qualities: one, to be a terrifically well-made weaving, and two, a strong undeniable history as to where the piece had been, and this had to be iron clad.

Ridgemount could thank Trevor for giving him the idea for having a fake made. The turn-of-the-century photograph he had stolen out of his file cabinet was a picture of Goulding's Trading Post near the ancestral home of Randal Begay. The old tattered photo clearly showed a first phase hung over a rail in front of the post, with lots of Navajos standing by. An old trader had his hand proudly placed on the masterpiece of old. The caption in India ink now fading read "Old Chief's Blanket."

All Ridgemount had to do was have a reproduction first phase made by his new friend Randal Begay, and a bogus provenance letter drawn up attached to a notarized document stating such said provenance was verified true. For good measure it should be notarized on the Navajo reservation. Darryl had gently broached the idea with Begay in Santa Fe when he bought the rugs from Bloom's, testing the waters. Randal was up for forgery if it meant big bucks and Ridgemount took the risk of saying it was old. No real numbers had been given but Darryl had hinted it would be basically twice the usual pay, around $30,000. Begay's mouth had started to water at the thought of all that cash.

Ridgemount had hoped he could find a genuine piece but with Trevor pushing Gusher's buttons he had to act now. It would take time to have the piece woven, six to eight months. He hoped he didn't have to deal with mounting competition from Trevor but if he did, then Trevor was toast. Timing was critical. The beauty of the fake was he could simply pay off Begay and some old rancher who was in money trouble who Begay had suggested would testify as to the piece's provenance, and he was golden. He'd have huge profit margins and then time to disappear. Find a new team to root for, maybe the ducks of Oregon, though he hated their school colors-green.

CHAPTER 28

AN OPPORTUNITY PRESENTS ITSELF

Four months had passed since the last time Buck Wilson had seen the Daisy Taugelchee. He was surprised when Doc Riddly dropped by with the rug out of the blue.

"Hi Buck. I promised Mr. Johnson I would have dinner with him sometime and that sometime is tonight. I thought you might like to see the Daisy again. Mr. Johnson suggested I bring it back over here, as you would never tire of looking at it."

"He's right. That weaving's pretty special." Buck's eyes never left the textile as he talked to Doc Riddly.

"I could leave it again for the night if you want to baby sit again, just bring it back tomorrow?"

"That would be great. I would love a date with a pretty thing. It's been a while."

Carson left the rug with Wilson to revisit days gone by.

Buck, like a lover, brought the rug back into his room for a long look. Having the Two Grey Hills lying on his bed for the first time in nearly half a century made Buck Wilson wonder how he could have gone so wrong in his life. When he originally bought the weaving it was only $1,000. It was 1954 and he could have afforded to put it away, but he sold it. One of many mistakes a man can make in a life if one can't see beyond tomorrow. He knew the weaving was a masterpiece at the time and it would be doubtful he'd get any more like it in his lifetime yet he still sold it.

His entire life was summed up in the missed opportunity of that one rug. His only child Elmer was a screw-up who would if given the opportunity probably run the ranch into the ground, if he didn't do it first. His wife's dead voice talked to him as if it was yesterday, encouraging him to keep the rug. "Buck, make it a gift to your son. You know it will only go up in value."

In 50 years of marriage she had never been wrong. She was his guiding force. She was right and he knew it, but now the rug was owned by a rich doctor who didn't have a clue as to its importance in his life or the true value. As Buck studied the weaving's intricacies his eyes filled with tears. He wished he had recognized its importance 50 years ago. He wished his wife was still alive to help him through his financial mess. If only he had a genie to make all his wishes come true, the first one would be to own the Daisy one more time. He stroked the fine silky wool; a long-lost love suddenly rediscovered. His mood changed from depression to anger: "I was young! I thought I had all the time in the world to make more money and get more rugs. There are no more! All my chances for success and wealth are gone just like this rug!" He was surprised something of such great beauty could cause such negative, angry feelings in a man who rarely showed emotion. He rummaged for a throwaway camera that he had had for years, never finding enough images in his life worth remembering, and took a picture of the blanket like he should have done 50 years ago, back when he didn't understand the meaning of time.

He would never develop the roll of film. As with his own life, the film's potential would never be realized. Sitting on the side of the bed quietly stroking the silky rug, eyes closed, visions of his life running through his mind like a B movie, he was startled and almost fell off the bed when a man's voice shouted from inside the house.

"Buck? You there, it's Randal."

Buck wiped his eyes, ashamed at his self-pity, hiding the cheap box camera under his pillow. "Yes, Randal, I'm in my bedroom. Come on back." Buck was sitting on the end of the bed, his hand still touching the Daisy rug.

"I thought I might find you with your old friend. Grandfather said Doc Riddly was going to bring it back over for you to enjoy. It must feel good to see such a treasure again."

"Lot of thoughts, Randal, about how an old man wasted part of his life and could have done better. My life is more like this rug than I like to admit." Buck was surprised by his openness.

"I've got to ask you something, and I don't want you to take it the wrong way." Randal was fidgeting at broaching a very uncomfortable subject, forgery.

"Go ahead, Randal. After today, nothing's going to bother me."

"I know your son Elmer isn't of much help right now and things are tough, but I may have a way to make a bunch of money. It involves both of us doing something not so good."

Buck looked up from the rug for the first time, staring intently at Randal. "I'm listening. In my financial state, I'll listen to anything short of murder."

"Well, I got this rug buyer of mine with tons of money. He bought my big rug over in Santa Fe a few months ago and paid almost $15K for it. He wants me to make him a weaving that looks just like an old blanket, a first phase. I don't know what he wants to do with it and I don't want to know, but probably it ain't good. Here's the part where you come in. The man wants a letter saying it came out of an old ranching family and the person who writes the letter has to have it notarized as truthful. He's got an old photo of a blanket taken around Goulding's Trading Post showing an old chief's blanket and a white guy—it may be one of your relatives—and he wants the letter to say that's the same blanket and it's been in your family for like a hundred years. He asked me to find someone who would vouch for my blanket and who would keep his mouth shut."

Buck didn't say a word. He just sat on the bed looking at the rug and stroking it like his wife's hair. "Randal, how long have you known me?"

"All my life."

"That's right, and have you ever known me to do anything dishonest during that time?"

Randal looked down at his feet. "Nope."

"Well, son, you have now. The genie is out of the bottle!"

Randal looked Buck in the eyes, smiling ear to ear, wondering what the hell was a genie.

Buck added, "You know your grandfather would kill us both if he knew what we were about to do. The truth is my ranching life is finished if I don't raise some cash soon. My hogs are eating up what little money I have and I don't see any way to sell them soon unless it's at a bargain-basement price which also doesn't help me. So how much are we looking at?"

"He's going to give me $35K for the blanket and he will give you $20K. I'm not really breaking any laws 'cause I'm Indian and can always just say I made a nice rug. But you are breaking the law and taking a big risk. I don't want you to think bad of me if this thing somehow goes in the outhouse."

"Son, I've lived long enough to understand how to take responsibility for my actions, even shitty ones like this." Buck looked intently at the Daisy rug next to him, knowing his selling it was one of those screw-ups that led him to his current state of financial instability.

"I'm not proud of doing this but if I hope to have a chance at keeping my father's father's land, I have to, no matter what the cost," Buck decided. "Besides, if someone is dumb enough to buy a blanket strictly because it's got a piece of paper saying it's old then they deserve what they get. Hell, it's still going to be a killer Randal Begay blanket. They just won't know it."

Both men started laughing. For the first time all day, Buck Wilson felt hope.

CHAPTER 29

NEW DIGS

The clouds on the horizon were building. It looked like a huge front was going to blow in sometime that day. The Hampton Inn, in which Carson had been staying, was comfortable enough, but his hotel days would be over tomorrow according to the letter he'd received earlier in the week in its foreboding official green and white I.H.S. envelope. He was told his permanent accommodations were ready and had been inspected by an entomologist and been deemed bee free for six months. The I.H.S. could no longer afford the $49 dollar a day per diem rate. Carson was only supposed to be in the hotel for two weeks, but had managed to stay there for nine months. A good feat, which took writing numerous compelling letters to the I.H.S. explaining his extreme reaction to and fear of bees, which had colonized the little house he was meant to be stuck in for two years. He went as far as to have his friend from medical school who was now a practicing psychiatrist write a letter on behalf of his phobia of bees. Carson figured this was payback for being sent to Kayenta to begin with.

Ironically, he now wanted desperately to stay in the town of Kayenta. The thought of being 30 minutes away from all civilization, even a town as small as Kayenta, was not something he cherished. He would have to drive an hour every day if he wanted a cheeseburger or to look at a pretty girl.

But the official order had come down. He had to check out of his hotel tomorrow morning. There was suitable bee-free housing next to North Clinic. He made his hotel rounds today, saying goodbye to the hotel staff. He would miss Ms. Smith, his favorite maid. She had always left him a small mint on his bed with a happy face card. She was probably 50, but of late she had started to look attractive, a bad sign in Carson's mind. Two years was a long time in isolation.

Being on call at the Kayenta hospital had not been bad. It was only once a month and generally he was never bothered. He would just make a couple of quick hospital rounds and then tool on back to the Hampton's (as he had started referring to his economy hotel.) Technically he was always on call for the North Clinic, but no one came by afterhours unless they were really ill and usually if that was the case they would go directly into Kayenta for its advanced facilities. Otherwise they would have to wait for Dr. Riddly to drive out to see them. The hospital nurse would call when his patients would arrive in town, and he could just hop over and see them there.

With the move into the new digs, Carson Riddly expected all that to change. His housing was located next to the clinic trailer. His could see it unfolding. All his patients would come, day or night, and knock on the door like he was a 7 Eleven—open any time for any one. There might be visitors who would want him to open up just to see the Daisy. The thought of constant access was frightening for a man who liked his down time.

He didn't hate the North Clinic, surprisingly, and even found he liked the isolation in moderation, with no noise of cars or stray dogs. Work was generally easy and except for the serious language barrier he enjoyed his Navajo patients. Most were old and still respected a medicine man even if he wasn't traditional.

The usual patient had diseases associated with old age. Heart disease was the exception, which surprised him. The general diet almost always included meat, usually mutton and lots of fry bread. Carson figured it had to be a combination of low stress, exercise, and some genetic peculiarity, possibly the same one that made the Navajo more susceptible to the ravages of alcohol, which he also encountered. Most of the drinkers were individuals who were sick and generally young. They were also susceptible to sniffing paint. Carson came up with his first rule of reservation medicine: patients either succumbed to alcohol early or lived to an advanced age. Not much in between.

Dotty had gotten used to Carson's habits. She liked the *bilagaana*. They made a good team. She translated and gave her own recommendation, which often involved some bad spirit. Carson accepted Dotty's insights and did not dismiss the effects of traditional healing by Navajo medicine men. He had seen with his own eyes how Hastiin Johnson, close to 90 years old, had survived a rattlesnake bite which should have killed him; he wondered if Johnson's own medicine and power had had as much effect as the clinic's antivenin.

The Daisy rug, as his father had predicted, was a hit among the locals. It had opened doors with the people. Even though the great weaver had lived over two hours east of Kayenta and woven in all natural colors in the Toadlena/Two Grey Hills style, weavers still knew who she was and respected her talent that Spiderwoman had given her. She was the Tiger Woods of the weaving world—a force to be measured against. He originally hung the weaving in his office but found its presence a distraction, as he would get knocks nearly every day from some old grandmother who would come in and have a seat to look at the magnificent rug, wanting to talk about the great textile. They might stay for an hour, speaking in Diné and standing uncomfortably close to Carson as he tried to work. He finally moved it into the waiting room and put a sign up that said 1954 Daisy Taugelchee, courtesy Dr. Riddly. Word had gotten out on the rug and occasionally he would get offers to buy it. Carson thought these might have been originating from Buck Wilson, who also dropped by periodically to make his own special pilgrimage.

He knew the piece must be very valuable since Randal's rugs would bring what a nice used truck would. Carson didn't have any insurance for the weaving and didn't know if his father's homeowner's policy would even cover such a thing, especially in a public building. He decided on his next free weekend he would get an appraisal, then insure it, just in case it was ever damaged. The

Navajos respected the piece, so he didn't worry about it being stolen, but others were finding out about its location. One never knows. Carson would get Randal's dealer friend Bloom to take a look at the textile and get a formal appraisal the next time he was heading to Albuquerque, now knowing Toadlena was east of Kayenta.

Brenda, the hot receptionist who he had completely turned off his first day of work, occasionally subbed for Dotty. Their relationship had not thawed in nine months, even with Carson's great sense of humor, which he tried unsuccessfully to interject periodically. He had bombed so badly his first day it was simply a lost cause. His timing was off as he was afraid of making some unknown faux pas. He found working with her distracting, as trying not to stare at the flawless body was nearly impossible. Brenda's *Playboy* figure was memorable and sent Carson's testosterone level skyrocketing dangerously high. His last female encounter had been when he was a happily naïve family practice resident. He wished Dotty would find a different replacement.

Carson's main fun besides reading was his own personal golf course of sorts, which he had set up adjacent to the North Clinic. It was a three-par executive course, which he christened Riddly's Ranch Range. A sign was commissioned out of a juniper plank made by the same man who had made the clinic sign. It hung prominently over his trailer's porch as if it were the clubhouse entrance, announcing to all where to check in for their tee time. There was no grass, just fine red dirt and lots of it. It was a challenging three-hole course that started from the clubhouse's front porch. Hole one's tee box was an old, faded green welcome mat located on the small patio. Occasionally when Carson would declare a tournament day he would lengthen the hole by moving the mat to the clinic's entrance. This gave the hole versatility, allowing for two courses that played between 150 to 100 yards. The landing area was the same for both holes and was tough: an abandoned sheep pen that required clearing the broken-down juniper fence. If you hit it short the ball would ricochet off one of the poles and recovery was impossible.

Hole two was a difficult 145-yard shot. It required landing on a small, narrow mesa which had a natural depression in the million-year-old sandstone. If you could land the ball gently on top, a hole in one would result as the ball would naturally drain to the old Anasazi grinding mano which was the designated cup, an important hole if you wanted a good overall score. Accuracy was again the key. Too long and you would hit a large boulder backstop, which would viciously send the ball directly at one's head.

The finishing hole was the hardest on the course. Pars were rare. They required a perfect high-pitch shot over the only sizable tree within a half-mile, a 300-year-old juniper whose dead branches seemed to grab the ball out of the sky as the ball attempted to fly over. A stack of small dead branches was rapidly accumulating on the ground underneath the massive tree trunk, casualties of Carson's errant ball hits. The bonus was the hole got a little easier with each felled branch. Currently he was not worrying about getting over the tree with his ball, but instead was taking direct aim at a particularly nasty limb that was the bane of his golf shot's existence. A couple of hundred more direct hits with his old range balls and the evil branch would be history. Currently about 20 balls had managed to hang up in the old tree, so it had an odd Christmas tree-like appearance from all the white, yellow, and pink golf balls. Carson would retrieve these after every big storm. Today's impending storm should free up much of his ever-decreasing golf ball inventory. "The limb must go," he thought as he looked at the looming afternoon storm. "Added ammunition by tomorrow morning."

The course record was nine, which was quite good considering the level of difficulty. He had threatened to break the score yesterday, having gone into the last hole with a score of three, to only be destroyed by the juniper's outstretched limb. Carson pictured himself as President Eisenhower who battled a grand old tree on #17 in Augusta. Eisenhower hated the Augusta tree, a Loblolly pine, and petitioned to have it removed (unsuccessfully). Carson, on the other hand, loved the ancient juniper, for it gave him a reason to continue to compete in a land with no opponents.

Driving back into town for his last night at the Hampton's, he decided to take advantage of the unusual warm snap for late March, mountain weather being so unpredictable. The sky was still overcast, but it actually seemed warm enough for a dip in the pool. Yes, he would have a special-occasion Mexican night, his own private celebration. Celebrations were going to be rare at his new home in the wilderness, a trailer with no sounds or lights other than those of nature and certainly no place to stop for a takeout dinner on his way home.

His goodbye feast tonight would be composed of a six-pack of ice-cold Negra Modelo dark beer which he had smuggled in with him from Phoenix and two Bashas' burritos covered with leftover Taco Bell fire sauce, which he had saved from better days. The plan was simple: Float in the pool with a good buzz, and pork out on cheap, tasty Mexican food. Tomorrow was the big move. Alcohol on the reservation is against the law, so the buzz factor would have to occur in his room first. Carson had already seen the damage alcohol wreaked on many of his patients and understood that it was a serious problem for the Diné. He had made one serious faux pas already with his Kit Carson stumble. Getting caught with alcohol would not be his second. Whatever he didn't drink tonight he would dump.

The buzz was on. It was 7 pm when he was settling into the pool, his 99-cent burrito in one hand and a packet of hot sauce in the other, laying comfortably on an iridescent blue rubber raft, gently drifting around the deep end of the eight-foot pool. This was his last chance to indulge in the pool, and neither the impending storm nor winter's suddenly dropping temperatures were going to stop him.

Winds of force are known to come suddenly out of nowhere on the rez. The Diné instinctively hunker down when the Nilch'itsoh spirit blows through, and do not come out until the fury has passed. Carson, who was anything but hunkered, was caught off guard as the first 50 mph mini-tornado made its presence felt.

The fine red dirt from the nearby canyon walls had become air born and engulfed Carson's open burrito, destroying it in its opening act. The wind capsized the rubber raft, taking Carson's now red-green burrito to the pool's bottom. Coming up gasping, still clutching the soggy burrito, kicking furiously to stay afloat in the pool's deep end, Carson thought, "I wonder if I'll get lucky and my new digs will get blown away!" Carson was for the most part an optimist. Mexican night was over, but he hoped for some good from the Nilch'itsoh.

He quickly headed to his room, 2B, struggling to keep the door from ripping off the hinges. Hurricanes have nothing on a big windstorm blowing through the rez. The wind was topping 80 mph with gusts reaching nearly 100 mph within five minutes of Carson finding safety. The toilet water took on a life of its own, gyrating up and down from the massive pressure changes. Outside, the loud clanking of the metal pool furniture chimed against the buzz of the wind, the noisy symphony originating from metal on metal collisions, the individual pieces being picked up off the ground and thrown back down. Only the heavy metal chains, which Carson had original assumed were to keep it from being stolen, held it earth bound.

The outdoor parking lights were completely obliterated with sand, causing a strobe effect while looking out the window as the blinding sand came flying through in waves. Carson thought it had to be a tornado and turned on the TV to hear any information about where he should go for safety. The local news out of Flagstaff reported "some high winds for the next couple of days coming off the Mogollon Rim."

Carson looked as if he had been dipped head to toe in red chile powder. His entire body covered in fine Arizona sand, he stood staring at the television in disbelief, hearing the weatherman's nonchalant wind report. He began to quarrel with the television as if it could hear: "Nothing at all? How about take cover—the roof's going to come off shortly? What the fuck am I doing out here? Aren't 100 mph winds worthy of mention? They just ended my Mexican night! This is not a place for civilized humans!" His protests could barely be heard over the now deafening hum of the wind.

Little did Carson know the Nilch'itsoh were the least of his troubles. He would soon be in real danger and it wasn't coming from Mother Nature. It was something much more sinister: man.

CHAPTER 30

MOVING DAY

North Clinic opened at 8 am. Carson left his cozy Hampton Inn at 5 am before the sun came up to negotiate his way north past downed trees and finally move into the I.H.S. trailer/hogan, otherwise known as Riddly's Ranch. Departing the last vestibule of civilization which had fast food and retail establishments with names he could pronounce was a sad but inevitable task best attacked while still fresh. Carson figured he would rather have a shitty day from start to finish than leave the Hampton's any sooner than he had to. Now he understood why the rich East Coasters hated to leave the Hamptons. He felt the same way.

His new housing was 300 feet from the North Clinic. It was a metal 30-year-old trailer. His front door (his only door) faced east. The odd configuration of homes in Tuba City was now understood by Carson. He had learned that all traditional Diné homes face east to greet the morning sun. The trailer had both plumbing and electricity and at this point no bees. It was a one bedroom, with two windows. Heating was from a wood-burning stove, and the floor was recycled fifties white linoleum tiles, which were undoubtedly laden with asbestos. He had considered getting one of the tiles tested to see if it did have the dreaded asbestos, but he figured from a health standpoint it was probably better to leave things alone. If he found the dreaded material, they would simple rip it out and leave a fine dust of the mesothelioma cancer-forming particles everywhere. He might get to stay in the motel a little longer, but the risks outweighed the rewards. The entire structure took on a Frankenstein-like appearance with its multicolored metal panels fashioned together to form an odd but pleasing design, a modern sculpture of sorts. The trailer/hogan could be described as rural modernism to anyone who visited him, which of course they never would. Even though he had been working for months at the North Clinic and the first hole of the golf course started off his porch, he had never before ventured inside the trailer. What if the bees weren't gone?

Opening his new home's creaky door in the dark for the first time was bad enough, but a small creature scurried past his feet as he peered in. He let out a loud girlish scream, a sound at least an octave higher than most male voices, a trait he was not proud of. He frantically looked for the only light switch, which he found at a level a midget would have been happy with. It was not that Carson was afraid of wildlife. In fact, just the opposite, but the sudden unexpected movement triggered a bee attack response. He instinctively grabbed for his EpiPen, which he kept on a leather strap around his neck along with a small bear-stone fetish Hastiin Johnson had given him for good health. He was surprised at how open-minded he was to the possibilities of the medicine man's gift. He had started wearing the green stone bear around his neck. Extra bee protection. Carson thought maybe he was going Native, just like the art dealer that lived at Toadlena. He wished Brenda could appreciate his slow transformation. Brenda, who he still had a crush on, presently referred to him as Col. Riddly, a constant reminder of his first-day blunder. Though lately a smile accompanied the ridicule, a positive sign he thought.

His housing was illuminated by two large florescent lights that hummed as they warmed up. The one-bedroom home had no decoration except for a calendar from 1959 that featured a Navajo weaver on the cover with the caption, "A master weaver at work." The month was April, which was ironic as Carson realized it was almost 53 years ago to the date when the calendar was made. He decided he would keep it up and hang it next to his animal calendar, which now had nine months filled with X marks, this month's animal being a roadrunner. His high-school poster of Kathy Ireland was then proudly hung next to the faded Santa Fe Railroad calendar, using some additional upholstery tacks left in the wall. There were no other signs any other soul had lived in the desolate little home. His great Daisy rug was left in the office waiting room, to avoid the grandmothers who would want to come over unannounced to his house and visit it like some old friend.

The single piece of furniture was a World War II solid iron single bed that took almost all of Carson's entire five-foot-ten frame. He turned the mattress over four times, looking for any bed bugs or scorpions that might have set up residence. He decided it would be money well spent to purchase a king-sized bed with a nice foam pad. He still hoped to find someone to share his bed, though it looked like slim pickings except for Kathy Ireland. He wished he had looked inside months ago. Now he would have to struggle with a bad bed for a week.

The kitchen was adjacent to a wood-burning stove, which also appeared to be the only means of heat, as his breath was visible during the inspection of the so-called residence. The outside temperature had fallen 40 degrees since yesterday. The heat inside the residence had not been on in a long time. Clinic appointments would start soon and he was already tired from the morning move. Carson lay on top of the exposed mattress and dozed until Dotty's truck rolled in precisely at 10 till eight. She saw Carson's Mustang in front of his trailer and the light on, and knocked on the door. The sound made him cringe, as he knew this would be the new normal, total access all the time.

"Come in," Carson yelled.

"Hi Doc, how you like the new Indian digs?" Dotty giggled at seeing the rich *bilagaana* doctor living like his patients. She would have to share the moment with his recruiter, who was originally from the area and kept in touch.

"Great. I wish it wasn't so big. It feels odd to have so much room, not like back home in Florence," Carson quipped sarcastically, referring to Florence, Arizona—the state prison, which he felt was equivalent to his current fate.

"Oh, you'll get used to it. You're going to love the silence and all the stars. It will make you a better human. Learn to listen to Mother Earth instead of the TV. Besides Doc, you save yourself one hour a day driving. I know time is important to you *bilagaanas*. Plus there are no other prisoners here to bother you," Dotty teased him, knowing how he worried about time and she'd caught the prison jab.

"I'm sure you're right," he sighed. "But I also need a little me time. You think you can make sure my patients understand I need down time? Try and keep normal hours?"

"Afraid we're going to bother you too much 'cause we like *bilagaanas* more than our own families or tending to our sheep?" Dotty retorted.

Carson cringed, realizing he was overreacting. His patients would respect his privacy and he was acting like he was Mr. Important. In fact what he had observed was most of his patients were private people who tried not to bother him even at work unless it was to share the Daisy rug with a relative. "I wish I had a family, on second thought. Hope more people come by."

"OK, Doc, I'll let them all know to come on by. They would love to use your restroom, it's indoors!" Dotty said, grinning.

Carson knew she was kidding, or so he hoped.

She nodded toward the clinic. "I got to do some notarizing for old Buck. He's coming by this morning. He likes to have his blood pressure took. We do it for him even though he's not officially supposed to get any medical treatment. But to us he's almost as much Indian as white."

"I'll be happy to help out. Just keep a chart on him so I can cover my butt."

"Already done," she responded. "He's listed under the W's for white or Wilson, you pick. No other W's."

Buck Wilson arrived right at 8 am, and went directly into Dotty's reception area with some papers for her to notarize. She was one of only three notaries in the county, and she handled everything north and west of Kayenta. Not a lot of need for notarization on the rez.

After Buck finished, Dotty took his blood pressure, which was quite high. Not usual for him. She ushered him back into the examination room and got the doc.

"Buck, Dotty tells me your pressure is up. Anything stressful going on in your life? Sounds like this is new for you," said Carson.

"Well, I been having some trouble with finances and I ain't seen Elmer in two months. He was supposed to take over the ranch so I could retire, but the hog business isn't so good and now he's working in Flagstaff as an auto mechanic. Can't say I blame him, good steady pay check."

"Nothing else going on, which could have you under stress?"

Buck had been hesitant, and Carson picked up on it. There was something else, but Buck wasn't in the sharing mood.

"No, just the usual. So Doc, you think I need medication or just wait and see?" Buck asked.

"Probably a mild diuretic for right now will be all you need. I'll recheck you in a week, how's that sound?"

"Fine. If I need a pill, make it for the morning or you will have me peeing all night long. I'm nearing 80 and nights are hard sometimes."

"No problem, here's the scrip. It's once a day in the morning."

"Doc, your great rug—any chance you would ever part with it? It would have to be for great money, of course."

"No, 'fraid not. As you know my dad gave it to me as a present so the only way would be if I was in real financial trouble, which I'm not."

"I understand. I had to ask. I wish I had never sold it 50 years ago. I'll see you next week. I'm sure I'll be better by then," Buck said.

Carson could tell there was something on the old rancher's mind and it was probably money related, but exactly what he wasn't saying. He wondered if cash was a problem how Buck could ever come up with the money to buy his Daisy? Carson definitely needed to know the rug's value. It was time to visit Randal and get his Toadlena dealer's phone number and find out what his rug was worth.

CHAPTER 31

AN UNEXPECTED VISITOR

Carson walked out of the clinic at 5 pm to go see Randal Begay. He wanted to get there before nightfall. The roads were bad enough during the day. He had to travel slowly with his poor road vehicle—his '68 Ford Mustang which now had a constant covering of fine red sand on it. He had considered selling it in February at Barrett's auction in Scottsdale, but he couldn't bear the thought of losing his baby even if it was totally impractical in the harsh desert environment. The hotel had some covered parking, which he always used, but the trailer was lucky to have running water. There was no shade or garage for 20 miles. It was only a matter of time before another big wind blew in. By next year if the elements started to take their toll on his cherished ride, he would have to get rid of her. He couldn't fathom thinking of her damaged, with a bent frame, sand-blasted paint job, or simply turned to rust.

The washboard dirt roads took twice as long in his car as in a decent truck. When he finally arrived at Begay's, he waited the customary few minutes before knocking on the door. Little forms of Diné etiquette had been imparted by Dotty as part of her plan to educate her Doc Riddly.

"Hi Doc, what you want? I'm kind of busy," Randal yelled through the closed door after looking out the window and seeing the Mustang convertible, a totally unsuitable car for the rez.

"I'll just take a minute, Randal. I need to get a phone number and some directions."

Randal didn't answer but two minutes later came out the door, slipping out like a cat would, and closing the door firmly behind him.

"OK, what you need? Directions to the hot spot in Gallup? Time for a little Navajo action?" Randal was somewhat abrupt, a very un-Navajo characteristic.

Carson explained, "Nothing like that, though I may be up for it soon. I wondered if you thought that Bloom guy at Toadlena could do an appraisal on my Two Grey Hills rug? I need to figure out how valuable it really is."

"It's a good one, I can tell you, but I don't know exactly. I think Bloom or the old dealer Sal Lito who is the trader there will be able to help you figure her out." Randal gave Carson all the pertinent information. He waited for Carson to get back into his car, commenting, "Well I need to get back to things. I would invite you in, but my house is really a mess."

Carson found this extremely odd as he had been in the house once before and it was a mess then, but Randal never seemed concerned. Plus, Carson couldn't help but notice the new pickup truck with Arizona plates in front of Randal's house. Carson knew Randal had the reputation of always being broke and an on-again, off-again gambler. Randal had always driven a beat-up green Ford. "So where does Randal get money for a truck like that? Maybe he won at the tables?" Carson wondered to himself as Randal disappeared back inside. Carson yelled, "OK Randal, I understand. My house is a mess too. I'll give Bloom a call. Thanks."

Carson wondered if Randal's odd behavior was related to Buck's similarly unusual attitude earlier in the day.

What Carson didn't know was there was a completely pristine first-phase reproduction chief's blanket on Randal's loom just a few feet away from the door entrance. He had just finished the masterpiece a few hours ago. It was the best weaving of his short but stellar life and he was proud of it, even if it was made as a fraud and could never be shared. No one had been inside of Begay's house in six months and he wasn't about to screw it up on the last day on the loom. He would take the blanket off the loom today and secretly store it at his grandfather's hogan for safekeeping until he met with the man from Texas at the end of the week.

At least that was the plan. Right now, Randal's resolve about this mission was flagging. He needed to talk to Buck one more time.

CHAPTER 32

TOADLENA GETS A VISITOR

On Friday, Carson had the day off. It was his week of the month to get a three-day pass from rez hell as he thought of it after long stints of work. He had three things planned. See Bloom, drive to a big city, say Albuquerque, the better to get a buzz on, and finally, find some nice-smelling girl to dance with. Golf was now secondary to the female persuasion. With this springtime cold snap, a set of warm feet seemed like a better choice. It was a sophomoric weekend plan but his sex drive was still that of a 28-year-old, and his pin-up poster was getting to him. He hadn't even thought about where he would store the Daisy while looking for strange women and cold beer in Albuquerque. He was more of a girlfriend kind of guy, but this weekend all bets were off.

Carson had called ahead to make sure Charles Bloom would be in, and arranged an appointment for Bloom to see the textile. Bloom hadn't been dealing long in Navajo textiles but he understood the importance of a Daisy. Her presence was legendary at the Toadlena Trading Post. Bloom particularly wanted Rachael to see the piece, as her grandmother Ethel had been friends with Daisy. Unfortunately, Rachael was teaching classes at the high school today, although she had decided to give up teaching at the end of the year to become a full time weaver.

On Friday morning, Carson was up at dawn. He went over to the clinic and took down his prized textile, leaving Dotty a note so she wouldn't be worried when she came in. He threw his packed bag into the car and hit the road to be at Toadlena by the time the trading post opened. Dotty would run the clinic in his absence, as there were no other doctors available. If an emergency came up they would head into the Kayenta Clinic.

Arriving at the historic trading post which still exuded charm, Carson wished there was some nearby clinic he could get assigned to. Toadlena was practically in a city with Gallup only 60 minutes away and Albuquerque just three hours. Randal had given Carson the typical Navajo description of Bloom: "He's *bilagaana* and older than you. Not the old white guy though, he owns the post. Bloom is their younger hired gun."

Bloom saw Carson's blue Mustang slowly creep up the dirt road and wished immediately he could afford a new vehicle. His time on the rez had made him think only about trucks, a much more practical vehicle than the old Mercedes he still owned.

Charles stepped out to greet Carson. "Hi, you must be Dr. Riddly. I'm Charles Bloom. Come in and I'll get you some coffee. Nice car! Surprised you haven't gotten a truck yet. Still hanging on to your old life?"

"I'm afraid so but I'm starting to wear down, just like my car." said Carson. "I hope the coffee is Starbucks and not that cowboy coffee everyone seems to drink around here."

"You'll get used to it. Soon you won't touch a $6 dollar latté," laughed Bloom, who now could only imagine drinking Rachael's fine brew.

"If you say so, but right now I'd kill for a perfectly foamed latté and *The New York Times*."

"Well," Bloom offered, "I've got a *Navajo Times*. It's about as good, though a week old, plus there is no business section to worry about."

The two well-educated *bilagaanas* who found themselves living in the same foreign environment felt an immediate kinship. Bloom gave Carson the extended tour around the old trading post, spending additional time discussing the numerous rugs in inventory.

During the tour, an elderly Navajo woman came in that Bloom stopped to help. Carson watched in fascination as she sold her little brown rug for credit at the post's general store, which Bloom also helped fill. It seemed to Carson as if he had entered a time machine and gone back to the old West. Squeaky worn-out wooden floors and skeins of brown and white wool thrown over the post's ceiling beams seemed straight out of a movie, complete with Indians bartering for food with the white man.

Finally the moment Bloom had been waiting for came. Carson pulled out the Daisy from its garbage bag. It did not disappoint. As tight as anything he had ever seen or could imagine. It was huge by today's weavings standards: over 4 X 6 feet. The rugs Bloom had sold during last year's Indian Market were very, very good, but this one was the definition of great. He understood it required a true textile genius's touch to accomplish such a feat. Randal Begay was close and someday might surpass the master, but for now he was still second fiddle.

"Carson, you want to do a little 'Antiques Roadshow' or maybe trade it? I can offer you a hell of lot of soup for that one," Bloom said, knowing it wasn't likely.

"Don't want to trade it, unless of course you have Campbell's White Beans and Pork?" Carson joked.

"We're out, I'm afraid, so it will have to be `Roadshow' time. So Dr. Riddly, any idea what the Daisy Taugelchee tapestry weaving would be worth in today's market?" Bloom inquired, trying to sound as proper as one of the highbrow East Coast appraisers.

"I know my dad paid a lot when he bought it at the Heard Museum, so I guess $3,000 or $4,000," Carson suggested.

"Well Doc Riddly, it was worth at least that when your dad bought it in the early eighties. However..." Bloom paused, doing his best to bring tension to the moment. "In today's market I would estimate at auction on a good day it would bring close to $100,000!" Bloom watched for the inevitable "oh my God" reaction and got it.

"Oh my God! I'm truly shocked! I had no idea it would be that valuable. That's like an S-class Mercedes," Carson said, putting the value into the only thing he could imagine being worth that much money, a great car.

"Yes it's valuable but it should bring even more in my opinion. A secondary Warhol print can bring that much. Somehow it doesn't seem fair that they should have an equivalent value." Bloom the contemporary art dealer now found himself acting like all his Texas clients, judging what art's true value should be. "Now if you do want to sell it, Carson, I'm more than happy to help place the piece, which I know I can. I have a guy in Texas who I'm sure wants one and would pay that number if I pushed him."

"Wish I could," Carson sighed, "but it was a gift from my father and he really loved this piece. It would devastate him if I sold it. He probably has no idea of its current value."

"I can't say I blame you," Bloom agreed. "I would keep it too if I were you. I don't know if you have time, but my girlfriend Rachael Yellowhorse is a Toadlena/Two Grey Hills weaver and she would go crazy to see this piece. She's a teacher and had to work today. Think I could talk you into hanging out till she gets off? If you want, we got a little trailer in back. You could stay the night."

Carson had no intention of staying in another small town on the rez, having been in its vise grip for months, and especially not in a trailer. But somehow it seemed right and he always followed his gut. "OK. You talked me into it. Your girlfriend doesn't have any single girlfriends, does she?"

"Afraid not. The pickings here are slim for single girls, and if my woman has her way she won't be that much longer either."

Carson and Bloom both started laughing simultaneously, recognizing the male code for dive, dive, dive...

When Rachael arrived home, she opened the hogan door to find a handsome, blonde *bilagaana* with a magnificent rug draped over his shoulders, drinking what appeared to be one of Charles's famous deadly margaritas. Bloom knew Rachael wouldn't approve of the drinks, but hoped the visitor's presence would blunt her displeasure at alcohol being served in her home.

"Hey, you're home early. I've invited a friend, the only other young *bilagaana* within a hundred miles, Doctor Carson Riddly," Bloom announced. The "Carson" didn't faze Bloom, who still had the mentality of a white man, but Rachael caught it immediately.

"Carson, huh? Any relation to Kit?"

"No way, I hate that guy," the slightly tipsy Carson replied, trying to overcompensate for his Brenda screw-up. "My dad was a Johnny Carson fan, the old late-night talk-show host and comedian. I'm funny like him, can't you tell?"

"Yeah, you're hilarious. I can tell you been around us Navajo long enough to know the Carson thing is still close to the surface—140 years in Navajo time is like yesterday, we don't wear watches," Rachael threw in her own joke about the Navajos' little concern for the white man's clocks.

Eager to change the subject, Carson suggested, "Just call me Doc, everyone does. Care for one of your boyfriend's ripping margaritas?"

"No thanks, I'm not a fan of the white man's fire water. You mind if I hold the blanket you're wearing?" Rachael's interest in touching a piece of Navajo history was obvious.

Carson, as carefully as possible without spilling margarita all over the piece, handed it to Rachael, who plopped down on a chair to examine the masterpiece.

"Wow, a Daisy. One of her major works." A small tear started to roll down Rachael's cheek. Being a weaver she realized the time and expertise needed to make such a work of art. "No way I'll ever be this good, no matter how long I weave."

Her heartfelt confession made Bloom's heart sink, as he knew how devastating this feeling could be to any artist who strives to be the best and feels that a silver medal is all you can hope for.

"Rachael, you sit here and I'll get you some sun tea. I'll put some nice lamb chops on the stove and you can examine the weaving closely and figure out her weaving tricks," Bloom proposed, trying to lighten her heart at seeing such a magnificent weaving, one she would not be able to duplicate.

"Sure, I'll play with it. I already know her tricks. They're called pure genius mixed with tremendous patience and a long life, none of which I have, but I'll still look. I remember grandmother Ethel telling me about her friend Daisy and her special gifts. I met her a couple of times as a kid but didn't realize her tremendous abilities or her importance as an artist. Now I understand."

Later, the three sat down for a meal, margaritas put aside, each learning more about the others' lives and how they all ended up on the rez.

CHAPTER 33

SHOWTIME

Randal Begay had taken his blanket and hid it under his grandfather's bed. The 90-year-old would never look under there as he had a hard enough time just getting off his rickety old cot. Randal wanted to speak with the medicine man because he had felt something was very wrong with his *hozho*. Randal had not been eating or sleeping well, both problems he had never experienced before. He knew something was off when he made a couple of mistakes finishing up the blanket and completely forgot to put a spirit line in the piece.

The spirit line, which is found in most Navajo rugs both old and new, is a small separate thread of color often very subtle which takes the weaver to the outside of the textile and allows the weaver's spirit to exit the rug. Randal had always done a spirit line, as this was how his mother had taught him. He had completely forgotten to put it in this piece and now it was too late. In two days he would sell it and collect his $25K paycheck. He had talked Darryl up from the original $30K into paying him $35K for the rug, and had already received $10K in advance.

The deal was almost done. But forgetting to include a spirit line was a warning sign from Spiderwoman telling him not to complete the transaction. Randal needed guidance from Hastiin Johnson. His grandfather was a powerful medicine man and would be able to advise him. Randal knew he couldn't tell him the exact details, but would talk in generalities to see if there was a sing his grandfather could perform to cure him.

"Grandfather, I think I have lost my *hozho*. My weavings seem to be changing," Randal began.

"If you are pure of heart, it will return. You must be patient and follow the Navajo path."

"What if I have veered from my true course and am on the wrong road?"

"You will know," his grandfather advised. "You must listen to your heart and soul to help guide you from the dark side. You should go take a long, hot sweat. Don't come out until you see a clear vision of your correct path. This will tell you how to conquer whatever bad *chindi* have possessed you. Do not wait. Let me know what you see and then I can help, if I need to perform a sing or make a sandpainting."

"Thank you, Grandfather, for your help. I promise I will listen to my heart. Please Grandfather, be careful this year as the snakes will be out soon and I cannot lose you yet. We have many sings we need to do together." Randal knew April was the first month in a normal year that rattlesnakes emerge from their hibernation dens.

"Some may already be out, my son. We both must be careful. But snakes are our friends. Always remember that."

Randal had only two days before the Texan came for his commission. He was now having severe second thoughts about the transaction even though he desperately needed the money. If he didn't get the cash he would lose the new pickup, which he had bought using a down payment for the first phase. Luckily he had not gambled any of the proceeds, a first for Randal. He decided to visit Buck Wilson before the sweat to get Buck's thoughts, which might influence what Randal's sweat told him. Buck was old and had seen a lot. He was also a friend and in this case an accomplice who had the most to lose.

Randal went over to Buck's house to give him an update on the weaving and let him know about what his grandfather had told him.

"Buck," Randal admitted, "I'm having second thoughts about selling my rug. It's bad *hozho* for me to sell this blanket, which we both know the Texan is going to sell as a great old weaving. I think my ancestors may be angry. You know if it goes bad, you could lose more than your ranch. "

"I know Randal, but I have no options," Buck shrugged. "If I lose my ranch, than I might as well be dead or in prison. This is my only home. Besides, you don't have to worry. You can always say you made the rug for me and I screwed you. I needed the money and told everyone it was old even when I knew it wasn't. You're Navajo and a weaver. You'll be fine. Your ancestors will not care. They will be happy the whites are getting what they deserve. You let me worry about me. The Texan will pay us both, he will go away and place the blanket in a big-shot *bilagaana* collection, and no one will ever know."

Buck further rationalized, "I'm sure no one can tell it's not old. You made it with Churro wool and have all the old indigo dye. It would take some fiber expert to be able to tell, and even then they would probably question his opinion with my sworn ironclad affidavit and the real antique photograph. Our Texan sent me a copy of the photo. Turns out the man in the picture is my great uncle who use to run Goulding's! So there is no way anyone will ever question the authenticity, not with your weaving skills. You're the best living weaver and as good as any of the old blanket weavers."

"OK," Randal considered. "I understand your point, but Buck I've got to take a sweat and figure out my path. I don't want to screw up anything for either of us. Until I do this I can't know the answer. The blanket is finished and safe. I hid it under grandfather's bed for now. But I can't promise you anything. We can talk tomorrow evening. I will have a decision by then."

"Randal, remember you will lose your truck and this guy could be dangerous, we don't know. He seems kind of rough from talking with him and he has money. He may come after the both of us if you back out on your deal. Remember, you gave him your word."

"I know. But I can't screw up my *hozho* either, Buck. This may be bigger than money or even my own safety. I need to make sure I can live with whatever choice I make."

"We'll talk tomorrow. I hope you make a good decision," Buck said in perfect Navajo to reinforce the idea that he too understood what it meant to be a Navajo and the ramification of losing one's way.

Buck Wilson needed the money and was afraid Randal was going to ruin what little life he had left. If the first-phase blanket wasn't an option, he would have to think about getting his hands on Doc's Daisy. It would be more than enough to get him out of trouble.

After Randal left, Buck made a phone call. It was to Austin.

CHAPTER 34

A BREAK-IN

Buck Wilson's life had been one of trying to do the right thing. Now he was put in a position where his family's ranch would soon be gone if he didn't get the blanket deal done. The call to Austin confirmed his worst fears. The man was not going to put up with Randal backing out. Buck had tried to explain what it meant to be Navajo and that this act of making a blanket for a dishonest reason was something Diné just didn't do. He had hoped he had talked Randal into keeping his promise, but until after tomorrow's sweat lodge he just wouldn't know.

The man told Buck he would be there the day after tomorrow with his cash "and to have the blanket waiting or else."

Buck could tell this was not an idle threat. The man meant business. The "or else" meant real trouble for Randal if he didn't hold up his end of the deal. Buck considered telling Randal about the conversation, but knew Randal's resolve was firm. Randal had to make his decision in Navajo fashion in the sweat lodge.

Buck decided the only course of action was to secretly retrieve the blanket from Hastiin Johnson's place and keep it safe until the man from Texas arrived. Buck had never met the man. His only correspondence had been by mail and phone. He knew if Randal didn't cooperate, the man would be coming his way as well. If Buck had the blanket, he would have the leverage to make the final decision if need be.

Stealing the blanket was not hard, as Buck knew Johnson's routine, which hadn't changed in 50 years. Both Hastiin Johnson's and Begay's hogans were visible from the high ridge where the Wilson home stood. Buck's six-power scope on his hunting rifle worked fine for spotting the perfect time to go down and get the blanket. Johnson left to check on his horse each evening around 5 pm. Using his own horse, so as not to be heard, Buck rode up quietly and walked into the unattended hogan. Once in, Buck crawled on his hands and knees to retrieve the blanket, which was wrapped in a black trash sack and pushed to the farthest edge of the bed. At nearly 80, the ordeal was pushing his own resilience. Buck wondered if God was talking to him to change his own ways.

Once Buck had the blanket, he secured it behind his saddle, then climbed back on his horse and rode full tilt across the nearly two miles of open pasture back to his ranch, only the red sand he kicked off attesting to his journey. His heart was racing from the excitement of the ride and taking the blanket, which he could hardly wait to see. He had not ridden that fast in a decade. For the first time in a long time Buck felt alive.

Dumping the blanket out of its black garbage bag onto the dinner table reminded Buck of all the great blankets he had owned when his family still had a trading post. The piece was magnificent. Its glossy, long Churro wool fibers glistened in the evening light. The indigo blue was iridescent. It truly did look like one of the old blankets he had seen in museums. It was a remarkable copy and no one would ever doubt its authenticity. Buck had found a photo of himself as a child with his great uncle. The man in the two antique photographs would solidify the ownership of the blanket.

In two days, Buck and Randal were to meet the Texan at a designated spot to make the hand off, a little area just outside of town known as Kayenta Crossing. It was where two straight dirt roads bisected and formed a Christian cross when viewed from an airplane, an ironic meeting place to finalize such an evil transaction. The marker had a single hand-lettered sign: "Mitten Rock Gospel 14 miles."

Tomorrow Randal would make his sweat-lodge pilgrimage and hopefully come to his senses. If not, Buck had the blanket and he would be in control. He hated to double-cross his friend, who was like family. But his real family's future was in peril and he needed the money. For Buck Wilson there would be a Kayenta crossing. It was up to Randal to choose which one.

CHAPTER 35

SOMETHING GONE VERY WRONG

The next day, all Buck could think about was watching when Randal took off for his sweat lodge and when he returned. The longer the sweat, the more likely some vision would occur which probably wouldn't bode well for Buck's prevailing common sense. Randal would opt for breaking the deal.

The sweat lodge was directly behind Randal's hogan. Buck himself had used it on occasion. The hut's thick, dirt wall was ideal for working up a good sweat. Unfortunately, Buck couldn't see the lodge since it was behind Randal's hogan, tucked into the canyon wall. Buck could only watch for its plume of gray smoke, used to heat up the rocks. Randal got an early start at 7 am.

Buck sat on his front porch with two bags of chips and a pitcher of lemonade and waited. You get good at waiting on the rez. Every so often, Buck would place his gun on his white picket fence and aim the scope at Randal's hogan to see if Randal was done. By 3 pm, Buck was pretty sure what the outcome of the sweat lodge would be. Randal was taking it very seriously and he would embrace his Diné ancestry. Randal would not allow the blanket to be sold and Buck would be screwed. As Buck pondered what his next move would have to be, a brown Impala quietly eased in front of Randal's home and made the decision for him.

A tall man with an orange University of Texas cap stepped out and headed for Randal's hogan door. Randal had started locking the door ever since he began weaving the blanket, in a very un-Navajo way. Apparently he'd locked it that day as well, as the man could not open it. The man walked around the hogan and tried its one window, and looked under rocks around the hogan searching for a key. Buck was mesmerized by the events unfolding. He was sure this was the Texan he had called to give the heads-up as to a possible problem. The man was a day early and that could only mean trouble for Randal. He had been able to find his hogan and he knew from his conversation with Buck that Randal was taking a sweat, so he would find Randal shortly. Buck thought over his position. Randal was going to say they couldn't sell the rug. If Buck let the Texan find Randal, he might hurt Randal or even kill him. If this happened the blanket would be all his and the deal would definitely get done and probably at a much higher price to himself. It was like Buck was paralyzed as he watched the man head for the very small remaining wafts of smoke behind the hogan. Buck considered shooting his rifle at the man to warn Randal, but the dark force had overtaken Buck so he simply watched, paralyzed.

Randal Begay never saw the man in the orange hat. He never saw the hot round river rock as it impacted viciously on his right temple, shattering his skull and ending his life's forces in a single massive blow. His assailant had been patiently waiting for his prey to emerge and had made sure his orange hat's brim was down low so as not to be interfered with by the Arizona sun. Randal Begay's severely crushed cranium struck the dark reddish earth with a dull thud against the parched ground of his ancestral land.

Copious amounts of Randal's bright-red blood formed small rivulets which were immediately sucked up by the dry desert dirt of Mother Earth. Only the first inch of topsoil was warm enough in early April to accept Begay's delicious final gift of life, and it did so greedily. Randal Begay's body looked like a performance artwork, his glistening brown skin still covered in small droplets of sweat, ruts in the dirt filling with blood which flowed freely out of Randal's now exposed cavernous sinuses. The edges of the small blood trenches were covered with fine fatty deposits from the remnants of Randal's right temporal brain. Barely noticeable was the appearance of Randal's fingertips, which had a bluish hue, some sort of stain, and not due to his current state of anoxia. Soon the color clue to the cause of his death would simply blend into the rigors of death; a single blue hue of oxygen deprivation found in all cadavers.

The tall man with the orange hat searched Randal's clothes, which he had so neatly folded outside his homemade sweat lodge and hung on a tree branch. Finding the desired key, the man returned the now useless clothes to their original perch on the only pinion tree within a mile. The man with the orange hat watched intently for any hint of movement from Randal. Nothing. Randal was dead. The killer's blow had been strong and sure.

The killer opened his pants, relieving himself on the rock that was covered in blood and brains. He casually tossed the murder weapon back into the pile of rocks inside the sweat lodge. It would take some serious police work to figure out which stone had been used to kill the talented Randal Begay. The orange hat man was not a fan of any police, tribal or otherwise. Then as the murderer turned to leave the scene of the crime, he heard a familiar sound and a large smile came over his face. Nearby, a hungry family of coyotes was yipping to each other about their evening meal. Apparently they must have already caught the salty smell of Randal's fresh blood, still pooling around the sweat lodge's entrance. Their excitement was the calling card: we will be visiting soon.

As the tall man in the orange hat slowly exited Begay's remote desert retreat, his face was beaming, anticipating the coyotes' visit. "Yes, those Injun cops will have a fun one with this case. See you Randal. Sure was nice doing business with you."

CHAPTER 36

A NEW DEAL

From two miles away, Buck had watched the man with the orange hat open the door of Randal's hogan. He must have gotten the key from Randal and this could not be good. The Texan was in the one-bedroom house for 30 minutes. When he came out, his face was red—even from miles away. He reached into his black jacket and pulled out his phone and dialed. Cell service on the rez was spotty at best, but Buck's phone went off. It had to be the Texan on the line.

Buck's heart started to pound, but he told himself, "I'm in control here. I have the blanket and I know he has done something very bad. He needs me. I can see him and he doesn't know I can see him." Buck finally picked up the phone.

"Hello, this is Buck."

"Hi there, Buck. This is Darryl. You and I are supposed to be doing a deal tomorrow." No mention of Randal.

"Yes Darryl, I'm assuming we are still on for tomorrow at Kayenta Crossing?" Buck said, hoping the quiver in his voice was not noticeable.

"Well I got here a day early and was wondering if you had my blanket."

Darryl had called it his blanket, so he had an emotional commitment to the piece and may have just killed to get it.

Buck assured him, "I've got her, all safe and sound. Why are you calling me though, not Randal? How did you know I got the blanket?"

"Well let's just say Mr. Begay is out of the picture now and it's you and me. A bigger piece of pie for you, assuming you did get a notarized write up?" the Texan said.

"Yes sir, I got it. In fact, the photo as it turns out was one of my kin and I've got an old family photo showing that same guy with me as a kid. Your provenance is rock solid and so is the weaving. It's a masterpiece."

"Great, I can't wait to see it. How about tonight?" Darryl pressed, planning to eliminate the other half of the partnership as fast as possible.

"Afraid that's not going to happen. You and I got to renegotiate our original deal. The rules have changed since you have removed my friend and partner from the picture," Buck stalled, looking through the scope so he could see the man's body language change, as he knew he was about to get screwed out of some additional money.

Buck decided he was now in a stronger bargaining position, and he better take advantage of it. "I'm sure you can understand why I feel that way, Darryl. So for me to let you have the blanket and my family history I want more than the $20K. More risk now. Also Darryl, we aren't doing any business today as there are going to be cops all over this place very soon as I'm calling them shortly if you don't leave Kayenta by tonight. You see Darryl, I'm not a man to be fucked with. I'm not as naïve as my late Navajo partner and I know the kind of men we both are. So here's my deal, and it's not negotiable. You call me from the McDonald's in Kayenta in one hour. Stay next to the play area so I can hear the kids playing, and I'll let you know where and when we will meet for the exchange."

"What if there ain't no fucking kids, Buck?"

"Well you better round up a few, or I'll screw the pooch, and you won't make your plane in Albuquerque. And by the way, I've got my 36 trained on that bright orange hat of yours so if you're having any other thoughts concerning going it alone, you may want to think twice about that."

Darryl realized he was being watched and if the old man would allow his partner to be killed he wasn't a person to take lightly. Darryl would play it straight for now.

"Fine Buck, you and me are partners now. One hour. But you remember what I'm capable of and if you fuck with me, you will be real sorry."

The phone went dead on Buck's end.

Buck's hand was shaking as he put down the phone's receiver and watched the man in the orange hat calmly get in his car and leave the same way he came in. Buck knew good and well that Randal was dead. The conversation had left no doubt. The fact that Buck hadn't heard a gunshot meant Darryl had killed him by hand and at close range, which is a harder thing to do. Buck knew all too well what it meant to kill a man by hand, having served in Korea and disposed of an enemy soldier by stabbing him with his bayonet, face to face. The image was still clear in Buck's mind 60 years later.

Buck was now an accomplice to a murder, even if at this point no one knew it other than himself. Buck had made a decision by not stopping the man when he had the opportunity. He had embraced the dark coyote inside of all humans, and there was no going back. Buck would have to deal with whatever consequences might befall him. He was glad he wasn't a religious man, because if he was, hell had just opened up a prime spot for him.

Buck's home phone rang exactly one hour later.

"Hear the kiddies?" Darryl directed the phone towards the plastic cave's entrance so the reverberation of children's screams would be loudest.

"Yeah, I hear 'em. How much money you got with you, Darryl?"

"Don't worry, I've got the $20K in cash for you. That was our deal."

"It was indeed," Buck agreed. "Then you got greedy and figured you'd kill Randal, and I'm assuming, me too. But the blanket wasn't where you thought it would be, so now you need my help. Sound about right?"

"No it's not like that at all. Your so-called partner was about to screw us both. I did what needed to be done to get the deal finished. That's how I see it, Pard. You called me, remember, to tell me about our problem with Begay getting religion? I just assumed you wanted me to get rid of the problem and I did. So you're running the show right now, but as you know I'm not a man to be pushed too hard. Might have to grab a kid on the way out just to show you what kind of fellow I am," Darryl upped the stakes.

"I have no doubt you are the kind who could do just that, and I'm not greedy, but I also know there is a hell of lot more on the line for me now than some bogus blanket. We're talking capital punishment and maybe kidnapping if I read you right," said Buck.

"I'm listening, old man. How much?" Darryl Ridgemount summed up the situation, understanding this was a business negotiation.

"OK Darryl, I haven't called the cops yet so you know I'm willing to play ball. I'll give you plenty of time to get out of Dodge. You and I can't make any deals today. We need to wait a while. This whole area will be crawling with cops and they will be asking a lot of questions. You need to get back to Texas, hang loose for a month, and I'll figure out how to get you the blanket. Here's my proposition, and it's not going to cost you anymore. In fact, it'll be less. I want to make $100K on this. Now I know that weaving has to be worth triple that, maybe more."

"Sounds like it's costing me a hell of lot more than the $35K I was paying Randal and the $20K for you!" Darryl protested.

"Nope. Here's why. There's a great Daisy Taugelchee I know about and I'm going to get it and give it to you for next to nothing. It's worth at least $100K, and since you were going to spend $55K to begin with, you would actually come out way ahead on the deal. I need time—at least a month—to get the Daisy and also time for the cops to do whatever they do besides shut down hog farms, and stop asking questions." The sting of the quarantine was still burning in Buck's mind.

"A month," Darryl agreed. "No longer. The Daisy's a nice touch, real cute. You're sure it's a Daisy, not some look alike?"

"Oh it's the real thing. I bought it from her in 1954. I remember it quite well."

"Alright you got your month. Call me and keep me informed of anything you might hear about the cops. I would stay away from Begay's place for a while unless you want your fingerprints on a crime scene. Remember old man, I will kill you if you try any more of this Kayenta double-crossing," Darryl warned.

"Yes, I understand. By the way, Darryl, there is a trash can to the side of the building. It has a McHamburger head. The hat will come off if you pull hard from the back. Open it and leave me $10K, as a 10 percent advance. A goodwill gesture. We will plan on talking every week, same time," Buck instructed.

"Fine, it's your money to lose. If someone takes it before you get your happy meal that's your problem. You're just plain McFucked." Laughing, Darryl hung up.

Buck got in his old truck and headed into Kayenta to pick up a hamburger, fries, and a cool $10K.

CHAPTER 37

YOU ARE THE CORONER

Most of Randal's body wasn't found until noon the next day. The coyotes had been hungry. Hastiin Johnson had worried when his grandson had not come over to discuss his visions and went looking for him. The hogan door was wide open. This was never done in a land of wild creatures and Johnson knew immediately his grandson was in serious trouble. He found most of Randal's body just where it had fallen at the entrance to the sweat lodge. The old man had seen many coyote kills in his long life, and knew it was not their doing but one of man. He couldn't imagine who could want to harm such a loving and talented person as his grandson. It had to be a very bad spirit. Even at 90 and living a hard life, which included surviving three rattlesnake bites, it was hard to stomach finding the partially devoured murdered body of your only grandson.

Johnson's shock reduced him into a kind of Parkinsonian personality. His walking became shuffled and a mask-like face appeared on the usually jovial man. He went to his nearest neighbor and longtime friend, Buck Wilson.

Buck had been watching anxiously all day through his monovision scope. When he saw Johnson's truck pull in, he knew it would be catastrophic for the old man. Buck felt terrible for him, knowing what he was going about to experience: the death of a child. Buck had been driven into a world of dark forces and felt he had to embrace these emotions if he was going to survive the next month's ordeal. He fully understood Johnson would seek him out and he had been practicing his lines so they seemed heartfelt and spontaneous.

"Buck, it's my grandson. He's...." The old medicine man didn't know how to say it in English, so he used the Navajo word for dead as he burst through the front door without knocking, something he had never done in 50-plus years of knowing Buck.

"*Yá át ééh*, what's wrong? What's this about Randal?" Buck said, trying to sound as concerned and shocked as possible.

"They have killed him, and coyote has done his part too," said Hastiin Johnson.

"What? Who has killed him? Where is Randal?"

"He took a sweat yesterday. A bad *chindi* had been haunting him. He was trying to clear his mind and find his way. The bad spirit found him first. Somebody bashed his skull in and left him like a rabbit's intestines to rot." The old man had streams of tears running down his face. Buck also started to cry, for Randal and himself.

"We need to call the police. Leave everything the way it is and let them handle this. These are the things they are good at," Buck said, thinking they were also good at ruining rancher's lives by shutting down their hog pens and telling everyone not to eat Wilson's pork.

"Can you call them?" the medicine man asked. "I don't feel very good. My head is light, too much for an old man to see. I wish I had died last year with the snakebite. I should have died and never had to see what I just saw."

"You can stay here with me for now. We will see what they know. Do you have any idea why someone might do this?" Buck asked, at this point fishing for any information the old man might know about the first phase.

"No. He was having problems eating and sleeping, and was on the wrong path. I don't know why he felt that way. He never said."

"Did you look in his hogan? Was anything gone?" Buck questioned.

"Nothing too out of place, though his loom was empty and I didn't see a rug. He usually had a rug going and it would be up, so he either just finished one or maybe somebody took something. I don't know."

"Are you sure he was weaving something now?"

"No, but he was a weaver and that is what they do. I think he would have something going, he always did. But he hadn't talked about weaving in a long time so maybe something had changed in his life. Maybe his *hozho* had been changed by not weaving, I don't know." The old man started to sob and was not able to talk anymore.

As a possible homicide on Navajo land, the coroner is called to the crime scene. In the case of Randal Begay's death, the man on duty was Dr. Carson Riddly.

Dotty got the call. "Dr. Riddly, I got the Navajo Tribal Police on the line. They need to talk with you."

"Hello, this is Doc Riddly. How can I help you?"

"Dr. Riddly, we have had a homicide out at Randal Begay's place about 30 minutes from your clinic. We need you to come out and remove the body for an autopsy."

"Can you repeat, did you say Randal Begay? Is he dead?" Carson was shocked.

"This is of course classified information at this time, but since you are the acting coroner and will need to know shortly, yes sir that would be correct."

Carson was stunned not only at the death but to find out he was the coroner, a title he never wanted or asked for.

"Shit, I know him. A nice guy. I just met with his art dealer this weekend, Charles Bloom."

"Where was that, sir?"

This sounded like the police were fishing for information as if Bloom or even he were involved in the case.

"It was near Toadlena in New Mexico. On Friday and Saturday. The rest of the time I was in Albuquerque. Just got back last night around midnight," Carson clarified.

"Good, I'll write your statement up and have you sign it. We want to make sure everyone who knew Randal is checked out, nothing personal, but since you're acting corner we have to make sure there are no problems."

"I understand, officer?"

"Lieutenant Ricky Wildhorse."

"Lieutenant, can you repeat what you said about me being the coroner in this case?"

"Yes sir. Our flow map shows you as the physician in charge of all potential homicides north of Kayenta. Your North Clinic is in charge. You."

Carson could just see the recruiter who sent him to this clinic chuckling, knowing Carson would get called for extreme duty sometime during his two years. His voice saying, "This will teach you to screw with my form 16160. Six lines only, no exceptions."

"I need to warn you, I need guidance. I have never been involved in such a case. I'm a family doctor fresh out of residency and I have to plead stupid," Carson admitted to the officer.

"Thanks for your honesty. I'd rather hear that than you try to B.S. your way through. Main thing, Doc, is to come out to the crime scene and carefully observe and make notes if you notice anything odd, medically. We have taken all the necessary steps already on our part, but your medical training will give you a more sophisticated understanding of the scene. Take the body back to the North Clinic for an initial evaluation. I will arrange to have Mr. Begay's body sent to Flagstaff from there for a detailed autopsy. You're more like a pseudo-coroner."

"I like the sound of that a whole lot better," Carson confided. Grabbing his doctor's bag that he never used except during nursing-home rounds, and adding a few extra jars and vials just in case he found something unusual, he headed outside to meet the patrol car that would take him over to Randal's hogan. He remembered how Randal had acted oddly just last week when he saw him and wondered if this was related to his death. Possibly.

As a doctor you learn how to prepare yourself for unpleasant visual situations. It first happens when you work in the emergency room and see trauma cases come in. Kids are always the worst as they are so totally helpless. The brain switches to complete autopilot as you know you have a job and if you get emotional you will screw it up.

This was Carson's mindset as he rode in the tribal police car. A large roll of yellow police tape had encircled the old hogan and disappeared into the distance to where the body was found. The desert winds would take care of flimsy tape in short order. It was obvious to anyone who had spent time in the windy environment that it was more for show than function. It was a message along the lines of, "Take the photos, show we're real cops. See, we have a crime scene."

The first crime scene a rookie experiences is always the toughest, or so the cops say. Carson hoped it would be his last as the official northern Kayenta coroner. The fact that he knew the deceased and had visited his home twice made the experience very unsettling on many levels. Randal had just been joking about finding a girl for him, and now he was bits and pieces in the desert.

The hogan's door was open, unlike the last time he had visited. Randal's new truck was still out front and the police had dusted for tire tracks. The lieutenant described the location of Randal's body and exactly what to expect.

Walking the 200 yards behind the hogan, Carson visually skimmed the surroundings looking for anything unusual, as if he would know. He saw a pile of cans, mainly skim milk in various states of decay, and a broken chair with a packrat nest living under its blue-and-white metal exterior. There were various tracks of animals along with some human shoe prints, but nothing unusual. Once he crested the hill, he saw the little brown dirt building and in close proximity, what appeared to be Randal's broken body. Even Carson could tell he had been ambushed: his torso had fallen face down and remnants of the skull were turned to one side. The body looked like a grotesque fruit roll-up: Randal's corpse was half white and half blue. The top where all the blood had drained was ashen white. The lower half was dark blue where the blood had pooled. A large amount of blood had apparently drained out of an open head wound. Several animals had eaten on the body. A large portion of one side of his face was gone. Teeth and claw marks were apparent. The damage was limited primarily to the cranium. Randal's long black hair had matted into a thick organic salad of dried blood. The sight of Randal's broken body —when Randal had always been so nice to him—in such a pitiful condition made Carson's stomach queasy. The smell was to a minimum as it was still very cold for April and Randal's abdominal cavity had been spared. Large sections of Randal's triceps, hamstrings, and flank had however been stripped away by hungry carnivores, most likely coyotes.

His body was in a complete rigor mortis, which meant he had been dead for around 12 hours. His arms were crumpled underneath. It was obvious Randal hadn't seen his assailant coming. The police took numerous photos and finally the body was turned over. Carson looked carefully like a dress designer might examine their spring line. Every detail was scanned and mental notes made of any irregularities or signs of additional trauma. No entry or exit wounds were seen. The body was basically nude except for some underwear, which would be consistent with a sweat lodge. The fingertips of Randal's right hand appeared to be bluer in coloration, which he could not explain. All of his arms and hands were cyanotic but the right hand fingers definitely had a more intense blue color. They almost seemed as if they were stained. This was impossible to delineate without a microscope, which he made a note to do when he got back to the clinic.

The entire process took two hours. Then the body was taken away by an ambulance for closer inspection at the North Clinic. Carson understood everything he saw might someday come up during a trial. His notes could become evidence in a murder case. Doctors today are well trained for the rigors of litigation in the practice of medicine. It's a given you will be sued sometime during a medical tenure as a physician. It isn't that doctors are careless, but there are more lawyers to doctors in society's ratio. Carson approached his evaluation already thinking what questions the lawyer might pose to him as he sat squirming on the stand.

Back at the clinic, the front waiting room was packed. For a reservation the size of Ohio, it didn't take long for word to spread about Randal's death and it wasn't by telephone. Somehow the word flew. Numerous locals were waiting when he arrived with the body. Carson was shocked at the appearance of so many Navajos mulling about in one place, all looking upset. He prayed no one knew his first name.

"*Yá át ééh*," Carson said to the crowd as he exited the patrol car. His greeting was weak and unconvincing. He sounded like a little kid at his first paper presentation in front of a live audience. The crowd did not respond kindly. They wanted information.

"I'm sorry, I don't have anything I can tell you other than there was a death. Officer Wildhorse will brief you. The clinic will be closed today except for extreme emergencies. All others should reschedule or go down to the main clinic in Kayenta. I'm sorry for any inconvenience," Carson told the crowd. He then had Dotty reissue his statement in Diné for those unable to understand the white doctor.

Carson walked quickly past the crowd, who all seemed to be saying something in Navajo about him. He heard the word Kit uttered in the crowd, undoubtedly by one of Brenda's family members.

Lieutenant Wildhorse shared the fact that the deceased was Randal Begay and it did look like it was a homicide. If anyone had information they should contact him and he gave out numerous cards. An older man in the crowd yelled to the lieutenant that a *yee naaldlooshii* (a witch) had been stealing sheep and wondered if it was after weavers now. This upset many of the grandmothers in the crowd and it took 10 minutes to alleviate their fears. Wildhorse promised he would look into it and took the man's name to check on the sheep loss.

Even though another ambulance was on its way from Flagstaff to relieve Carson of the dead body, he did want to take a closer look at Begay's remains under more civilized conditions since he was the acting coroner. Randal's mutilated corpse was taken into the back room and placed on a long steel table. His arms were still at odd angles, hanging straight off like a broken kite. The body examination revealed nothing remarkable other than the very large crush injury to the temporal frontal region of Randal's right cranium. The right thumb, first, and second fingers were examined under microscopic magnification and bright light. Carson's first impression appeared correct. The coloration was not due to blood, but some kind of stain. The dermatologist in Carson yearned to escape his current skin evaluation and return to Scottsdale and look at teenage pimples or wrinkles for Botox treatment. Anything but examining the mutilated body of someone he knew.

He scraped a sample of the blue resin off Randal's finger using the end of a scalpel blade and placed it on a slide, covering it with a glass cover slip for further evaluation. A voice in Carson's head told him, "This is something to pay attention to, not an artifact." He decided to take a second sample, one for him to evaluate in case the real coroner felt it was of no interest.

Randal was hiding something, the closed hogan door and his unusual behavior must be connected to his death. A murder was in the neighborhood and Carson was one of the prime investigators of the crime. Tonight he would lock his trailer's door assuming it had one. For the first time since arriving at the reservation Carson felt afraid living in such a remote location; the coyote's howling no longer had the same enchanting connotations it once did.

CHAPTER 38

BLOOMED

The phone call came as Bloom walked into his house after working all day at Toadlena. It had been a good day for the post. He had sold three nice rugs and was feeling great about his newfound abilities selling Navajo textiles. The smell of Rachael's homemade chicken potpie filled the small room. As he helped himself to some of the crusty side drippings, the phone rang. He ignored it, busy slurping down the treat and trying not to burn his mouth. After the third ring, he picked up.

The voice on the other end was Navajo, as it usually was. Bloom had started answering all calls "*Yá át ééh*" and in a pretty decent Navajo accent. He loved it when he could fool a Native speaker into rambling in Diné. The person on the other end now was upset. Not knowing the language didn't prevent him from feeling their distress. He stopped the person in mid-sentence from having to repeat whatever was bothering them.

"It's Bloom. I can't understand you. I don't speak good Navajo yet." This was of course a massive understatement as he spoke only a few words: rug (*diyogi*), wool (*aghaa*), and sheep (*dibe*), as these terms were common daily words for a trading post.

"*Yá át ééh*, Bloom. This is Rachael's great-aunt Doris. I heard bad news and I want Rachael to know."

"*Yá át ééh*, Doris. Do you want me to get Rachael?"

"No, you tell her. I don't want to."

"Alright, I'm listening."

There was a pause before Doris spoke as she thought carefully about how to phrase the tragic news in English.

"Tell her, that weaving friend from Kayenta was found murdered today. They don't know anything more. I heard this from a good friend who knows his grandfather, Hastiin Johnson. He's a powerful medicine man near Kayenta and used to know her grandfather very well. Rachael will remember Hastiin Johnson."

Bloom had been around enough elderly Navajos by now to know they didn't want to say the name of someone deceased so he would have to say Randal's name for her.

"Is this friend Randal Begay? The weaver Rachael did a show with last summer in Santa Fe?" Bloom's own voice now showed his own signs of distress.

"Yes, that's who it was."

"OK, I'll let her know. Thanks." The phone went dead on the other end.

Bloom's first thoughts were of Willard Yellowhorse, Rachael's late brother and Bloom's onetime superstar artist. He had felt this same feeling 20 years ago upon hearing Willard had been found dead hanging from a rope. Both Randal and Willard had been murdered, and both had also been represented at Bloom's.

He remembered his old fear that the word *Bloom* was now going to be used as an adjective to describe bad luck with artists. People would say the artists had been *Bloomed*, or cursed. Maybe he had the black touch instead of golden.

The irony of Rachael's enthusiastic voice singing along to a recent Beyoncé song in the background and the tragic news he would now have to deliver made his stomach flop. He knew the sizzling potpie coming out of the old wooden oven and the wonderful intimate dinner was about to be ruined. *Bloomed*.

Walking into the small kitchen area which was barely separated from the living room, he could see the back of Rachael's shapely butt bouncing along to the hip-hop tune. She was licking her fingers of some of the excess juice, which was flowing over the potpie's edge when she spotted Bloom. She saw the look on his face and immediately knew it was bad news.

"What's wrong? Are you OK? Are you hurt, sick? What's wrong?" He walked over and hugged her, whispering in her ear which had been enjoying the music, "It's Randal Begay. He's dead. Murdered. Your Aunt Doris just called."

Rachael was stunned. The tears started to flow full force down her high cheekbones. Her favorite Beyoncé song, "Single Lady," would now and forever be a marker for Randal's death news instead of the song she was going to play at her wedding.

"How? Why? I don't understand."

"Honey, I don't have the answers. They just found him today but I will find out. Maybe he got into something, drugs or gambling, I just don't know. Tomorrow I'll try and talk to Carson Riddly, see if he knows something. He may have some answers."

The hot potpie was never touched. They both lost their appetites and went to bed early holding each other. Another great Indian artist lost too early.

CHAPTER 39

CARSON AND CHARLES

Early the next morning, Bloom headed out the door for his daily run. His exercise helped him with his own *hozho*. The rush of endorphins lifted his spirits and seemed to help him think more clearly about life's many obstacles. He looked forward to every run, even today.

This morning's goal was more to try and forget the horrible news of Randal's death and come to grips with losing another gallery artist. Charles and Rachael were supposed to be getting ready for spring break: taking a vacation to discuss their own lives and future. Their two-year anniversary of living together was next week, a watershed mark for both. Bloom was feeling the matrimonial pressures on a daily basis and understood the week together would be a time to discuss each other's expectations. It would be a critical point in their relationship, possibly life changing.

Usually Bloom left his cell phone behind when he exercised, but with yesterday's bad news he figured he should take it in case Rachael needed him.

The call from Carson surprised Bloom as he was going to try to touch base with the doctor later in the day. He figured Carson would be getting hammered with inquires and he didn't want to be the first person to bother him that day.

"Charles, I have bad news. Randal Begay was found murdered yesterday outside his hogan. I know you represented him in your gallery. This must be a terrible blow."

"I appreciate the call, Carson. I heard last night. News travels fast on the Navajo pipeline. Do we know how and why?" Bloom slowed to a fast walk, panting.

"You OK? You sound winded."

"I'm fine, just running to clear my mind. Anything you can share would be greatly appreciated."

"What I can tell you, which is more than I probably should, is that it looked like he was ambushed coming out of a sweat lodge. His grandfather had recommended the sweat to work out some problems he was having," Carson said.

"Problems? What kind?"

"I don't know. I do know when I went out to Randal's to get your number last week to have you appraise my Daisy, he did kind of act weird."

"Weird in what way? Drugs?"

"It wasn't that kind of weird. Drugs and alcohol I can recognize. He didn't want me to go inside his hogan, like he was hiding something. The first time I met him last summer he invited me in and proudly showed me the rug you sold in Santa Fe. He was very friendly. Last week was different."

"How so?"

"He didn't invite me in. He said the house was a mess and he didn't want anybody to see it. I can assure you the first time I saw his hogan it was a pig sty, and he could have cared less. He also seemed distracted this time, and he had lost weight. I think he was possibly depressed about something and appeared to be hiding something or someone in his house."

"Have you been in the hogan since his death? Did he have a rug on the loom?" Bloom had learned the ways of Navajo weavers and knew there was almost always something in progress. This was how you made your money. Santa Fe's Indian Market wasn't that far away in terms of getting a rug ready, and one should have been well along.

"The loom was there but nothing on it that I saw. Not much yarn around either, just a couple of little balls of wool. I believe they were natural colored."

"Carson, that seems odd to me. Last year when I was at Randal's hogan he had me come in without hesitation. Maybe he was working on a commission. He didn't share any information with me the last time we talked. I got the impression I would be lucky if I got anything significant for Santa Fe this year. He must have just finished whatever he was working on if there wasn't much wool spun. Randal liked to spin all his wool first and then weave," Bloom reasoned. "Maybe his commission went bad or was stolen. I'm guessing, but I can't think of anything else. The word on the street is he liked to gamble, so maybe he had a bookie he owed some money to and when he didn't pay they took his rug and killed him. If you get a chance, you should go back out and look. If your cell will work out there, call me from his house and describe what you see. Murdering for a rug doesn't sound like something another Navajo would do to a Navajo. You don't steal rugs. Too many people can spot a great weaving and start asking questions like who's the weaver. Only a couple of weavers have his skill, so if it was stolen it has to be by an outsider."

"I noticed a new pickup truck that was apparently Randal's, so I wonder if the gambling idea could be right?" Carson pondered out loud.

"I don't know. Every time I saw him he asked me for money. Maybe he sold the rug and bought the truck. You could check on how new it is."

"I'll tell the lieutenant, a guy named Wildhorse, to look into the truck angle. Also I told him you and I had met last week and Randal had given me your number. I imagine he will call you to see what you know."

"That's fine. I have nothing to add other than I think it's strange there was no rug and he had a new truck. I've only talked to him by phone once this year, when he called me from Goulding's last month to tell me he wouldn't have much for this August's show."

Carson decided, "I'll go out tomorrow to his hogan and try to call you. Any other advice? This is my first murder case."

"You got any Navajo fetishes?" Bloom asked.

"As a matter of fact I do, a little turquoise bear Randal's grandfather gave me for good health."

"Keep it on at all times. Call me tomorrow." Bloom figured Carson could use all the help he could muster.

CHAPTER 40

RATS

By the next day, Carson Riddly knew a lot more about what the title Kayenta Coroner entailed. He had fielded interview requests from two radio stations, one TV station, and three newspapers, including the *Albuquerque Journal*, all regarding Randal's death. Nothing in medical school or residency had prepared him to answer questions regarding a murder case. He did his best to answer questions as obtusely as possible, limiting his liability to lawsuits from who knows who.

Every person from 50 miles around came to see Doc Riddly, all complaining of some minor malady so they could see the doctor and pepper him with questions. His pat answer was, "We have no suspects as far as I know. You will need to talk to Lieutenant Wildhorse."

Bloom knew from his own experience that being in the middle of a storm of press was no fun. It would last for the next couple of days, then the worst would be over. He had seen Carson's face on television and heard him on the radio already once today. Bloom waited until the late afternoon to follow up on yesterday's call.

"*Yá át ééh*, this is Charles. How you holding up under the pressure? You must be drained."

"I am. This doctoring stuff is not for the faint of heart. I'm really convinced I should have been a dermatologist," Carson said, managing a little laugh at his wish to be transported out of the rez into private practice. "I'm heading out to Randal's place in a couple of hours after I close the clinic. I'll try and call from there to see if you can walk me through what I should be looking for."

"OK. If you don't get cell reception, make notes, take photos, and we will talk when you get to a land line."

Carson finished up with the last patients and retired to his trailer for a quick cup of instant coffee and some biscuits one of his patients had brought him. The day had been brutal but he felt if he was to find any additional clues he needed to act quickly.

Randal's hogan was still partially covered by yellow police tape although most of it had been blown away by the *Ma'ii* winds. The unlocked door was closed now, unlike when he first had arrived on the scene and the door was wide open. No signs of life, which Carson was thankful for. The sun would be down shortly and he wanted to get in and out quickly, as being so isolated he feared the murderer could still be around. The first signs of spring were also around along with the usual influx of bees.

The interior was as he remembered. Untouched. There were weaving tools next to the loom, which he had not noticed when he first saw the crime scene. The tools looked ancient, as if they had been used for generations. The oak wood was dark from hundreds if not thousands of hours of human touch. The smallest wooden implement that looked for all purposes like a smooth stick had a darkish blue tint to one end. Its color looked fresh. Carson picked it up and examined the hue. It was similar to what he had scraped off the Randal's fingertips, an indigo blue color. He took a scalpel from his doctor's bag and made a scraping from the wood and placed it into one of his sterile bottles, leaving the tools as they had been found.

Carson tried his cell phone and on the third attempt got one bar of power. He managed to get a poor-reception connection with Charles Bloom.

"Charles, I'm out here looking around. There were some weaving tools I hadn't noticed before. I took a scraping off one of the small sticks. It has some kind of blue coloration. This is something I also noticed on Randal's fingertips. Any idea what it could be?"

"The weaving stick was probably stained from stirring up some dyes for wool preparation. I'm not sure what the significance of the blue color might be. Maybe he was preparing some yarn right before he died, or was eating blueberries? No bluish yarn anywhere?"

"No. I see a couple of small balls of brown and white yarn next to the weaving tools, otherwise nothing unusual. I see just a few pieces of rustic furniture and the empty loom. Nothing out of the ordinary."

"The loom, are there any strings on it? When a weaver gets ready to start a rug they string yarn. It looks similar to a harp."

"No rug or strings. Just a metal loom and weaving tools and two small balls of yarn."

"Carson, go around the hogan. See if there is some little shed or holding area. Maybe there is a rug or yarn there."

That was the last of the cell phone service. It went down with the last cloud, not to return that day.

Carson walked the perimeter of the property, finding no structures other than the sweat lodge. Reluctantly he stuck his head and flashlight in the last place Randal had ever taken a breath. Nothing was found other than the piles of river rocks in the center, which should have been confiscated by the police as possible murder weapons.

What Carson did find were a few fresh rat droppings in the hogan, a pack rat no doubt making a new home. As he started to leave, the scientist in him thought about the rat feces and knowing about pack rats' behavior from following his Gila monsters for his senior year high-school science project, he decided to take a cursory look around the hogan looking for their dens.

Pack rats are notorious for getting into homes, cars, anything that can be chewed on and taken back to the home nest. He found a large active nest under an old engine block and one under a chair. The one under the engine block was substantial, filled with mainly human refuse: tin foil, cactus parts, old sticks, gum wrappers, and something unusual—little pieces of handspun sheep yarn. The yarn was blue. It was the same blue color as Randal's fingers and the weaving stick. Carson concluded that the yarn must have been wool that Randal was working with. Carson collected all of the fragments he could find and stuck them into another vial for identification.

With the sun going down, the temperature plummeted. Carson was happy to get out of the area. The skin walkers—as his patients called those personified elements of evil—would be out tonight as there was unrest north of Kayenta. Carson clutched his bear fetish. He was a *bilagaana*, but he wasn't stupid.

CHAPTER 41

COLOR ME BLUE

"The blue-colored yarn, Randal's stained fingers, and the blue resin on the weaving stick must be related," Cason thought to himself as he drove home. "Was he weaving a rug with blue dye he had dyed himself? If so, where was the yarn or rug?"

At the time when he was at the hogan, it seemed like a good idea to collect the evidence, but he now realized what he had taken was from an active crime scene and he was not a cop. The fact that the rocks were still in the sweat lodge and Randal had most certainly died from head trauma worried him. Should he tell the tribal police to go gather the sweat lodge rocks, and if so what about his unauthorized yarn-and-stick resin collection? Maybe they were planning to make a thorough search of the perimeter? It still had most of the yellow tape and since he had walked all around the perimeter, his footsteps would now be evidence as well. He saw himself getting grilled at trial, an O.J. type moment. Brenda would be the prosecutors' first witness. He could hear her voice: "Yes, Doctor Riddly claimed, even boasted, he was the direct relative of Kit Carson during the first encounter I ever had with the man." A Navajo tribal judge would throw the book at him, or possibly look to him as the murderer.

The more his mind raced about his stupid investigation, the more he was sure he had broken some law. He didn't have a clue if the reservation had separate tribal laws. Criminal charges could be filed. Carson's analytical brain was adrift in *what ifs*. He tried to reason to himself, "I was the Acting Kayenta Coroner. I needed samples to help figure out the coloration on the deceased. Yes I should have had supervision, but as I told Lieutenant Wildhorse this was my first time as a coroner." He would practice these lines of reasoning instead of, "How could I have been so stupid?"

Back at the clinic, Carson stared at his little vials. He considered tossing the stick scrapings and Mr. Pack Yarn in the dumpster, never to be seen again. He knew this would be a worse mistake. He had chosen this path and must see it through. He saw a correlation with his childhood act of throwing the Black Cat firecrackers into dry grass. After calming down, he exclaimed to himself, "I know I can solve this riddle, after all I am Doc Riddly!" laughing at his play on words, one he had heard thousands of times during the Batman movies. "Bloom got me into going back to look for this stuff; he can help me get out," Carson reasoned.

So Carson called Bloom for some more guidance. Bloom was at home just finishing last night's warmed-up chicken potpie.

"Charles, it's Carson. I think I may be onto something. Got time to talk?"

Charles wiped the last of the delicious chicken from his mouth. "Sure, just finishing dinner. Wish you could taste Rachael's chicken potpie. It's so good, even reheated."

Carson had not had a home-cooked meal since last June at his folks' home. The thought made his mouth start to water. "I walked around the hogan. I didn't find any hidey-holes with a rug or yarn, but I did find some yarn scraps in a nearby pack-rat nest. They had the same iridescent blue I found on the stick and on Randal's fingertips. Think they could be related?"

"Maybe. I asked Rachael about the color on the stick. She told me it was not uncommon for the end of one of the tools to be used to stir up dyes. She had never seen a blue color but she's a Two Grey Hills weaver. The only color they use is pinion pine pitch, which is black. The yarn you found: what was the texture? Was it similar to the balls of yarn next to the loom?"

"Yep, best I could tell, but just snippets. Probably already chewed up by the rat."

"I would have to guess Randal dyed yarn blue and used it in a weaving. Do you have it where you could look at a piece?" Bloom asked.

"I've got a strand in front of me," said Carson.

"Unravel the yarn and look for any kind of fading, even just the slightest amount and do it under bright light. Also, does it have a shimmer to the color like indigo?"

Carson carefully dissected the small piece of wool, periodically looking over his shoulder as if breaking another law. "No fading and it does shimmer. What in the hell does that mean?"

"Indigo dye is a color used in most early Navajo blankets. Occasionally you will see it used today making a revival piece. Maybe Randal was working with indigo. It's also possible the yarn is from an old weaving blanket. Pack-rat nests can literally be around for centuries, just being reused over time."

"Is there any way we can test the yarn to see if it's old?"

"There are a few textile experts that can do spectrophotometric tests to determine the color spectrum of the yarn. With a powerful microscope, the yarn's composition can also be determined to some extent. I know Sal at the Toadlena Post has had this kind of analysis done before. I'll find out who the go-to person in this field is and we can send it out for them to take a look."

"Great. Can he also check scrapings from human skin for color analysis?"

"I don't know why not. I'll get you the textile expert's name tomorrow. By the way, Rachael and I have next week off for spring break. Maybe we'll come out your way and visit Monument Valley. Any good motels around Kayenta you can recommend?"

"I expect you to come and see me if you're in town. I want to share my margarita mix. Not like yours, but it did help me get through gross anatomy. You'll have to bring the alcohol since I'm out. As for the hotel, stay at the Hampton Inn. Ask for room 2B. I miss it so."

CHAPTER 42

LET'S MAKE A DEAL

The tribal police visited Buck twice in the week following the murder, trying to solidify his story of how often he saw Randal and when. Lieutenant Wildhorse didn't view the old man as a suspect in the investigation. There was no motive and Hastiin Johnson had confirmed that he was like family. The tire tracks the police had lifted from the crime scene didn't match his vehicle or any other trucks in the vicinity. The tracks seemed more typical of a passenger car, so they were checking out the local rental-car facilities for anything suspicious. Randal apparently did have a bookie and was in debt for $2,000 but had been paying off his debt on a fairly regular basis. He had paid his debt down by half approximately eight months ago but it had built back up with the 40% interest. The police didn't really think the bookie was the murderer as he seemed to have a good alibi, but he was definitely still on the list of suspects.

Buck had used Darryl's $10,000 advance to pay down his own heavily mortgaged property. Lieutenant Wildhorse never found these records as Buck used an out-of-state transfer from his son's account. Buck was concerned about having the valuable blanket hiding at his house. It was new but it would sell as an original first-phase blanket. Randal's masterpiece truly did look like the real thing. Buck decided the only component missing was a little wear, as a blanket of this vintage would undoubtedly have. Using it as if it were a common saddle blanket, he took his horse for a long ride to help solidify its age. Nothing like horse sweat for a realistic instant patina.

Buck decided he needed to complete the deal sooner rather than later. He didn't trust going to Texas. He needed the home advantage of his own back yard. Darryl was not a man you turned your back on. Randal had taught him that. Buck decided to place the call to set everything in motion.

"Hi Darryl. This is your friend from Arizona. I'm ready to make a trade," Buck announced.

"I thought you wanted to wait a while and see what shakes out. Any prime suspects?"

"Yes, apparently Randal had a bookie. He was into him for a couple of thousand. The police have talked twice to me but don't seem interested beyond what I know about Randal's comings and goings and any visitors. It should be safe now for us both to get what we want. I've given the blanket a little age and I must say it looks outstanding. You should do fine."

"Well that sounds peachy. You got my Daisy as you promised? I'd be disappointed if you couldn't keep your word. I'm counting on that if you want the kind of cash I'm supposed to be bringing," Darryl checked.

"I know where it is. I'll have it when you get here. It's a timing issue," Buck hedged.

"Doesn't sound like you exactly have it. I'd hate to be disappointed. Randal disappointed me."

"I'm old, but not senile. I'll take care of it and it's a beaut! Darryl, let's meet in five days. You can call me from Mr. McHamburger head and I'll tell you where to meet," Buck proposed.

"Sounds cloak and dagger to me. I don't like this unknown shit. Remember, $90K more coming to you, that's it. As you know I'm not a man you want to screw with, Pard. And that fucking Daisy better be part of the deal. We on the same page?"

"Darryl, I may not have a lot of hair, but I want to keep what I've got. Don't worry. It's a straightforward deal. I'm too old to start trying to do a double cross. I don't know exactly where we will meet because it depends on how I acquire the Daisy and I won't know till that day."

"I'll call you in five days. Let me know if anything changes."

"Till then. By the way, about how much room does $100K take up?"

"One can of house paint." Click.

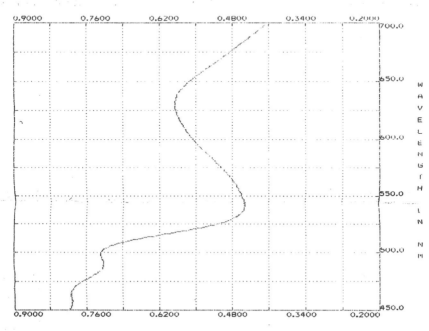

CHAPTER 43

A SMALL WORLD

The yarn expert that Sal used for analysis was located in Austin, Texas. He was the head of a small private museum that specialized in textiles: Trevor Middleman. Bloom called Trevor to explain the specifics of what they needed evaluated and how it was time sensitive since it was an active murder case.

Trevor was intrigued and realized who Randal Begay was as he had wanted to get a piece for Ms. Hughes's collection. He knew Begay's weavings, which were already hard to come by, would now become impossible to find.

"I'm sorry to hear about Mr. Begay's premature death. He was a gifted individual. I was familiar with his work. Did you know him well?" Trevor asked.

"I represented him in my gallery in Santa Fe. I had a two-person show last year and sold a lovely piece of his for a good sum of money," Bloom recalled.

"Your client was fortunate whatever they paid. It's probably worth double now. Randal's last weaving will be especially valuable. Was that the one you sold?"

Bloom of course understood this concept of dead artists bringing a lot more money, especially if they died young. "Yes, as far as I know it was Randal's last big rug, the one he did for me last summer. He was supposed to be doing one for this summer's show but no rug was on his loom when his body was found. I shouldn't say this about a client, but the guy who purchased Randal's rug from me last year probably would be happy about the increased value even if it meant a great artist died tragically. You may know him, he was from Austin. Likes his University of Texas team. Darryl Ridgemount?"

"DARRYL RIDGEMOUNT!"

"I'll take it you know him?" Bloom was concerned by the visceral response Trevor had to Ridgemount's name.

"I know him all too well. He was my ex-boss's so-called art expert. I would not trust this man, and I'm also not the kind to talk behind a person's back. I think he set me up at my last job to get me fired. We are talking serious stuff. I think he actually may be a psychopath."

"I can assure you, Trevor, I wasn't too fond of him myself. He seemed like the kind who would go behind your back at the first opportunity. In fact I thought he probably did so at my show though I don't have any proof. Just a feeling from the way he talked to Randal and took him out for dinner directly after the show."

"I could see him doing that, trying to cut you out and get more for himself. He is currently working for my old boss's ex-husband. He probably bought the Begay textile for him. He's still buying weavings for him as far as I know."

"Well thanks for the heads-up, Trevor. If he looks to me for anything else I'll keep my guard up. I figured he was dirty when he paid for the weavings in cash. Not normal to have accumulated that much cash to spend on art. One of the samples I'm sending you is human skin with what looks to be dye material that was on Randal's fingertips. I know you specialize in yarn, but can you evaluate that too?"

"I can do a dye analysis easily enough on any sample, but I can't tell you anything else other than what kind of dyes were used, if any," Trevor explained.

"I think the dye results are all we need. It's possible the three samples might be related. Please call me when you have the results," Bloom requested.

"I'll call you the same day I get the samples. I'll put this as my number-one priority." Trevor didn't believe in coincidences, and Ridgemount buying Randal's rug was most likely related to Randal's death. Trevor's puzzle-solving abilities told him so. It had to be.

Trevor Middleman got the three samples the next day, overnighted by Carson as Bloom had promised they would be.

The spectrophotometer required a very small sample and was exceedingly accurate for dye analysis. The results were the same for all three specimens: indigo dye.

Trevor called Bloom on his cell phone. Bloom had just checked into the Kayenta Hampton Inn, room 2B. It was supposed to be a vacation with Rachael, their spring break, but Bloom wanted to do some detective work regarding who killed Randal. Bloom didn't appreciate seeing one of his best artists killed. Again.

"Mr. Bloom, please let Dr. Riddly know all three samples are indigo. My guess is from the same batch, though I can't say for sure. The yarn that I looked at under microscopy is definitely Churro wool and exceptionally spun. Only a master weaver could spin the yarn that fine. It's impossible to determine age from visual inspection. We might learn something from carbon dating, but my gut tells me it was recently made, as the fibers were smooth and individual strands laid down evenly. No microscopic injuries were present, which would be very unusual if it came from an old textile. Indigo generally was no longer used in Navajo weavings past 1880, so I wonder if it's possible that Begay or someone nearby could have been making some kind of revival piece and was trying to be as accurate as possible using indigo dye?"

"To my knowledge, Trevor, there are no other weavers within five miles of Randal's place and I have never known Randal to make any pieces with natural or vegetal dyes though he did like making his own interpretations of old blanket styles. But he used aniline dyes. I guess it's possible he was experimenting with indigo trying to be authentic. Dr. Riddly said Randal didn't want him in his hogan recently. It seemed like he was hiding something. Maybe he didn't want him to see some new style he was working on," Bloom speculated.

"I guess that's possible, Mr. Bloom. I do see a lot of textiles from Navajo weavers. If something unusual comes through my hands I'll let you know. Good luck finding Mr. Begay's murderer. I hope he doesn't go after more weavers. And remember, be careful dealing with Darryl Ridgemount. He is bad news."

CHAPTER 44

LEAVING TOWN

Gusher was thrilled that Darryl had finally tracked down a great first-phase blanket and it would be his shortly. He was happy it was only going to cost him $500K for the blanket and a $100K finder's fee to Darryl. If it was as good as Darryl said it was, then it would be money well spent. A bargain, though the collector insisted on a cash deal. The collection would be pretty much complete with the addition of a first phase.

Darryl hadn't told Gusher about the Daisy as it wasn't in the bag yet and he figured he would spring it on Gusher at the last moment.

Darryl's plan was simple. Get the two weavings. Have Gusher wire money to Darryl's recently opened Anguilla account. And blow town for good. If Gusher ever did figure out the blanket was bogus or the Daisy turned out to be stolen, Darryl would be long gone and with the money he would have, he'd be set, especially living in Costa Rica where the houses were cheap and the hookers cheaper.

Darryl needed quick transportation for the deal, so he requested, "Gusher, I hate to ask because I know how expensive it is to fly your plane, but you think I could borrow it to go get the blanket? It makes things a lot easier and I've got to pay this guy in cash. I don't feel comfortable carrying that money on me. I'd have to ship a damn box of cash ahead. I was also hoping you could advance me my $100K fee and I'll cover the rest with my own money till you reimburse me when you're satisfied with the blanket."

"Sure, it makes sense. Hell I don't want you to have my blanket on some commercial airplane's overhead compartment. You never know what could happen. My boy Harold will be ready when you are. Just let me know when and where. Darryl, I'm a little worried about you putting out all that cash and me not seeing the piece yet. What if I don't like it for some reason? You got all your money tied up in something I don't want. I'm sure I'll like it, but what if I don't? Getting that much cash again in your lifetime might be hard," Gusher reasoned.

"How about this, Gusher? If you don't buy it, I get to keep the $100K finder's fee and I'll worry about the blanket. It will be my problem, not yours."

"OK, I can live with that. If you had to keep it for some reason, at least your cost would be much less than what one of these damn things is worth. And I can't imagine I won't like it."

"Then it's a deal. I'd like the $100K in cash and to leave tomorrow, as early as possible."

"OK, Darryl. I can make it happen. Come by the office around 3 pm, and I'll have your money. Where do you need the plane to go?"

"Farmington, New Mexico. I checked, the airport can handle your plane."

"Not a problem. Glad to hear it's coming out of Navajoland, better history. What is the blanket's history, Darryl?" Gusher had suddenly remembered Trevor's warning about getting a rock-solid provenance with a piece of this importance.

"It's coming directly from the original family, an old rancher," Darryl assured. "I may need the plane for a couple of days. I have a feeling this guy will want to jaw a bit before he lets go of the family heirloom. This one's been in his family's collection as best we can tell for over 120 years, so I don't want to rush anything I don't have to."

"Makes sense," Gusher agreed. "Take your time. Get the damn thing, and I will need a receipt for the piece, cash or not. Make sure you have all the provenance. Gotta be rock solid."

"Don't worry, I've got it all: old photos showing the weaving in the family's possession at the turn of the century, and a sworn notarized affidavit swearing to the history. It doesn't get any better than this."

"Great, I can hardly wait. As soon as I see it and give you my approval, your money will be transferred to your account. Wish us both luck."

"No luck needed. Just took a go-getter to ferret it out. Needed a true Texan instead of your pretty boy Trevor."

"'Fraid you're right. I liked Trevor. He meant well, just didn't have what it took. Too bad. He could have had his name associated with this outstanding feat. But now it's you Darryl. Good job, boy."

"Thanks! Yes sir, I'm happy to be able to put my name to some of my best work."

CHAPTER 45

1 + 1 = 2

Trevor couldn't sleep the night after he told Bloom about the results of the indigo test. Indigo once was an important export for the New World colonists, but after the invention of coal tar-based dyes by the Englishman Perkins in 1856 the use for natural dyes became passé. Trevor's readings were unequivocal: it was indigo, the same dye for all three, and it required effort to obtain. Available, but not readily.

The murder of a famous weaver who Ridgemount had had direct contact with caused Trevor great distress. Something didn't add up and he knew it. Trevor could figure out puzzles with the best of them and had even won a quiz contest on Sunday's NPR puzzle breakers. The answer was here, he knew it. It was a puzzle he needed to crack, and fast.

Trevor settled in his favorite chair as he would on Sunday mornings and attacked the present problem. He wrote down all the information he knew from Bloom and Carson regarding Randal's death, setting up a chart with known facts and his impressions.

Fact: Randal's last rug was seen in August eight months ago, about the same amount of time required to make a great weaving.

Impression: Weavers make rugs. How was Randal supporting himself, with no next rug? Maybe there was a rug and he had just finished the piece, a possible reason for Randal's death?

Fact: Indigo was found on three objects. The Churro yarn, Randal's weaving tool, and Randal's fingers.

Impression: Randal was working on a rug and used indigo, his fingers stained from stirring the stick. He probably didn't know indigo could leave stains, having never worked with the dye.

Fact: Ridgemount knew Randal, having met him eight months ago.

Impression: Ridgemount was building Mr. Hughes's collection. Maybe he wanted some special rug from Randal.

Fact: Gusher's collection only had a few holes and he would be trying to fill these holes.

Impression: Had Darryl helped Gusher fill his most important hole, a first phase?

Trevor's heart was racing as he followed the line of reasoning. He knew he was close. He talked it out with himself. "Ridgemount couldn't find a first-phase blanket, so he *made* a first-phase blanket by a great Navajo weaver to fill Gusher's hole in his collection! Does Gusher know it's not old? Maybe he doesn't care. Randal's dead, so something went wrong in the deal. Ridgemount must have had a hand in Randal's death. He's out of control. Who might be next?"

Trevor decided he had to talk with Melinda Hughes regarding the blanket collection. He had promised Mr. Hughes he wouldn't tell her that her ex-husband was the one who had bought her collection, but he saw no choice now. Ms. Hughes probably wouldn't be involved in this deal with Randal, but she might have some insight into what was going on. If he called Gusher, he would probably do as he had last time and immediately inform Ridgemount, and that was real trouble. Trevor knew it was a risk talking to either Hughes, but felt Melinda would listen. Also, Trevor wasn't as afraid of her actions. Although he realized it could have unexpected consequences he couldn't predict, it was a gamble he was willing to take.

CHAPTER 46

AN UNEXPECTED CALL

It was a particularly glorious April morning. Melinda lived in a huge house on top of a mountain overlooking the Barton Creek Golf Club just west of Austin. Her overbuilt home was perched where the distant capitol building was visible on the Austin horizon. Melinda was lying near the pool, having an early morning Bloody Mary and reading the *Austin American-Statesman*. Melinda had always been a social drinker and could hold her alcohol with the best of them. With her divorce and no more Darryl her life was off track. Her daily combination of Bloody Mary followed by vodka martinis followed by margaritas seemed to be the only thing that helped pass the time. The unexpected call broke the morning peace.

"Hi Ms. Hughes, this is Trevor Middleman. May I have a moment of your time?"

Melinda's pulse picked up. She had not talked to her ex-curator since before he left on his vacation over a year ago and his memory had quietly faded away along with a few of her alcohol-affected brain cells.

"Trevor, this really isn't a good time, maybe later we…"

Trevor did something he had never done before. He interrupted Hughes in mid-sentence and called her by her first name, which stunned the tipsy Hughes. "Listen, Melinda, we have something in common. I don't know what cock-and-bull story Ridgemount told you to get me fired, but I can tell you he has hurt both of us. It's important for your own safety to listen."

"I'm listening."

Trevor left nothing out. He told of his talk with her ex-husband, of Gusher surreptitiously buying back the rug collection, and how Trevor had promised he wouldn't say a word but he was telling her now because of the frightening developments in Arizona with Randal Begay. He laid out his reasoning for believing that a pseudo-first-phase blanket had been made and that her ex-husband might be at danger or involved some way, but how he was afraid to talk with

Gusher because of his relationship with Ridgemount. For her part, Melinda shared the finding of marijuana and pornography and the wool moths. She hadn't really heard from her ex, which she was happy about, other than he was still with Tiffany. Ridgemount and she had gone their separate ways as he was taking care of his mother, or so he had said. She apologized profusely to Trevor for her poor judgment in men and then downed a stout shot of vodka to help ease her growing awareness.

Trevor promised he would keep Ms. Hughes informed of any developments as everything was still only tentative, but he knew when it came to figuring out puzzles he was rarely wrong. Melinda promised she would keep the information confidential and not call either Gusher or Ridgemount.

Melinda Hughes would have kept her word, but she was too far gone for the day in her alcoholic binge. She couldn't resist calling Ridgemount to confront him, still not wanting to believe Trevor's warning.

"Hi, this is Darryl." When Darryl realized who was on the other end, he knew it was trouble.

"Darryl, you are a bastard. I just got off the phone with Trevor. He told me everything. I can't believe you sold my blanket collection to Gusher and you set up poor Trevor. I loved you." Melinda started to cry as she slurred the word *loved.*

"Hold on now, Melinda, you got everything wrong. You know I love you too and would never do what you're saying. Poor old Trevor must be in trouble again and trying to get his old job back. He probably heard about me helping out my mother and figured it was his opportunity to get back into your life," Darryl protested.

"Did Gusher buy my collection? What about that?"

"I know I sold it to a Japanese company. You saw the bank account information. All of it came from Japan and I believe it was transferred from yen to dollars. It's possible that Gusher got wind of the transaction and bought it from them, I couldn't tell you. I can call Gusher if you want?" Darryl offered.

"I don't know what I want, I'm confused. You make sense but Trevor seemed so convincing. He told me he thought you were involved with killing an Indian weaver and making some first stage…" Melinda was still drinking and found clear thinking difficult.

Ridgemount knew he had a serious situation that had to be dealt with quickly. He was scheduled to leave in a few hours for Farmington. He now had Melinda and Trevor to deal with. It was obvious Melinda would be the easiest.

"Melinda, my love, how about I come over and help you figure this out? Sounds to me like you're having some difficulties right now. Trevor, remember, is not the person you think he is. You and I both know in our hearts he is not a good Christian. He likes men, for God sakes!" Ridgemount was smiling on the other end, knowing the Christian card always worked on God-fearing Texas women.

"OK, come over. I'll leave the back door open," Melinda agreed.

"Great, I'll see you shortly. You need anything? It's Saturday. Yay. Your maid's off, right?"

"No, I'm fine. I'm alone. You might pick up some Grey Goose on your way. I'm running low."

"No problem." Ridgemount was more than happy to bring in a half-used bottle of Grey Goose he had sitting in his house. He wiped off his fingerprints and headed directly over to his first victim for the day.

CHAPTER 47

SWIMMING, ANYONE?

Darryl's car was packed, ready to meet Harold in just a few hours to fly to Farmington. He carefully parked where no one could see the car as he entered Melinda's open gate. He loved how Melinda was so trusting. Most of the homes in this part of Austin had cameras at the entrance and electric gates. Melinda's gate was set up with a code, but she always chose to keep it open. Today Darryl was happy to be free of any additional traces of his presence. The cops would be looking for answers shortly.

Slipping in carefully, carrying the Grey Goose bottle in his gloved hand, he found Melinda stretched out on an expensive iridescent blue lounger next to the black-bottomed pool, her weight likely having hit 200 pounds, her best dancing days well behind her.

"Hi, Honey. Can I pour you a glass of vodka? Got your Goose you asked for."

"Please. No ice and make it stiff." Melinda's words formed long slurred passages.

Darryl careful placed the bottle on the bar near the pool, left the top off, poured a drink and removed his gloves. The drink he picked up with a napkin and gave to Melinda. He sat next to her and placed his hand on her arm.

"Melinda, tell me everything again. Let's see if we can make sense of why Trevor has this sick grudge against me and wants to try and take advantage of you again."

Melinda again explained the entire conversation she had had with Trevor.

"How long ago did Trevor call you?"

"Maybe three hours, hard for me to say exactly."

"Do you think that Trevor has spread this gossip to anyone else? Maybe he's talking to Gusher, or even is so psychopathic that he has gone to the police?" Darryl asked.

"No, nobody knows about it. He said something about getting some samples of blue stuff from the coroner in some little town in Arizona. Krenta, I think? This is why he thinks some first stage is being made. He thinks you did it."

Darryl had all the information he needed. No one else was involved except the coroner in Kayenta. Darryl would be there by the end of the day. He could wrap everything up in one clean sweep. Trevor would be next, but first it was time for a nice morning dip.

Darryl smoothly slipped back off the lounger and onto his haunches. He got a good, firm grip under the sides of Melinda's iron couch. Like a weight lifter doing the clean and jerk, he picked it up, stomach clenched, and heaved it forward, flipping both the lounger and Melinda over. The 200-pound Melinda Hughes bounced off, cracking her head as she hit the edge of the pool, then gently slid into her watery grave like an elephant seal going back to sea. "Trevor was right," Darryl couldn't resist muttering. Discussion over.

Darryl looked around. No clues that he had ever been there. "Now that was neat. I can't believe how she whacked her head. How great is that. It's the perfect murder. I hope she's got a good grip on that glass. This was just too good." Darryl was beaming ear to ear. It had been easy. The Austin coroner's report would read, "Accidental drowning secondary to alcohol and head trauma. Case closed."

CHAPTER 48

CURATORS NEED TO STICK TO CURATING

Since it was Saturday, hopefully Trevor Middleman was still at home and hadn't made any other calls. Trevor lived in a quiet neighborhood. Killing him in broad daylight was going to be tricky. Darryl had brought his .45 magnum, but planned on using his old Blackjack baton to take care of things. Quieter. First, he would need to interrogate Mr. Busybody.

It had been nearly one hour since Melinda's demise and it would more than likely be Monday before her body was discovered by the maid or pool boy. Still, time was ticking. This had to be wrapped up quickly. Darryl first stopped by Gusher's office to pick up his money. It was an odd feeling. He had just killed off Gusher's wife, which is some ways Gusher might enjoy. Once he was safely in Costa Rica, Darryl thought, "Maybe I'll write a confession saying Gusher set up the whole thing—he paid me to kill her. How fun would that be. I'll take down the rich fat cat."

The cash was waiting at Gusher's office as promised. Darryl was amazed by the super-rich. How they could throw away $100K without a blink of the eye. The more Darryl thought about how hard he worked and even killed for money, the more he thought it would be only right if Gusher went down for murder.

Of the $100K he picked up from Gusher, $90K of the money would go to Buck Wilson. Darryl would keep his end of the bargain; some honor between thieves. Besides, he was getting a free Daisy and pseudo-first-phase blanket. He would then get $600K more for both from Gusher. With the original cash he had gotten from Gusher, he would be worth well over a million. That would go a long way in Costa Rica.

Darryl still had to deal with Trevor and the Kayenta coroner. At least he knew no way was Buck going to turn him in. Buck would go to jail as an accessory to murder if he did, and it was obvious he needed the cash. If Darryl tried to kill off Buck, his only source of critical provenance for his first phase and Daisy blankets, it could raise serious suspicions. Darryl rationalized it was one down and two problem individuals to go, then the money was his.

Darryl parked his car a half block away in a location he had noticed the last time he had visited Trevor. He knew the layout of the house so all he needed was the element of surprise. He had his tools for a robbery and they would suffice to work over Trevor as well.

He slipped in the back yard. He could see Trevor cleaning up in the kitchen. No one else was around except a black cat sitting near the window. Darryl easily picked the lock of the front door. Pulling out his gun, he headed into the kitchen for a little interview.

"Hi, Trevor. Bet you weren't expecting me! Don't try anything foolish, or you will be cat meat."

Trevor could see in the cold blobs of Darryl's pupils that he was to be taken at his word. Trevor's puzzle-solving skills had apparently been correct. He had to think fast. Darryl must have talked to Melinda.

"Mr. Ridgemount, what are you doing? Please put down the gun," Trevor calmly suggested.

"Don't *Mr. Ridgemount* me, you fucking ass! You have been snooping around and have some explaining to do! Tell me everything you know, and make it quick!" Darryl demanded.

"What do you mean? I don't understand?" Trevor was panicking. He didn't want to lie if Darryl already knew everything.

"Listen dickhead, here's the deal: Melinda is fish food and you will be following in her footsteps if you don't start squealing like a little pig! Understand?"

At this point Trevor knew Darryl knew everything Trevor had told Melinda. Trevor hadn't mentioned Bloom and wouldn't add his name, as he now figured anyone he mentioned was a target for murder. All he could do was hope for the best and pray. He repeated what he had told Melinda, including the coroner information, and gave Darryl the name, which he would find out soon enough.

"That's what I like about you, Trevor. You always were straightforward and a very smart man, probably smarter than I gave you credit for. Turn around and face the window," Darryl instructed.

Trevor figured it was the end. He prayed and closed his eyes. His world went dark.

Darryl swung the Blackjack down onto Trevor's head from behind, knocking him out in one fell swoop, then he tied Trevor up and gagged him securely with his favorite, duct tape. He couldn't leave him in the house—too risky. Someone might find him. Darryl needed to talk to the nosey coroner, Dr. Carson Riddly, and find out how much information Trevor had actually divulged. Did anyone else know what Trevor suspected? Best to keep Trevor alive for now.

Darryl retrieved his hidden car and pulled it into Trevor's garage. He rolled Trevor's trim body up snuggly in numerous sheets, wrapping him tight as a mummy, then lashed the mass with more duct tape. His package was ready for delivery back to his own home.

※ ※ ※ ※

Darryl dragged Trevor's semi-conscious, hog-tied body into his own house and dumped him onto his bed. Darryl planned to torture his captive a bit, as it was Trevor's own fault that Darryl had been forced to kidnap him and soon would kill him. Darryl decided round one was to wrap Trevor up in even more sheets and blankets so he couldn't move, and turn on his favorite hunting and fishing channel to torment the art-loving gentle man. Around the bed he strategically placed an array of metal weights so even if Trevor got enough momentum to roll off the comfy bed he would likely get injured in the fall. He did open a breathing area in the sheets. He didn't want his victim to accidentally smother. As Darryl opened the breathing hole he saw that Trevor was quite conscious now. Darryl decided to start the intimidation process early.

"Well Mr. Trevor Meddler, seems you had to stick your nose where it wasn't needed. I'm heading off to get my chief's blanket and when I get back, you and I are going to have a long talk. If you don't answer all my questions truthfully, I'm going to bury you alive like one of my money paint cans, but there won't be any map to find you. Horrible to die a slow death underground, so I recommend you use this time to enjoy some interesting fishing shows and reflect on what you got to tell me when I get back. Also if you try to move off this comfortable bed, I assure you the results won't be pretty. You don't want to test me."

CHAPTER 49

HUNGRY FOR MCDEES

Timing was going to become critical if Darryl was to succeed. It was Saturday. He probably had three days tops before cops would start to get involved. He had a cadaver floating and a soon-to-be corpse stashed in his house. Trevor seemed like a loner, so hopefully as with Hughes, no one would notice he was missing till Monday. Darryl also still had to deal with the nosey coroner, then dispose of his body after a quick and brutal interrogation. If all went well, Darryl would have the two blankets and be back in Austin by Sunday night. He'd wrap things up with Gusher and hire his own plane for a quick escape.

Flying private was easy to get used to. Austin International Airport was not bad to navigate as most airports go, but private was cake. Simply drive in, leave the car, and go. Minimal questions asked. The trip was looking promising for Darryl.

The flight into Farmington Four Corners Regional Airport was much less bumpy than it had been into Santa Fe last summer. April's thermals are still minimal in New Mexico and Arizona. No thunderheads yet.

Farmington Airport was not much. While there was some big oil money in Farmington, it was doubtful a plane as nice as Bill Hughes's had ever graced its runways. Flying private and with so much cash made Darryl feel as if he were powerful and unstoppable. He was born to be rich and his killing spree added to his bravado. His only concern was about which kind of jet to take down to Anguilla after he got back to Austin. He decided to get a smaller one and save money. He still had to pay for a nice yacht to get him to Costa Rica for his new life as a patrón.

Darryl told the pilot Harold to hold tight for the day, get a hotel in Farmington, and he would let him know when to expect their departure. He figured no later than tomorrow, but maybe as early as tonight if everything went smoothly.

It was going to be his second time in Kayenta in less than a month. Darryl worried about renting a vehicle through the same car company he had used in Albuquerque for his first visit, so in Farmington he rented with Avis, using Gusher's credit card as he had done before. Every detail at this point needed to be thought out, as cops would soon be buzzing. The drive over to Kayenta was no less boring than before. Its long vistas of red striated mesas interspersed with scraggly trees were unsettling for the boy from Texas. Darryl had grown used to Austin's lush plants and rolling hills of oak trees. The flat, open horizons reminded him too much of his own poor beginnings in West Texas. Thinking of his abandoned childhood on the high plains made Darryl instinctively caress his gun, which was hiding in its special little pocket in his leather jacket.

Private jets make it easy to bring a loaded .45 magnum to any destination without worries. The gun was insurance in case old Buck decided to change the deal. If he played it straight, Buck would be wealthy. If not, Buck could follow his Navajo neighbor's lead into the netherworld. The gun shouldn't be needed on the coroner. If he were like most doctors, he would be all brain and no brawn, someone easily manhandled and broken.

The contact point was McDonald's, which was packed. Darryl felt uncomfortable hanging out in public. After all, Kayenta was a small town and he stuck out, especially being white and tall by local standards. He called Buck.

"OK, Buck, I'm here and I've got all your money in cash. Let's figure out a meeting place and get this show on the road. It doesn't do either of us any good me hanging out too long."

"I agree," Buck replied. "I'm still working on getting your Daisy and should have it all arranged by 7 pm tonight. Why don't you find some place to lay low and then I'll have us meet at my house. Don't show up early or you may screw up my Daisy deal and I'm sure you still want that rug?"

"You know I do. No Daisy, no premium paid to you," Darryl taunted.

"That's right. My deal, my problem. So give me the time to make sure it goes down. My house is two houses away from your late friend's. Don't take the first right at the fork, or you will end up at Hastiin Johnson's. He's Randal's grandfather and he would not be pleased to see a *bilagaana* at his front door. He's a powerful medicine man. He might recognize you as the killer."

"You mean, he would have some sixth sense or vision to know I bumped off his grandkid?" Darryl chortled at the absurdity.

"Darryl, let's just say he has a way of knowing and he would spot your coyote spirit quickly. He may be old, but he's not a man you want to mess with."

"Whatever, I'll take the second turn. I've done my research. I know where you house is. Even out in nowhere land, Google Earth's got your number. I'll be there at 7 pm sharp. Make sure you have both my blankets, plus the first phase's history. No funny stuff or you'll need a different hat size."

"I understand completely. You're not the kind of guy I want to upset. I've seen your work at close range. You'll get what you came for," Buck promised.

Darryl had three hours to kill, and he wasn't the sightseeing kind of guy. He did need to track down the coroner but wanted to wait until he had the blankets safely in hand. If Darryl brought up the complication of someone snooping around, Buck might back out and Darryl wanted him completely committed. For now Darryl would rent a room at the best hotel in town, clean his gun, watch the tube if they had porno, and take a nap. He wanted to be well rested for tonight. He was serious about his profession. No screw-ups because he was unprepared or tired.

Darryl knew he would be on the old man's territory and it was risky business, but he felt confident of his own powers of observation and was good with a pistol. Buck was old and had smarts enough to understand he was dealing with a cold-blooded killer. If Buck got cute, Darryl would just take both weavings and leave the old man in a heap no matter what the consequences of killing off his only source of provenance for the weavings might be.

The Hampton Inn was the best hotel in Kayenta. It was new and clean, and had a decent pool. Darryl called Harold and told him he would plan on meeting tomorrow in Farmington, early morning to mid-day. Darryl picked up a local Navajo paper with a headline that continued the saga of the local murder: "No Leads in Weaver's Death." The story went on to tell about Randal and how all the leads pointed to a gambling habit and possibly a skin walker had been seen by a resident near Begay's hogan. Two sheep had been killed and no tracks had been found, so many in the community felt a very bad coyote spirit was among them. Reading the paper Darryl started laughing, a hard gut laugh. "Boys, you don't know how right you are. I plan on skinning your coroner later tonight!

CHAPTER 50

DINNER AT SEVEN

Doc Riddly was plowing through his Saturday clinic schedule. It looked like he would be done by 5 pm. He normally didn't look at the clock as time flew with the daily grind of being the only doctor, but today was different. He was expecting Carson and Rachael for drinks at his so-called hogan, his first invited guests. The unexpected call came at 4:15 pm.

"Hi Doc, this is Buck Wilson."

"Mr. Wilson, what can I do you in for," Carson replied in attempted rancher humor, which he was not good at. Buck ignored the feeble attempt.

"I have a huge favor to ask. I hope you can help me. A niece of Daisy's is visiting me and I told her about your great rug. She remembered the rug vividly and said she had a picture of herself when she was a little girl standing next to Daisy, with the rug. She would love to be able to see it again and she's not in good enough shape to come over tonight. She's leaving in the morning. If you had a photograph of her with the rug as a girl and as an old lady, it would make your weaving more valuable. People love that added provenance of where things came from and the original owners. My guess, it would add an additional 20% value to the rug. She's old, so this will probably be your only chance to get a photo. So what do you say, Doc? Can you drop by with the rug for just a couple of minutes? It will be well worth your time and make an old lady very happy."

Carson had made that drive several times and it was 30 minutes of bumpy dirt roads that sucked the life and value out of his precious Mustang. But 20% on a $100K rug was a lot of money. He figured he better take the time and maybe get some bonus points with the old lady. Maybe she was related to Brenda. If he left right at 5 pm, he could be back by 6:30 and still have time to get the steaks on. He couldn't get the margaritas blended anyhow until his guests arrived, assuming Rachael allowed Bloom to bring the tequila.

"Sure, I can be there Buck. But I have plans tonight so I need to be gone by 6 pm. She will need to make a quick pilgrimage."

"Understood, don't make a huge production. Keep it on white man time. No problem. She will be so happy to see the Daisy."

Charles spent his first day of spring break wandering around Kayenta visiting Rachael's friends. She wanted to see one of her grandfather's oldest friends, Hastiin Johnson, but thought the added pressure of Randal's death and her visiting might be too much. She had visited the powerful medicine man many times as a kid. Her own grandfather, Hastiin Sherman, known for his visions, consulted with Johnson on certain medical cases. Rachael had even met Randal Begay once when she was 10, but he would never have remembered. Boys aren't interested in girls at that age. Rachael on the other hand remembered well. The thought of Begay's murder still gave Rachael chills. She had her grandfather's sensibilities.

The happy couple got back to the hotel. They were getting ready for tonight's dinner at Carson's. Bloom was looking forward to seeing Carson's place and determining if it was as remote as his own digs. He liked the intellectual stimulation of the other *bilagaana* (as he had started calling Carson), and the Begay case was still weighing heavily on his mind.

What Bloom saw when he went down to the front lobby to get Rachael some shampoo stopped him dead in his tracks and gave him a shiver. It was like seeing a ghost. Darryl Ridgemount was in the lobby buying a pack of cigarettes. Bloom recognized him from behind, wearing an orange University of Texas hat and talking with the hotel clerk. Bloom slipped behind a potted plant before Ridgemount could spot him. He watched Darryl get the cigarettes and head for the elevator. Bloom waited to see what floor the elevator stopped on. It was the third floor. Bloom was paralyzed. He felt like he was back in New York, dealing with the crooked art-gallery dealer. "What could he be up to in Kayenta?" he said to himself, then looked around to make sure no one heard his out-loud question. "This has to be about Begay, what else it could be?" Bloom realized something was out of balance. This was no coincidence. Bolting to his own second-floor room, Bloom forgot to get shampoo and barged in on Rachael taking a shower.

"Rachael, that dick guy Ridgemount is in the hotel! I think he's staying here! What could he be doing here?"

"Maybe he's adding to his collection. There are quite a few good weavers around Kayenta. Maybe he wanted to buy directly from the weaver, not pay some overpriced dealer like you to sell it to him. I can understand that," Rachael giggled at her artist/dealer humor. It was always a battle about who deserves what.

"You don't *understand*, Rachael," Bloom emphasized. "I talked to a textile expert last week in Austin who knew Ridgemount. He said Darryl was a compete dick, cost him his job, and was very unethical. He told me that he thought Ridgemount was capable of very bad things and to be exceptionally wary. Now Darryl's in Kayenta! I had bad vibes when I dealt with him in Santa Fe. Remember, he wanted to deal only in cash and tried to get me to come down more? He's a bad guy. I can feel it, something's wrong. Maybe he got wind of Carson's great Daisy and he's here to get it? Remember, Randal was viciously murdered and he had no weaving on the loom."

"Call the yarn guy in Austin again. Tell him what's up and see what he says." Rachael's good mood was now gone and fear was starting to creep in.

"Great idea." Bloom tried the two numbers he had for Trevor. Nothing. He left messages at both.

Bloom knew that Ridgemount's visit meant trouble. He had to warn Carson immediately. He called the clinic but it was after five. Carson was gone. He tried Carson's cell, but no answer.

"Rachael, nobody's answering. We have to go. I'm afraid Ridgemount may be trying to steal Doc Riddly's Daisy rug or maybe worse."

"Are you sure? That's a very bold accusation to make. I know he was a jerk, but maybe he just offered him a lot of money and he's making a sale. You know people do sell these things sometimes." This was a reference to his wanting to keep her first rug and Rachael saying she was an artist, not a collector; you made things to sell and share.

"Let's go now," Bloom urged. "We need to get to Carson's and warn him. We'll show up a little early, that's all. If we find out he's selling it then fine, but I don't want Carson to get ripped off because we were afraid of arriving early."

Rachael's long, black un-shampooed hair was slightly matted, having just been towel-dried. Her perky breasts were looking Bloom directly in the eyes. His mind was trying to focus on helping Carson, but the primitive parts of his brain only saw Rachael's very large breasts, which seemed more inviting than ever. Bloom's bigger head prevailed as he focused on the man from Texas.

There was no sign of Ridgemount as they headed back through the lobby, then out to Rachael's Ford. So far, so good. Rachael knew the road to the North Clinic, so she took the wheel. Driving on dirt washboard roads is an art form, one a Navajo learns like walking. You have to drive at just the right speed and watch the rhythm of the road's surface, gliding to and fro as the bumps naturally form. When Rachael drove it seemed effortless. Bloom on the other hand would have sore wrists after half an hour. It was after 6 pm and the last rays of light were disappearing behind the red mountains. No other cars were sighted as they drove north. Pulling up to the North Clinic parking lot, Carson's Mustang was nowhere to be seen. However, a large blue note was taped to the door jam on the building next door, which had to be his current residence. It read:

"Hi Rachael and Charles, I had to make a quick stop at Buck Wilson's. If you get here before I do, make yourself at home. Also, excuse the pin-up poster as I was going to take it down but you got here first. C.R."

Rachael and Bloom walked in the unlocked door and looked around. No Carson. "Don't you think he would be here by now?" Bloom quizzically asked Rachael, hoping for some magical answer.

"I guess. We are still like 15 minutes early. I know Buck Wilson. He lives right next to Hastiin Johnson and very close to Randal's hogan. His house is an old out-of-place-looking colonial home on the hill. Remember I told you to look for it when you visited Randal last year? It's a great marker to know you're in the right place."

"Yeah, I remember laughing about it having the only grass yard in a hundred miles."

"That's the one."

"I'm going to go over and look in the clinic window," Bloom decided. "I know that Carson kept his Daisy in the waiting room so all the old grandmothers could come and see it. Probably the best art of any doctor's waiting room in America, for sure on the reservation." Bloom used his flashlight app on his iPhone and peered into the clinic windows like a burglar. He felt strange about his actions and hoped no one was watching.

"I don't see anything. If it was in there, it's not now. He has it with him or he's moved it or Ridgemount stole it! Rachael, we have to go to Buck's. My inner voice is talking to me and it's always right. Carson is the kind of person who would be home getting ready for his expected guests. He even documented the time on the paper, see there it says 5 pm."

"I see it. You're right."

"He could have easily gotten back here by now. Ridgemount is dirty and he's in town and the Daisy is not where it should be."

"Your inner voice saved you once and it knows the right path," recognized Rachael as she swiftly gathered up her purse and jacket. Rachael had gone from twentieth-century educated woman back to a religious Navajo who understood many things in life cannot be logically explained. One trusted one's instincts. A bigger force was often guiding those who were willing to listen.

The couple jumped into the Ford, and Rachael took the wheel again, spinning out of the parking lot, leaving a cloud of dark red dust as they headed for Buck's. Little did they know Ridgemount was already on the loose in Navajoland.

CHAPTER 51

AWFUL HOT IN HERE

Ridgemount arrived 10 minutes early at Buck Wilson's. His heart was picking up its pace in anticipation of the unknown. The .45 was safely tucked under his leather jacket in his special gun holster pouch. He wiped the sweat off his palms just in case he needed the gun. Touching it through the jacket reassured him. The house lights were on and Buck was at the door sitting on his front porch swing.

"Hello, Darryl. Little early, but that's fine. I was able to get the Daisy as I hoped. Can I get you something to drink before business?"

"What's with the blue Mustang? Looks out of place here." Ridgemount's level of caution was high. The car was unusual on the rez.

"Well I splurged," Buck demurred. "Had that $10K you advanced me and I figured with the extra cash coming my way I could afford a gift for myself. I always wanted one."

Darryl looked suspiciously at his host's eyes, searching for any sign of deception. He saw nothing.

"So what can I get you? Beer, water, coke?"

"Nothing. I'd just as soon do our business and hit the road. I've got a lot on my plate and I'm not a big fan of returning to crime scenes, if you know what I mean."

"I understand completely. Let's go into my parlor and you can get your weavings. I'm assuming that can of paint in your hand contains the rest of my cash?"

"That's right. It's your own piggy bank. All yours if you have kept your end of the bargain."

"Oh, I have." Buck showed Darryl the way to his large room that was his family's generational parlor. It had a large antique pool table in the center of the room that was covered with a gray protective cloth.

"Care for a game of pool first? You look like a man who knows his way around a stick."

"You're right there, Buck. I can play a mean game of pool and under other circumstances I would be happy to take your money but not now. I will take some water after all. You got your house here awful hot, like a sauna."

"Sorry about that. You'll see when you get old, you never seem to be able to stay warm enough. I'll turn down the heat and get you a glass of cold water." Buck left the room. Darryl started to relax.

Darryl scanned the room for any other people or anything odd. He spotted the two weavings across the room. Both were carefully folded and placed in an old antique lawyer's bookshelf with a glass front. The glass had small bubbles of imperfection and a grayish tint that exposed its true age of antiquity. Darryl could see the two weavings through the glass and they looked magnificent. He decided he would help himself before the old man came back.

CHAPTER 52

BE CAREFUL, WAIT FOR ME

Rachael and Bloom decided they might need help if Carson was in trouble. Rachael would drop herself off first at Hastiin Johnson's hogan. He knew the intricacies of the land and could guide them if necessary. Rachael and the medicine man would meet Bloom at Wilson's house. Hopefully it would be a big misunderstanding and nothing would be wrong. Bloom gave Rachael a kiss and passionately told her, "I love you! Please hurry. Something is wrong. I feel we could be in danger. My *hozho* is out of whack." Both he and Rachael were surprised by his use of the Navajo word for balance. Bloom was beginning to understand the Diné sensibilities even if he still used the word whack.

"I love you, too! Be careful! If something seems wrong, don't go in. Wait for me and Hastiin Johnson. We can go back down the road and find some cell coverage and get the police, let them handle it." Rachael's concern was real. She was not only worried about him but also their unborn child… which she was planning to tell Bloom about at the right moment on their trip.

"I hope the medicine man is as powerful as your grandfather was," Bloom said as Rachael exited the truck. Hastiin Sherman, Rachael's grandfather, had been a great medicine man and he had saved Bloom's life once.

Bloom drove off in Rachael's pickup. As he got close to Buck's house, he turned the lights off. Then he shut off the engine. He walked up the dirt road the rest of the way in the dark. Growing up in the West, he instinctually scanned the ground looking for rattlesnakes, keeping his pace, not too fast. In the West you don't take risks walking fast at night in rattlesnake country.

As he approached the house, he saw three cars. Carson's Mustang, a pickup that must be Buck's, and a Chevy Malibu that looked like a rental car—a car that defined the word average. His inner alarm began ringing louder and adrenaline coursed through him quickening his breath. Maybe Ridgemount was here to buy Doc's rug and Buck was simply the middleman making the deal happen? Maybe not. Rachael's cautionary advice echoed in Bloom's mind.

Bloom decided to sneak around the side and look through the window before ringing the doorbell. He found a large, open window letting the cool evening air in that he could peer through. He saw an unbelievable drama unfold.

He could see Ridgemount walking over to a case that held two nicely folded rugs, one on top of another. The upper textile appeared to be some sort of early Navajo blanket with blue stripes, and the other was Carson's Daisy. Ridgemount slowly opened the glass case door and reached in to retrieve the top blue-and-white blanket. Then all hell broke loose.

"Aahhh," Darryl screamed as a stout six-foot western diamondback snake lunged at his neck from behind the two weavings. His hand had grabbed both snake and blanket. The snake's deadly venom squarely hit its mark: Darryl's neck just above his heavy leather jacket, which could have saved his life if the snake's aim had been just a tad lower. "God I'm bit, I'm bit," Darryl screamed, knowing a rattlesnake just bit him. Darryl fell backwards grasping his neck and clutching at the pool table as the impressive snake quietly escaped, sliding under the pool table's covering, its black-and-white tail slightly buzzing.

Both Buck Wilson and Bloom witnessed the event unfold. Buck was just out of range watching with anticipation. Bloom, completely shocked, had nearly screamed himself at the spectacle and had to cover his mouth so as not to make his presence known.

Buck strode back into the parlor. "Well, I see you and Lulu have met," he remarking, pointing his 12-gauge shotgun at Ridgemount, who was now going into shock. The snake's hemolytic venom had pierced Darryl's subclavian artery and was being pumped directly into Darryl's heart with each racing beat.

"That's a bad bite, my friend," Buck warned. "You have very little time if I don't get you to a doctor. You need antivenin. Without it, you'll be dead in an hour, maybe a little longer if you quit breathing so hard. It's funny how active a snake can be when it gets warmed up a bit. Normally a snake like this should just be coming out of hibernation, but I've known old Lulu for 10 years so I woke her up a little early as a surprise. I try to leave her alone and that way she leaves me alone. First time I ever needed her help and she performed like a champ. I bet she hasn't eaten in at least four months, so that was a seriously dangerous load of venom you just got hit with."

"What do you want Buck," Darryl gasped. "I need a doctor! The money's in the paint can. Look inside. It's all there and I can get you more. You've got to help me *now*!" Darryl's hands were shaking, his eyes completely dilated. Beads of sweat were running off his face in small rivulets. He collapsed onto the floor even though he knew his killer, Lulu, was no doubt in the vicinity.

"Listen Buck," Darryl pleaded, "you don't know everything. There are others involved—a nosey Austin curator figured out the first phase. He has to be disposed of. He's tied up in my apartment right now. Your local coroner has talked to this guy. He has to go, too. That takes a man like me."

"I want to let you in on a little secret of mine," Buck replied, keeping the gun pointed at Darryl. Buck flipped over the pool table's long cloth, revealing his other company. Doc Riddly was tied up and gagged. Right next to his face was Lulu's long body, lying completely stretched out trying to gain heat from Riddly. Carson's eyes were transfixed on the snake that was opening and closing her jaw as she reset her fangs for her next victim. Carson's face had its own streams of nervous sweat dripping off. The snake was using its forked tongue to catch some of the precious water after its long hibernation, which Buck had so rudely wakened her from.

"That's Doc Riddly tied up there lying next to Lulu. He's the local coroner. I don't need your help for shit. Too bad about the boy you've got back in Austin, but that's not my problem," Buck said, peering downward at the snake's precarious position. "Assuming she doesn't bite Doc, he should have enough antivenin back at the clinic to save your sorry ass if I let you both go."

"What do you want, you crazy old man!!" Darryl was starting to become short of breath as his lungs filled with his own fluids from his now failing heart.

"I want to know who you were going to sell the blankets to and for how much, for starters," Buck said.

"Guy's name is Bill Hughes. He's my client in Austin. Doesn't have a clue about all this shit. I was going to sell it for $400K," gasped Ridgemount, lying about the price even in his death throes.

"And the Daisy?"

"Doesn't know about it yet. I figured $100K if I was lucky. Is that enough information? Get that damn doctor to help me before the snake bites him, too!"

"Almost." Buck kicked a piece of paper and pen over to the now laboring Ridgemount.

"Write out a confession for Randal's death. Make it convincing. No mention of the blanket, only how you were settling an old gambling bet. Do it, or Doc's not going to make a house call," Buck demanded.

Darryl's hand, which was shaking, started to write. He had the .45 magnum, but it was tucked into a hidden pocket in his closed jacket and he couldn't go for it without Buck shooting him first with the shotgun.

At this point, Bloom had seen and heard enough. Carson was obviously traumatized and trying not to move, Trevor was in serious trouble back in Austin, and Bloom had just witnessed a soon-to-be murder by a rattlesnake placed by Buck Wilson. Bloom was about to run for help when a 90-year-old man and young woman came riding up to the house like the cavalry, both of them bareback together on a 10-year-old bluish-looking mare aptly named Lighting.

"Rachael, Rachael," Bloom croaked in his quietest yet terrified voice. "Buck's got Carson tied up in there, and released a snake that bit Darryl, who looks like he's dying! Buck has a gun on them!"

Hastiin Johnson, who at 90 looked 60, slid off the horse, took one look in the window, then calmly walked in the back door seemingly completely aware of the situation. The drama continued to play out now in front of Rachael's and Bloom's eyes as they both stood at the window paralyzed by the operatic play of life and death.

"You, Buck Wilson! I have known you all my life! I knew your parents and their parents. We have lived as neighbors and brothers for all our lives. You have lost your way, my old friend. Stop now and we can save this man. He must pay for whatever he has done to you, but you must stop," Hastiin cautioned.

"No, you don't understand. That man on the floor killed your grandson, and I'm taking both our revenge. Do you really want to help this *bilagaana coyote*?" Buck said *coyote* in Navajo to emphasize his righteousness.

"What about the doctor who saved my life?" reasoned Hastiin. "Why is he tied up with a rattlesnake next to his face?"

"I needed him to help catch this man. He would not have come voluntarily. I had no choice. The man just admitted to killing Randal. See the paper."

The old man looked at Carson's eyes that were blinking furiously to keep the copious amount of sweat from falling into his stinging eyes. He then looked at Darryl, whose confession was next to him. Darryl's mouth was wide open now, drooling, and his eyes dilated as his consciousness faded. Only his blinding white teeth still had the deceptive appearance of health.

Hastiin Johnson simultaneously picked up the rattlesnake and pulled the gag out of Carson's mouth. From outside the window, Bloom watched in horrific amazement, wanting to react but stunned by the complexity of the situation: one man holding a gun, another with a live rattlesnake, two individuals down. All Bloom could do was watch in perverse fascination.

"He's lying," Carson said, gasping. "They have a blue blanket they were trying to sell as an old chief's. Buck asked him about who he was going to sell it to and for how much. There's a can with money in it. Buck stole my Daisy!"

"Buck, it seems you have told me only a half truth. Talk now you must if you ever hope to live a good human life again," the medicine man warned.

Buck Wilson realized he had chosen the wrong path, but how can one backtrack from such a position? There was nowhere to turn. He saw Ridgemount soon to be dead in front of him, and he had killed him. How to handle his old friend and the doctor who had been kind to him?

"I needed money," Buck tried explaining. "I was stuck. The white banks would take my ranch. Your land is safe, it's Indian. But they can take my land. My whole life. Can't you understand! I didn't kill Randal, it was this man. He is the killer!"

"Buck, you must put the gun down and untie the doctor. This will tell me your heart."

Buck Wilson could see his life passing in front of him. He had to choose.

"Sorry, I can't do that. I'm old and I'm not losing my ranch."

The agile medicine man turned on a dime and tossed Lulu directly at Buck Wilson. "We let the snake decide who the bad coyote is," Hastiin Johnson yelled as he launched the six-foot-long snake.

Wilson shot at the snake as it flew toward him, shooting his gun wildly, missing. But Darryl, who had regained consciousness, did not miss. His .45 slug hit Buck squarely in the chest as the rattlesnake flew harmless, untouched, over Buck's right shoulder, hitting the floor with a thud and slithering into a corner of the room.

Finally Bloom knew it was his time to enter the play. He burst in the back door and jumped on Darryl, wrestling the gun away from his ever-weakening grip.

"Where's Trevor? Where?"

"He's at my Blueridge condominium untouched. Help me," Darryl begged.

Darryl slipped back into permanent unconsciousness as Buck Wilson's blood flowed down the floor and covered Darryl's head.

Hastiin Johnson went over to the old man, his friend of 70 years who was gasping with his last few breaths. He held Buck's hand as the rancher passed to another world. Buck pleaded, "I'm sorry, my old *compadre*. I lost my way, forgive me. Keep me close to you in death. Pity me and bury me in a Diné grave overlooking my land. Take the money in the can. Do with it what you like. Please be my friend in death."

"I will take care of your burial. I hope we meet again, only the gods know for sure," the medicine man responded.

Buck Wilson died after hearing Hastiin Johnson's words.

CHAPTER 53

FINAL RESTING

Darryl Ridgemount also died shortly after killing Buck, Lulu's potent winter venom proving too much for any man. Hastiin Johnson started chanting almost immediately after Buck's hand went limp. He gently picked up the old, traumatized snake and in Diné said: "Thank you for your help, mother. You have chosen wisely. Please forgive my friend Buck. He was blinded by the white man's money. Go in harmony and find a nice pack rat while you're warm and hungry." He walked outside the back door and placed the snake next to an active rat's nest. She slithered away as she had a hundred times before, her tail just slightly rattling, its sound disappearing deep inside the dark hole.

Bloom meanwhile untied Carson, who sat up, his breath starting to slow after the ordeal.

"I thought I was toast! I'm allergic to bees, God knows what a snake bite would do!"

"Nothing," Bloom assured, laying his hand Carson's shoulder. Bloom had learned some things in his longer time on the rez.

"What are you talking about? I watched it kill that man who just shot Buck! It was definitely very poisonous."

"Don't you remember in your medical training, Doctor, a rattlesnake needs time to replenish its venom? She was harmless. Could have bitten you a dozen times and it wouldn't have done much damage." Bloom looked over at Hastiin Johnson, who smiled slightly, knowing snake behavior better than anybody in the room.

"Shit, you're right," exclaimed Carson. "I totally knew that, 40 to 50% of all rattlesnake bites are dry bites because they just ate. I just freaked. I'm not used to being knocked unconscious and tied up waiting to be killed!" Carson rubbed his sore skull, where Buck had ambushed him as he came in the parlor.

Hastiin Johnson walked over to the first-phase blanket, which was on the ground where it had fallen from Darryl's greedy grip. He stroked the soft woolen weaving as tears came to his eyes. He knew the blanket was what had killed his grandson. Randal had used Spiderwoman's talents for deceit and he had paid for it with his life. Looking at Rachael, the only other Navajo in the room, Hastiin chanted in Diné.

The *bilagaanas* and Rachael stood frozen. Still clutching the blanket, the medicine man announced, "This is my grandson's weaving. It was his last. I will bury it with him in his grave on the mountain. No one can know about its presence or it will cause more harm. It can only be used for his burial. It must be returned to Mother Earth and become one with my grandson."

Rachael went over and hugged the old man. Hastiin Johnson grabbed the paint can as he walked toward the door, wrapping the chief's blanket over his shoulders just as his great, great, great grandfather would have.

EPILOGUE

Eight months had passed since the ordeal north of Kayenta. The local tribal police quietly closed the murder case of Randal Begay. Darryl Ridgemount was named the sole perpetrator. Randal's last magnificent blanket, never discovered, was now forever hidden in a small crypt alongside his body high above an unnamed canyon floor, his ancestral graveyard. Only Hastiin Johnson knew Randal's final resting place. As promised, the Navajo medicine man buried Buck Wilson in traditional Diné fashion not far from where his own grave would be in the near future.

The local police chose to keep hidden from the general public the duplicitous actions of Buck Wilson. Lieutenant Wildhorse had made the suggestion to Doc Riddly not to press charges for what had happened to him at Buck's house. Many in the community had known the Wilson family for generations and there was a period when that name had been synonymous with goodness. Tarnishing Wilson's reputation in the small community might become a dividing point and make Riddly's job that much harder. Doc Riddly, who had about a year left on his contract, wanted his remaining time to be enjoyable and not a focal point of contention with his patients. They had become important to him.

Lieutenant Wildhorse, whose niece was Brenda Wildhorse, was informed of Doc Riddly's upstanding moral fiber and helpfulness to the Navajo community. Brenda was impressed with Carson's new Navajo sensibilities and decided to let him teach her how to play golf on the Riddly Ranch Range. She in turn taught him what it meant to be Diné, in every sense of the meaning. Doc Riddly was now enjoying his humble clinic and his new Navajo girlfriend. He was even seriously considering signing on for an additional year of service.

Rachael was expecting her and Bloom's first child, a boy, in a few short weeks. Her condition made it impossible for her to travel with Bloom back to Austin, Texas, for the dedication of a new wing at the Blanchard Museum at the University of Texas campus. A foundation had been set up in the name of Randal Begay and Melinda Hughes for Navajo textile preservation and cultural awareness. A yearly scholarship had also been funded for one Navajo student to attend a full-ride scholarship to Baylor University in Waco, in Randal Begay and Melinda Hughes's names.

Bill "Gusher" Hughes had funded both the foundation and scholarship for $10 million dollars. He had also given his entire Navajo textile collection to the museum under the name of Melinda Hughes. Her name alone would grace the elaborate marble entrance, Bill being too ashamed of his role in her death. The textile gift and endowment had been widely publicized. A local U.T. donor who lived near the university and only a block from Gusher had heard of the generous donation. The donor was from an old Texas family that also happened to own a cherished heirloom, a first-phase chief's blanket. The family had never shared the piece with the world but believed the timing was right to help round out the Melinda Hughes Collection, which was missing this blanket type. The press release about the donor was written by the new curator of Navajo textiles, Trevor Middleman.

Trevor was now the curator for life of the Melinda Hughes Collection. He was selected personally by Bill Hughes. Thanks to Bloom's quick questioning about Trevor's whereabouts and Bloom's follow-up, Trevor had been found at the Blueridge condominiums one day after the Kayenta incident, traumatized but largely unharmed. Trevor—who was forever in Bloom's debt—offered him free dye and yarn analysis of any textiles for life, a very valuable consultation service for someone dealing in Navajo weavings.

Trevor's good fortune continued when the house next to his became available, which he was able to purchase as a guest home. The timing was perfect, as he had just come into some serious extra money. Trevor the puzzle master had remembered Darryl's final words and thought about them carefully. Darryl had warned Trevor he would not have a map to find his buried body unlike with his paint cans. Trevor found said map in Darryl's Blueridge apartment floorboards a month after his ordeal. Darryl always left easy clues. It was a nice bonus. Trevor's mother had been right: good things do happen to those who are truly good.

The End

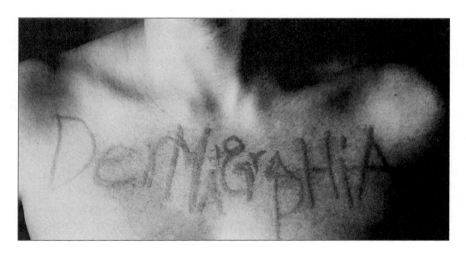

HIDDEN CANYON

BY MARK SUBLETTE

CHAPTER 1

#2 PENCIL PLEASE

Prison forensic psychologists recognize the fastest way to spot a true psychopath: ask the other cons. They all know. These broken individuals are loners, people to fear, with no gang or personal affiliation of any kind. They *think* their emotions, unable to experience feelings.

All languages across the world have a word to describe a psychopath, except for the Navajo. Psychopaths are exceedingly rare. Their ability to blend in and seem normal while being anything but, makes detection difficult and destruction of unsuspecting lives a given. Specialists in this psychiatric field believe these individuals are outliers in man's genetic code: unique humans born mentally deranged.

Fallon Scriber was such an individual. His physical and social environment only helped accentuate an inherent tendency toward destructive behavior.

His mother had exceptional intelligence and if not for her alcohol addiction, could have been a good mother to Fallon, though it probably wouldn't have mattered. Her only child was damaged goods from the start. Fallon's father was a non-issue. He came and went, an odd man with a bad temper whose only interaction was always some puzzle to be unraveled. He was never a stable component in either of their lives and by 1970 had disappeared for good.

Growing up in a rough neighborhood in Oakland, California, didn't help. It undoubtedly fostered Fallon's perverted outlook on life at a young age. Fallon was a short white kid in a sea of athletic color. He might have skated by on his personality, which was chameleon-like, if not for an unrelenting medical condition. His untreatable disease caused him to stick out, resulting in extreme taunting and pain.

Fallon's porcelain-colored flesh was cursed with one of the most severe cases of dermatographia ever recorded. Usually this condition is just a benign problem, more an oddity than an affliction. With dermatographia, the slightest touch of the skin causes red welts to emerge. These eruptions generally remain for only a couple of minutes and are associated with some transient mild pain in the affected area, but not for Fallon Scriber. His skin was so reactive the slightest scratch would cause deep welts lasting thirty minutes or even longer. The deeper the scratch, the more painful and long lasting the welt. He was a human Etch A Sketch, and everyone on Oakland's poor side of town in the rebellious sixties and seventies wanted to play.

Children can be downright vicious, especially ones with little parental supervision. A victim is singled out and taunting goes on until something breaks the cycle. Fallon was such a victim, which is ironic as he was already a full-blown psychopath who could have easily been the tormenter, making notes on whom to punish severely later in life.

The game he was subjected to was called Red Man Writes and the object was to see which contestant could write the most words on Fallon's skin that were readable. Each participant was allowed one minute to accumulate points. The game started when Willy Bellows would scream: "Red Man Writes!" Points were awarded for the amount legibly written and multiplied by the minutes for which they remained visible. It was like blowing soap bubbles and watching them pop. Great transient fun for all, except Fallon, who was never a willing participant.

In the game, curse words scored double as these were guaranteed to get Fallon in serious trouble with the teachers as well as give him severe discomfort. Fallon always wore long-sleeved shirts no matter how hot the weather. The cloth dampened his skin's reactivity and served as a weak attempt to ward off bullies who loved to see the painful lines appear instantaneously on his albino-like skin. Contestants of Red Man Writes would overpower the small kid, pull up his sleeves, and lift Fallon's shirt over his head, using his stomach as a human chalkboard. Let the game begin. Part of the fun was watching Fallon struggle to defend himself. That added a physicality certain boys loved.

The first semester of eighth grade was the worst. Fallon's saving grace was growing seven inches over summer break, pushing his new height to six feet. Bullies were now less likely to pick on a tough, tall white kid, even one they had tormented for years. The game took a new turn. Fallon decided he would no longer be the object of terror. He would stop being tormented no matter what the cost to his own freedom. Fallon's life force which had grown with his height would now embrace the dark side, something he had kept suppressed for far too long.

The aim of his anger was pointed at Willy Bellows, a mean child who was the official game starter of Red Man Writes. He viciously attacked Fallon under the school bleachers during the Halloween school party. Willy decided to give Fallon a red man's costume by making Fallon's skin into a single welt, one that would last all of the school day, which it did. Willy's sharp pencil tore into Fallon's fragile skin and left not only the usual reactive welts, but permanent scars, binding Willy the tormentor with Fallon the psychopath for eternity.

Fallon took time to work out his revenge plan. He would ambush Willy, who hadn't had the same luck of growth-hormone production. He waited until Valentine's Day. He would leave Willy his own heartfelt card, one for all to read. Fallon's calm demeanor was a great disguise. He seemed normal in every way, with no indication of his murderous side. This was unfortunate for his victim, whose only concern that morning was if he would get any Valentine's cards. He would. One he didn't expect.

Fallon showed up early to shadow Willy as he left his home in the projects. He ambushed his prey at his usual short cut, an isolated alleyway behind the ramshackle abandoned homes in the poverty-stricken neighborhood. At first Willy challenged him, "Get out of my way, fool, or I'm going write my name on your face!"

Fallon's unflinching black eyes told the story to a boy who had seen plenty of violence in his life, even at 14. Two yellow pencils, razor sharp, suddenly appeared, each gripped tightly in Fallon's gloved hands. He was as quick as a rattlesnake, fangs ready for action. Pencils would be Fallon's calling cards to the police if they could figure out the crime. Death by #2 lead, carried out by a young psychopath named Scriber, German for "writer." He was fulfilling his fate. The first in a long line of deaths by the boy whose skin was a painful piece of paper.

Realizing he was in serious trouble too late, Willy tried to run but tripped over his feet, the only part of his body that had grown during puberty. He fell hard. Fallon aggressively jumped on top of Willy, stabbing the boy in the neck and upper torso, the sharp lead breaking off as it hit cartilage and bone in Willy's still-developing cervical spine. Fallon's rage continued, using the dull pencil ends, plunging them violently into Willy's neck, deep into the blood vessels. Fallon was a pro at killing even his first time. He had worn gloves, knowing he would be murdering today, and had watched enough television to learn about fingerprints. He left none. However, Fallon purposefully left the two pencils sticking out of Willy's neck to see how well the police detectives would do their jobs.

At school, Fallon changed into a fresh set of clothes he had brought, cleaned his face with a wet towel, and then proceeded to have the best day of school ever. He could hardly wait for someone else to upset his natural order of life again. Fallon found himself exhilarated. He decided his lot in life was cast. No more the fool with the red, painful skin. He was in charge of his destiny and if anyone got in his way he would take care of them in his own fashion. Pencils, writing, and death were his new calling cards if anyone ever cared to look.

In the case of Willy Bellows, the police did not do their jobs well at all. They classified the killing as gang-related, like his deceased brother before him. Case closed. Another black child's murder unsolved, the Bellows name dying out with little Willy.

For the rest of eighth grade, Fallon took Willy's old short cut to school. He loved walking by the place he had become a man.

Unfortunately for his victims, Fallon Scriber would never go to prison. No easy diagnosis of psychopath would ever be rendered by his fellow inmates. The unlucky few who would encounter Fallon's dark side would not know they had experienced a rare breed of human, a true psychopath and the most dangerous type: a serial killer. The only question was could he ever be stopped.

To be continued in HIDDEN CANYON, *scheduled for release in 2014*

Photography courtesy Mark Sublette

Page 1: *Ancient Sweat Lodge*, Chuska Mountains, New Mexico
Page 4: *Monument Valley, Mitten*, August 2012
Page 11: Daisy Taugelchee, Navajo Two Grey Hills Rug, circa late 1940-early 1950
Page 17: *On the Road to Kayenta from Flagstaff*, Arizona
Page 24: *Kayenta Water Tower*, Arizona
Page 29: *Casita Canyon Road*, Santa Fe
Page 35: Stereocard of Sioux Woman with Navajo First Phase Chief's Blanket, circa 1875
Page 41: Navajo Second Phase Chief's Blanket, circa 1850
Page 55: Wool Moth
Page 61: *Paint Can*, Chuska Mountains, New Mexico
Page 73: *Going to Herd the Flock*, North of Kayenta
Page 79: *Side Canyon*, Monument Valley
Page 85: *Horses North of Kayenta*, Arizona
Page 91: *Ancient Hogan*, Northern Arizona
Page 95: *Indian Market Opening Day*, Santa Fe, New Mexico
Page 105: *Coming into Santa Fe*, New Mexico
Page 117: *Canyon Road Busy*, Santa Fe, New Mexico
Page 123: *Navajo First Phase Chief's Blanket, circa 1840*
Page 127: *Warren Trading Post*, Kayenta, Arizona, 1926 by Harmon Perry Marble
Page 140: *Ancient Juniper Tree*, North of Kayenta, Arizona
Page 152: *Red Sand of Monument Valley*
Page 155: *Toadlena Trading Post*, Newcomb, New Mexico
Page 164: *Mitten Rock Gospel / Oak Spring*, Northern Arizona/ New Mexico Border
Page 175: *Trash Heap*, North of Toadlena, New Mexico
Page 186: *Zuni Turquoise Bear, circa 1940*
Page 190: *Ancient Pack Rat Nest*, Arizona
Page 199: Spectrophotometer Recording of Indigo Dye
Page 206: *Early 19th Century Navajo Weaving Tools*
Page 216: *Farmington Accomodations and Dining*, New Mexico
Page 220: *Hampton Inn*, Kayenta, Arizona
Page 228: *Tiger Rattlesnake*, Arizona
Page 239: *Example of Skin Condition, Dermatographia*